Dragon's Fall

Book Three of the Dragon Spawn Chronicles
By Dawn Ross
© 2022

"Humanity is acquiring all the right technology for all the wrong reasons."
– R. Buckminster Fuller

Dragon's Fall

Book Three of the Dragon Spawn Chronicles

by Dawn Ross
Copyright 2022

Cover

Customized Dragon art commissioned from artist Dmitrii Brigidov. Spaceship from algolonline purchased under the standard license agreement through 123rf.com in 2021. Eclipse image and starry background from NASA. Images combined by germancreative on fiverr.com.

Special Thanks

I'd like to extend a special thanks to all the beta readers and editors who helped me make this novel shine. And additional thanks to my final editor, Grace Bridges, who has been instrumental in helping me with content and line edits as well as with pointing out opportunities for story improvement.

Reviews for StarFire Dragons

"A thoughtful novel that owes a debt to
Star Trek but works on its own terms."
—*Kirkus Reviews*

"A subtle space opera that explores the ethical
conundrums of intergalactic relations with main
characters who are worth rooting for."
—**Becca Saffier,** *Reedsy Discovery*

"Fans of epic sci-fi that look for realistic characters and complex
yet believable settings will find *Starfire Dragons*
a powerful introductory story that promises more, yet
nicely concludes its immediate dilemmas."
—**D. Donovan, Senior Reviewer,** *Midwest Book Review*

Dragon's Fall

Book Three of the Dragon Spawn Chronicles

by Dawn Ross

1
Falling Short

3791:050:18:37. Year 3791, day 50, 18:37 hours, Prontaean time as per the last sync. Bird calls, insect chirps, and shrieks from tree mammals created a maddening racket. Terkeshi sucked in air and scrutinized the wild scene before him. Tenacious vines strangled every limb and branch, but the trees defiantly sprouted varying shades of green. Short invasive scrub flourished under broad-leafed plants as towering evergreens barred all but a few dabs of sunlight.

Terk wiped a sheen of sweat from his brow. The sweltering jungle air clung to him but did nothing to alleviate the dryness in his mouth. His eyes followed the barely discernible path that disappeared into the bush as he evaluated the task ahead. An internal heat fueled his determination.

"You can do this," he muttered while flexing his fingers. *No more failing.*

With a few puffs of breath, he poised into a starting position. His muscles tautened, like that of a blackbeast ready to pounce on its prey.

His heart pulsed, flushing oxygenated blood throughout his body. Setting his jaw, he lunged into action. A giant green leaf slapped him in the face as he sprinted down the path, but he ignored the sting.

The gurgle and splash of rushing water filled his ears. After rounding a broad trunk, he jumped from an exposed root and landed on a wet stone. Without hesitation, he skipped from rock to rock over the wide stream until his feet squished into the mud of the opposite side. *Now for the harder parts.*

He scrambled up the slippery bank, grabbing at roots and rocks. The slope grew steeper and his breathing deeper. His legs and shoulders burned as he pushed and pulled himself up. With a grunt, he grasped the edge of an overhanging ledge and heaved himself over.

His strength wavered as he ran. Razor-thin branches and leaves cut across his bare skin. Sweat filled the slashes, overshadowing the fire of his spasming muscles.

Onward, he dashed—once hand over hand as he used a hanging vine to cross a swamp, twice ducking low to avoid limbs, and several times in bounds as he hurdled over rocks or dead wood.

The last leg of the course neared. His heartrate hastened. *Almost there. You can do it.* He huffed rhythmically until the path cleared and a ravine cut before him. His muscles tensed as he prepared to jump.

Now! He leapt from the edge and stretched his arms overhead, aiming for the thick, hanging vine. The instant it brushed his hands, he seized it. The vine slid through his palm and sliced into his flesh. He gritted his teeth and endured.

His momentum swung him over the gully, closer to the other side. *This is it!*

As he reached the tail end of the vine, he maneuvered his body to keep his power driving forward. His feet struck the lip of the ravine and—slipped.

He fell backward, falling only a meter before landing with a wallop.

The simulation fizzled out. The humidity dissipated and the jungle disappeared. Vines turned into ropes, rocks and hills became makeshift obstacles, and the ground reverted into an ordinary padded flooring.

Terk caught his breath, then rolled to his feet with a curse. "Chusho!"

He'd been at this for hours. Why couldn't he make it over that ravine? It was impossible. Whoever made this damned sim course was delusional. No one could beat it.

Except someone had—the one person he could never defeat. *Damn you, Jori.* Even dead, his ten-year-old brother continued to chafe his ego. He growled and punched his thigh. Stifling a sniffle, he swept away the liquid that had sprung into his eyes. It wasn't fair. Jori shouldn't have left him.

"Persistence will pay off, my Lord," a gruff voice said from the edge of the court.

Terk glowered at his mentor. Sensei Jeruko remained stoic. The silver hair streaked along his temples seemed to reinforce his steely physique. Even as he advanced through middle age, his bearing exuded a tranquil power.

Terk used to look up to him. Now he found the old man's steady temper irksome.

"It took me hundreds of tries before I succeeded," Sensei Jeruko continued.

"How many times did it take Jori?" Terk replied sourly.

"I don't remember exactly."

Although Terk's ability to sense emotions told him the man spoke the truth, he also detected evasiveness. It had likely taken Jori only a few tries to defeat this course. *Damned overachiever.*

His mentor's regret almost influenced Terk's own. He shoved it aside and deepened his scowl. It wasn't his fault Jori had gotten himself killed, nor could he blame Sensei Jeruko. They had warned him about what would happen if he helped those prisoners. As usual, he'd let his sentiment get the best of him.

Sensei Jeruko clasped his hands behind his back. "If you've completed your exercises, my Lord, your father wishes to speak with you."

Terk clenched his fists. *Wishes. Ha!* Ever since Jori's death, the man had made one demand after another. Terk barely had time to sleep anymore. Yet no matter how hard he worked, it was never enough.

He stomped to the dressing room, not bothering to tell Sensei Jeruko whether he'd comply. Father wouldn't praise him for promptness anyway.

He put on his nanite-infused uniform. The black garb of a senshi warrior contoured his body perfectly. He admired his muscles in the mirror, noting the broad shoulders and the cords in his arms. His tall and muscular physique was coming along well for a fourteen-year-old.

Then his emotions soured. His father didn't care about his young age. The asshole still expected him to perform like an adult senshi.

3

Terk abandoned the TTAC room. As he marched through the belly of the *Dragon* warship, giant senshi warriors veered around him. Most nodded respectfully because of his status as the last Mizuki heir, but a few treated him with just enough deference to avoid a reprimand.

Prince or not, he still had to prove himself before these men respected him.

The corridor on this outer part of the ship curved, revealing a mock viewport that spanned about ten yards. While much of the length displayed a sea of stars, one section was pitch black. A camera must be out. He tapped the MM tablet clasped to his wrist and checked the maintenance log to see if anyone had reported it.

While skimming over the list, a titanic object from the view outside loomed in the corner of his vision. He pointedly ignored the other spaceship. He needed no reminders of how he would have taken command of the *Fire Breather* if his father hadn't deemed him incompetent.

Adding menial tasks for the shokukin workers to take care of seemed all he was good for.

He jabbed his MM, closing the display, and entered the conveyor. "Command deck," he told the computer.

The closer the car brought him to his destination, the heavier he felt. He extended the reach of his sensing ability to check his father's mood. The man's anger stewed as usual, plus an added fleck of irritation.

What the hell's wrong now? Couldn't Father ever be happy about anything?

The conveyor doors opened to a narrow corridor bedecked with red and gold dragon banners. The glowering eyes of the Mizuki family symbol followed him as he passed. Terk shook off the weight of their judgment. He entered a more elaborate hallway, then hesitated before the ornate golden door to Emperor Mizuki's office.

Let's get this over with. He sucked in a breath and braced himself. A wintry draft struck his face as the door swished open. He stepped inside with his chin up and automatically fell into a stance of silent attention.

His father continued working. His brow crinkled, accentuating the modest wrinkles that betrayed his age. Although some grey streaked throughout his jet-black hair, his body was as robust as a man in his prime.

Terk peered straight ahead, resisting the urge to fidget as he waited to be acknowledged. The dragon picture on the wall behind Father's desk seemed to mock him with its fiery green eyes. Never had Terk hated that image as much as he hated it now. You're not good enough, it said. You will never be good enough.

Father raised his head, revealing flinty eyes with dark bags underneath. "I just read the report regarding the status of the emitter. It appears we've made no progress—none—these past several days."

Terk considered his response. Of course they hadn't made headway. The only ones who'd had any chance of reconfiguring the perantium emitter into a weapon were gone.

A mix of anger and hate swirled in Terk's gut. It was Father's own fault no one remained, but he dared not say it. "We're working on it, Sir."

"Not fast enough! If the workers don't understand the new technology, then they'd better study up on their off hours." Father's dark eyes glinted with madness.

The man's descent had begun with the death of Terk's older brother who'd lost his life in battle. The second eldest heir had died soon after. After that, one of Father's closest advisors betrayed him. The final snap had been when Jori got caught helping prisoners escape. Terk shivered at how his father's temper had spewed a destructive energy, leaving Terk as the only surviving heir to the empire.

"It might go faster if you allowed Benjiro to help," Terk said.

"No. I don't trust that idiot."

"He's not capable of being dishonest, Sir. I know he's an idiot in some ways, but he's a genius when it comes to engineering."

Father flicked his hand. "Fine. Just make sure he's watched at all times."

"Yes, Sir."

"This should have been done by now," Father mumbled. "Jori would have finished it already."

Terk's gut twisted. Not ten days ago his father had cursed his lost son. He refrained from pointing out the hypocrisy, though. No need to kick an angry blackbeast.

5

"If only Dokuri were still alive," Father said louder.

Despite the sting of the words, Terk wished it, too. He had hated Dokuri, but he wouldn't have to bear the weight of all this responsibility if he still lived.

"Incompetence. I'm surrounded by incompetence!"

Terk's cheeks burned. *Damn it, Jori. Why'd you have to die too?*

"I will speak to Malkai and make sure everyone is doing what they're supposed to," he said, hoping to divert his father's anger.

"Malkai is a fool," Father spat. "He has no more of an idea of what he's doing than you."

Terk bit his tongue to keep his attitude in check. "What else would you have me do, Father?"

The man rose, leaning over his desk on white knuckles. His face darkened as his brows twisted inward. "I would have you do your job and live up to the Mizuki name."

Terk resisted the urge to gulp and hardened himself instead. "I'm doing the best I can."

Father pushed away from the desk and advanced. "Your best isn't good enough!"

Terk's breath hitched, and he reflexively stepped back. Father's Herculean bulk stifled his breath. The singularity of the man's eyes flared like a relativistic jet. His dark hair and inflamed temper easily outmatched the biggest blackbeast.

"Tell me what to do," Terk said evenly despite his quivering chin. "And I will do it."

His father flicked his hand. Terk flinched, expecting to be struck.

"There's nothing you can do, boy," Father replied with a growl. "You give me no choice. I must contact the cyborgs. Maybe they will succeed where *you* have failed."

Terk's heart jumped. *The cyborgs?* When he'd first met them about a half year ago, their mechanical eyes and the computer ports in the back of their heads made his hair stand on end. It wasn't just their physical appearances or machine-like behaviors that unnerved him. The sense of their lifeforce differed from most other people. It had been... He wanted to say flat, but even that wasn't a good enough description. Stagnant, perhaps?

He shivered. "They're not natural."

"They're as human as we are."

"Barely. I can't sense their emotions the way I can with other people. And when I do, they feel wrong."

Father glowered. "If you don't like it, step up. Be at least half as good as your brothers."

Heat flushed over Terk's body. "I'll review everything again, in greater detail this time. I'll make sure the workers aren't slacking off."

Father puffed out heated air. "Fine. Go back to the *Fire Breather* and get it done. If you don't succeed, I'll have the cyborgs remake you into someone more worthy."

The truth laden in the threat struck Terk's senses, sending a quiver down his spine. Surely Father wouldn't break the ancient laws. *Would he?*

Father's growing madness tainted his essence more every day. *Yes, he would.*

Terk resisted the urge to swallow the dryness from his throat and tightened his fists. *No more failing.*

2
Dragon Emperor

3791:050:19:52. Emperor Kenji Mizuki released his fists and flexed his fingers. Micro sensations prickled as blood flowed through them again. He glanced at his deskview screen and tightened his knuckles once more.

What's that traitor up to? Another attempt to dismantle his legacy, no doubt. Fujishin wouldn't get away with this. Mizuki's ancestors had ruled for nearly five hundred years already. He'd be damned if he'd allow the Dragon Empire to fall now.

With a tap on his screen, he sent the video to his advisors. "Tell me who these men are."

As the three seasoned warriors standing before him reviewed their MM tablets, he replayed the footage for himself. The static distorted the two people, but the shorter one resembled the traitor well enough to make Mizuki's insides knot. Light-colored hair with a receding hairline existed in so few.

To think I allowed that chima to be a part of my inner circle.

He rubbed the back of his neck and stole a glance at the others. If one of the Five Talons had dared defy him, what was stopping these other four?

Sensei Aki couldn't. The senile old man had lived his last days under constant medical supervision. It seemed unlikely General Samuru and semi-retired General Nezumi would go against him, considering neither had ever displayed a hint of disloyalty.

He flicked his gaze to his final advisor. Colonel Jeruko's silver-streaked hair suggested his wisdom and his dark eyes reflected his honesty. Mizuki had known him since his teenage years, yet Fujishin's and Jori's treacheries raised his suspicions. Jeruko, after all, had been Fujishin's closest friend and the boy's sensei.

Mizuki leaned in and focused on the video. The man Fujishin spoke to was only discernible through a short, boxed beard, but a lot of senshi and lords wore that style.

"Who sent this, Sire?" Jeruko asked in his usual gravelly tone that only got rougher with age.

Irritation spiked Mizuki's temper. "What does it matter? Just tell me who they are."

"The one on the right looks like Fujishin, Sire," the giant General Samuru said. "I can't make out the other man."

"Agreed," Jeruko replied.

"It certainly resembles him," Nezumi added.

"Who is he talking to?" Mizuki tapped his foot.

As his advisors watched the video again, a hatred and a yearning clutched Mizuki's chest. His father had once ruled from this same chair, and that drunken chima was the reason he was in this predicament now.

He regarded the case of artifacts standing in the corner of his office. Most of the items had once belonged to his grandfather, Dragon Emperor Ryu Mizuki, the greatest Toradon ruler of the past century.

Mizuki's heart swelled as he gazed upon his grandfather's sword resting on top. According to his old sensei, his grandfather had last used it in the Battle of Abira. When the enemy had deployed new defuser technology to render phaser rifles and other energy weapons ineffective, he turned the tide with just his blade.

The reptilian-skin grip had since degraded. It might have once been dyed red, but now it was browned with age. If not for the subsequent failures of Mizuki's father, the sword could have been a symbol to carry on his grandfather's greatness.

Nezumi shook his head. "I can't make him out, your Eminence." His narrow face combined with his thin eyes and pinched mouth made him resemble a rat, but also reflected his cunning. Mizuki would trust a deceitful rat before Jeruko right now.

"It almost looks like General Sakon, but this man's not as wide," Samuru added.

Mizuki huffed. "It's *not* General Sakon." He eyed the ogre-like man. Samuru was the fiercest warrior he'd ever met, but hardly the brightest. The long scar running down his cheek had resulted from one such act of stupidity.

"The image is too distorted, Sire," Jeruko said.

Mizuki gritted his teeth. *Useless.* "Is it Lord Enomoto?"

Jeruko's eyes widened. "He wouldn't."

Mizuki scoffed. "Yes, he would. He's got the means."

Jeruko's expression returned to its normal flatness. "I can't imagine he'd be so audacious, Sire."

Mizuki's lip curled. *Of course he's defending Terkeshi's uncle.*

"Don't be so sure, Colonel," Nezumi said. "We all know what our spies have reported about him."

A heat swelled in Mizuki's gut. The thought of one more traitor both terrified and infuriated him. He bit the inside of his cheek to stem the flow.

"Creating dissent among the lords is one thing," Jeruko replied. "Conspiring against the Empire is another."

"I know the implication," Mizuki snapped. "It doesn't mean it's not him." *Just whose side is Jeruko on?*

"Where was this recorded?" Samuru asked.

"I'm not sure. Whoever sent it hid their tracks well."

"This sender's secrecy makes me wonder whether they meant to mislead us," Jeruko replied.

Mizuki narrowed his eyes. "Why do you find it so difficult to believe that Lord Enomoto would also plot against me?"

"It would be foolish and risky for him to ally with that traitor, Sire. And what reason would he have since Prince Terkeshi is his nephew?"

"He might do it if someone told him I exiled the boy's mother," Mizuki said with an accusation in his tone. After all, Lord Enomoto's sister had been sent to the same place as Jeruko's consort and sons.

Jeruko bowed. "I assure you, Sire, her location is too secure for word to get out."

Nezumi grunted as though challenging the colonel's claim.

Mizuki refrained from following suit. Even if he had reasons to doubt Jeruko's loyalty, Nezumi's attempt to discredit the colonel in a jockey for position annoyed him.

His eye twitched, threatening to trigger the involuntary muscle spasms he thought he'd gotten under control. How could he expect to control anything at this point? It was one disaster after another, and every rebellion Fujishin caused undermined his rule and inspired others to conspire against him. *Intolerable!*

He shifted his gaze to the dragon-styled helmet on the inner shelf of the case. Despite how menacing it appeared, Sensei Aki had said it possessed a fatal flaw. According to the story, its computer chip had malfunctioned when Mizuki's grandfather wore it during the Rebellion of Minashi. Instead of protecting him, it became a deathtrap. The faceplate blacked out, making him blind. Yet he fought on, his determination inspiring his senshi warriors until they'd won the day.

Mizuki relished the idea of winning a losing battle with his greatest warriors at his back—only many of those warriors seemed to want to stab him in the back instead.

Space dust had long since flattened the helmet's golden sheen and dulled its sharp edges. Pock marks flawed its smoothness. In Mizuki's younger days, the helmet had inspired his ambition. Now it served only to symbolize the decay of the Mizuki empire.

He wouldn't let this happen. "Even if that's not Lord Enomoto, Fujishin is still colluding with someone. It's imperative that we get the perantium emitter online before he discovers it."

He tapped his monitor. A mostly green planet expanded to take up a quarter of the screen. "I'd rather not get assistance from the cyborgs, so let's consider other options. What about Pulcrate? Will it have the resources we require?"

"I believe it's pronounced pool-cray-tee, Sire," Jeruko said. Mizuki made a face. Jeruko dipped his head as if apologizing for correcting him. "Their planetary defenses aren't that sophisticated, which indicates they won't have what we need."

"Doesn't the Prontaean Cooperative help them out with experts and technology?"

Jeruko bowed. "Yes, Sire, but the people there are still very much an agrarian society. Any specialists the Cooperative has sent will probably be in geoscience and biology."

"I agree, your Eminence," Nezumi said. His upper lip rose slightly, as though he had a distaste for agreeing with Jeruko. "If they have engineers, they are likely more skilled in building and maintaining industrial machines."

11

Mizuki cupped his chin. They needed physicists and aerospace engineers. The emitter he'd taken from Thendi a while back remained in pieces in his auxiliary docking bay. He'd rendezvoused with the spaceship to be used for housing the giant device, but Terkeshi's incompetence kept the project from moving forward.

Jori would've completed it by now.

A small figure caught the corner of his eye and his heart jumped. When he glanced at it, no one was there. *Of course no one's there. Jori's dead.*

He rubbed the ache lurking behind his eyes. How much sleep had he had since Jori helped the Cooperative prisoners escape? Not enough.

Damned little traitor. Those prisoners should have reconfigured the emitter.

"Sire," Samuru said, "if a Cooperative ship is there, we can attack them and take *their* people."

"We can't waste time based on what *might* be." *And we don't have the resources.* His *Dragon* was the best warship in Toradon, but the Prontaean Cooperative vessels were well armored.

"We can always lie low outside the star system," Jeruko said. "One of their ships is bound to show up."

"Another *might*." Mizuki eyed the man. Jeruko was usually adept at evaluating plans of action. Was he holding back?

Samuru tilted his head. "We don't need to go to Pulcrate, Sire. General Brevak is chasing down a Cooperative ship as we speak."

That's just another might, idiot. A pang ran up from Mizuki's jaw and stabbed into his forehead. The Cooperative vessel that had somehow convinced his young traitorous son to help them rescue their people was probably long gone, but he wasn't about to give up and let those chimas get away. "I don't have time. I need experts *today*."

"I'm sorry, your Eminence," Jeruko said. "I've run out of ideas."

The others remained silent. Mizuki expelled an exasperated breath and slammed his fists onto his desk. "Doesn't anyone have any viable suggestions? The longer it takes for this device to become operational, the more likely my enemies will discover and try to destroy it."

He popped his knuckles. Terkeshi certainly had no hope of getting the emitter working.

Mizuki suppressed a sigh. "I must contact the cyborgs, then."

Jeruko's brows twisted in a pained expression. Mizuki ignored him. The MEGA Injunction against enhancements meant contacting those freaks might undermine his rule, but that wouldn't matter when the weapon was ready. Not even Lord Enomoto's high-tech planetary defenses would withstand its power.

"Sire!" Major Niashi transmitted from the bridge. "An unidentified ship just showed up on our scope."

Chusho! Mizuki jumped to his feet. "Who's on tactical?"

"Captain Ching."

Mizuki dipped his head to Samuru, who rushed out faster than one would expect from such a giant man.

Mizuki and his remaining advisors followed in haste. He entered the bridge and froze with volcanic fury. On the viewscreen was a Rhinian mercenary vessel. *Hired by Fujishin, no doubt.* "Blast that ship to hell!"

"I'm on it, Sire," Samuru replied as he manipulated the weapon controls. The man could be slow witted, but he excelled at tactics.

Mizuki dropped into the oversized central chair. "What do we know?"

"Their ship is called the *Shadow Croc*, Sire," Niashi said. "They're firing at the *Fire Breather*."

Mizuki growled. This meant Fujishin had learned about the emitter already. How the hell did he find out?

He watched with intensity as his weapons dissipated harmlessly against the *Croc*'s shield. A few more shots should defeat it, but would it be in time? If the *Croc* damaged that ship, he'd have no place to house the emitter.

"Let's move! Block their line of sight. Our shield can take it."

"Yes, Sire."

"Sire," Jeruko said. "Your son is on the *Fire Breather*."

Mizuki frowned. He should have been worried but was too heated to think about anything other than Fujishin's audacity.

"The *Fire Breather*'s shields are down," another bridge crew member announced. "A blast from an energy cannon has struck its bow."

13

The *Shadow Croc* turned away. Mizuki slammed his fist on the armrest of his chair. "Pursue! I want that ship destroyed!"

"Sire!" Jeruko stepped into the peripheral of his vision. "We can't leave the *Fire Breather* behind. What if it's a ploy? Rhinians tend to travel in packs."

Mizuki bared his teeth and fumed. True or not, he couldn't let that vessel get away. This was more than just attempted sabotage. This was a personal affront.

"Keep firing until it's out of range, then." *Chusho.* That ship would be gone before he could penetrate its shields. This would allow it to return with reinforcements—which meant he needed the cyborgs now more than ever.

3
Nothingness

3791:050:20:16. Terkeshi glanced past the scaffolding, beyond gaping the maw gouged out of the unfinished spaceship, and out to the starry universe. Pinpricks of light gave the illusion of infinite possibilities, but all he noticed was the oppressive nothingness.

He sighed. The sound inside his suit whispered through the extreme silence of the surrounding space. His helmet visor adjusted as he brought his attention back to the *Fire Breather*'s illuminated inner corridor. Part of the outer hull had been removed, leaving a long crevice segmented by seemingly endless light and dark intervals.

The plan was to install the emitter here once they reinforced the surrounding bulkheads. Too much work and the lack of skilled labor slowed the process. Only four people from the shokukin caste had the knowledge necessary for today's job.

Terk reviewed the incomplete tasks on his tablet and his shoulders slumped. No way could he manage all this. The construction workers claimed they didn't have the right equipment. The electricians couldn't determine how to generate enough power. Every attempt to work around a problematic code created more issues.

The hollowness in his gut swelled. His lack of capabilities weighed heavily against the need to please his father.

He hated this damned ship. Even if Father changed his mind and allowed him to command it, *Fire Breather* represented much of what he'd lost. If only the cyborgs hadn't told Father about the perantium emitter. His mother wouldn't have been exiled to Hisui Island on Meixing, and Jori would still be alive.

He pushed off and drifted down the corridor, adding another connection point to his tether. "Malkai," he called to a shokukin through his comm.

The man in a white spacesuit ahead both knelt and floated as he used a pistol-grip tool to secure a panel. "Yes, my Lord?"

Terk grasped a leg of the scaffolding and halted his forward momentum. "How's this coming al—"

A piercing beep sounded from the main channel, followed by a verbal transmission. "The ship is under attack!"

"Chusho!" Terk's heart skipped a beat. A quiver from the scaffolding bolted up from his grip.

Malkai's mouth fell open and he stared dumbly as the metal braces vibrated.

Terk grabbed the shokukin's arm. "Move! Get inside and find an escape pod."

His attempt to shove Malkai toward an airlock failed in zero gravity. All he'd done was push himself away. Terk growled and grasped for the scaffolding.

To go forward or back? He glanced over his shoulder and noted the doorway he'd entered from. To head back would be easier. All he had to do was draw himself down his tether, but it was further. *Can I make it?*

With a grunt, he propelled himself over to the closer airlock and followed Malkai. As the shokukin hauled himself hand-over-hand, Terk carefully secured his own tether along the way.

A flash of a hazy glow erupted from the black sky above. His heart jumped as more flashes indicated the ship's shield being struck. He held his breath, hoping the meager defenses would hold.

Malkai reached the airlock. He turned with wide eyes and motioned to Terk with a wave.

"Go! Don't wait for me." Terk gripped the next bracing and wrestled with his tether's clip. His heart pounded as the mechanism fumbled from his hand. A brace bowed. A tremor ran through it. In a blink, it bent into a sharp, twisted angle.

Chusho! Terk kicked out until his foot struck the floor. He pushed off toward the airlock just as a soundless snap warped the scaffolding.

Everything jolted. Terk's helmet slammed into a beam, rattling his brain. His shoulder rammed into the opposite wall. His tether went taut as he flew back into the metal supports. A sharp twinge ran up his elbow. Pain seized his leg, manifesting in an agonizing buzz as he thrashed against the fortifications.

A thought about the inertial dampeners flickered long enough for him to realize that system wasn't yet operational.

His comm erupted with the cries and panicked curses of other workers. Piercing sensations overwhelmed his entire body. He lost himself in the chaos as blackness swirled in.

His arms and legs flailed. Bam! Bam! Darkness seared until he fell into utter oblivion.

4
Damaged

3791:050:20:51. Terkeshi stirred. A solid ache ballooned in his skull. His eyes fluttered open. Spots of light blurred until thousands stabbed like needles. He gasped and jerked his body, snapping to alertness with a blast of realization.

Trillions of starry lights encased in the vast nothingness of space surrounded him. His heart jumped to his throat. He windmilled his arms, looking for anything to grasp onto. His pinky finger clipped an object, but it floated out of reach. He turned in agonizing slowness as his limbs flailed, hitting emptiness.

Something resisted against his throbbing ankle, sending relief throughout his body despite the ache. He bent his knee, pulling the tether closer. When he grasped it, the rapidity of his breath lessened to a pant. He pulled himself around to face the ship, then hauled himself hand over hand until he reached the lip of the crevice. His fingers clutched the rim and he paused until his heartbeat returned to normal.

After verifying his tether remained secure, he took in the scene before him. The starscape rotated—or rather, the ship spun. Nothing about the vessel appeared damaged until he peered inside. The mangled scaffolding screamed ruination. Beams bent at awkward angles, resembling the arms of a twisted cybernetic monster. Debris floated nearby, most of it small. At least one panel four-times his size slowly spiraled away.

Someone in a spacesuit drifted upward from the crevice. Terk shoved himself inside, reining in the slack of his tether, and met him halfway. Malkai greeted him with round, green eyes. His mouth moved but no sound transmitted. Terk struck his helmet with his palm, sending a pang through his skull.

"Sir!" Malkai's voice shot from the shorted comm. "Are you alright?"

Terk took a mental stock of his body and flexed his limbs. Pain throbbed and pricked, but nothing was broken. "I'm fine. How severe is the damage to the ship?"

"Well…" Malkai lowered his head. "We'll probably need to start over."

A chill expanded over Terk like ice fractals. This would send Father's temper skyrocketing. "Can you fix it?"

Malkai's eyes swelled. "I-I don't know. If the structural backbone is damaged, this ship will be useless."

What the hell! Couldn't anything go right? Although this wasn't his fault, Father might be mad enough to turn him into a cyborg.

Malkai went over all the known problems this catastrophe had created. Terk half-listened as frustration and worry churned. Several months back, the cyborgs had come offering an alliance. As a token of goodwill, they'd infused Terk and Jori with undetectable defense nanites. It had been a good thing, too, because Jori used them in their escape from the Cooperative.

Those nanites had long since dissolved. If Father called on the cyborgs again, they might offer permanent technical augmentation. If those enhancements were also imperceptible, Father could turn him into a competent heir without triggering the lords into a revolt.

Goosebumps ran from his arms up to the back of his neck. It wasn't fair. He shouldn't have to deal with this shit. Nothing seemed to work in his favor, and it was all Jori's fault.

Hot tears hovered at the edge of his eyelids. No, his brother wasn't to blame. If Terk had outmaneuvered their pursuers, they wouldn't have ended up on that Cooperative planet. Then Jori never would've gotten to know the enemy well enough to want to save them.

Then again, Terk never would have gone into Cooperative territory if the cyborgs hadn't told Father about the perantium emitter. Those machine men were trouble. If only he could do his job properly, then Father wouldn't need them.

He gritted his teeth. A burning lurked behind his eyes, and he scrunched them shut to force it back.

"Sir?" Malkai said. "What do we do?"

The heat of Terk's shame sparked into annoyance. "I'm not the engineer, damn it. You are."

19

Malkai hung his head. "My apologies, my Lord. We've never done anything like this before."

Terk huffed. The shokukin was right, of course, but Father certainly didn't want to hear this excuse. "None of us have, but I expect you to figure it out."

"I'm trying, my Lord. I truly am," Malkai responded in a higher pitch. "But-but... I can't fix this. I wouldn't even know where to—"

Terk yanked Malkai by the arm, pulling him close enough for their helmets to bonk. "If you can't repair it," he said in a low and menacing tone, "then you're no good to me. Do you understand?"

Malkai shrank back. "But—"

Terk raised a fist, considering. Father would have struck the man to emphasize the threat. Why didn't he?

Because he was a coward.

"Yes, my Lord." Malkai's head bobbed.

The man's distress filtered into Terk's senses. His gut fluttered as though something gnawed at his insides. He released the shokukin and shoved himself away. Two doses of regret filled him—one for not having the courage to use force the way his father would have wanted him to and one for considering it.

Chusho. This was all so hopeless. If only Jori were still here.

*****

3791:050:22:03. Terkeshi maneuvered the controls. His shuttle touched down with a slight bump. A thump followed as the docking bay clamps took hold.

The artificial gravity of the *Dragon* tugged him to his seat, magnifying the soreness in his body. He dropped his head into the back of his chair and sighed. Father wanted to see him immediately, but he didn't want to go. The very thought knotted his insides.

He listlessly released his harness. Every movement sent a twinge to his temple, so he paused and massaged it with his thumb. A beep from the comm stabbed through his respite.

He answered with a growl. "What is it?"

"I'm checking to make sure you're alright, my Lord," Sensei Jeruko said.

"I'm fine."

Terk left the pilot's seat with a huff. Why Sensei Jeruko took such an interest in his well-being when he'd shown none for Jori was beyond him. If the man had expressed even half this concern before, Jori might still be alive.

He stormed off the shuttle and marched past Sensei Jeruko without so much as a glance. His mentor and the other personal guards followed at a silent distance. Terk's trek through the ship was a blur of brooding and spiraling doubts. By the time he reached the command deck, an imaginary two-ton pack weighed him down.

Father wasn't in his office, so Terk pulled back his shoulders and entered the bridge. The fury spewing from the man in the central chair seared into Terk's façade. He held his breath and planted himself before the looming figure of his father. "Sir, I sent the report you requested."

"Give me the highlights."

Terk braced himself. "The scaffolding is severely damaged."

Father's eyes flared. "How *severe* is severe?"

Terk shifted his stance. "We must start over."

Father shot to his feet and whipped out his hand. Terk's heart jumped. Instead of palm out as though to strike, Father held it out. Terk passed him his tablet. While his father swiped through the images and reports, Terk tightened his hands behind him to keep from fidgeting.

Father flung the tablet back to him and Terk scrambled to catch it.

"Who attacked us?" he asked tentatively.

"Who the hell do you think?"

"The Cooperative?"

Father plunged into his chair and a shadow crossed his features. "Don't be an idiot, boy. Who else has been a thorn in my side since..." He flicked his hand with vehemence.

Fujishin. Terk didn't dare say the man's name out loud. Considering his father's level of anger, he didn't ask whether he'd escaped either.

"How long after we repair the damage will the emitter be ready?" Father asked.

Terk hesitated. "Four months, maybe more—"

Father clawed at his arm rests and lurched forward. "Four months? You said you could get this done, boy!"

"The shokukin lack the education to proceed," Terk replied quickly, "so they need time to study up."

"You're supposed to motivate them to learn."

Terk's jaw tightened. "Sir, this kind of knowledge takes years to master. They're doing the best they can—"

"Damn it, boy! I don't want your excuses. Jori would have had this done already."

"No, he wouldn't—"

"Your level of incompetence is disappointing. You don't have Dokuri's strength, and you lack Jori's intelligence. Tell me, what good are you?"

Terk's cheeks burned. He avoided Father's glare and wished he could be anywhere but here in front of the entire bridge crew. "Dokuri was eight years older than me."

Father balled his fists. "Excuses, boy. I have no time for it."

"Maybe you should get someone else to do this then." Terk flinched inwardly at his unintended outburst but firmed his jaw.

Father growled. "Watch your mouth. If you weren't the last heir, I'd space you. Now go play on the aviation sim while I call in some *real* help."

The heat on Terk's face intensified. He marched out, avoiding the looks from the bridge crew. The soreness from the bashing he'd received on the *Fire Breather* was nothing compared to his shame.

I wonder if Father would've cared if I'd been killed? Probably not.

5
Rising Suspicions

3791:054:08:13. The ache in Terkeshi's temples sharpened. This was impossible, absolutely impossible. If only Father had meant it when he'd told him to practice on the aviation sim. Hell, even working on the sanitation level would've been better than trying to figure out how to put this damned emitter together.

He pinched his bottom lip as he studied the information on his tablet. Restlessness wouldn't allow him to sit still, so he strode through the bay instead. The exercise did nothing to activate his brain cells, but at least it inspired the workers to stay busy.

Terk did a doubletake at the straggly bearded man kneeling before a section of the emitter. Benjiro, or Makoto, or whatever the hell his name was, stuck his tongue out as he worked. Terk still couldn't fathom how this simpleton was his uncle. Known as Makoto in his youth, he became Benjiro when Lord Enomoto, Terk's uncle, had planted him here as an unwitting—and apparently dimwitted—spy.

Father had been pissed when he found out. It'd nearly cost Terk's mother her life. That she'd been confined to the harem and had no idea her brother was here almost hadn't saved her. This was the day Terk had realized his little brother needed to get away from their father's madness.

Malkai rounded the corner, his attention on his tablet. Terk cleared his throat, snapping the man's attention back to the present.

Malkai halted. His eyes widened then tilted in curiosity. "Is everything alright, my Lord?"

Terk inclined his head toward Benjiro and scowled. "Why isn't he being watched? Do you have any idea what my father will do if he finds out Lord Enomoto's brother is working on the emitter *by himself?*"

23

Malkai's throat bobbed. "I-I just stepped away for a moment, my Lord. A-and I don't understand half of what he does."

"If father catches him alone, he'll assume the worst and kill him." Terk crossed his arms. "Maybe you too... For your negligence."

"I-I..." Malkai's mouth opened and closed. His eyes darted. "B-but he's not capable of deceit."

Terk agreed. Benjiro had only one thing on his simple mind—fixing things.

"I can't watch him and do what I need to do, my Lord," Malkai continued. "Surely the emperor will understand."

Terk huffed. "Have you ever known my father to be understanding?"

Malkai wagged his head. "But *you* are, Sir. You know how hard we're working. And you know how far behind we are. We'd be spreading ourselves thin if we had to supervise him on stuff we don't even comprehend."

Terk agreed, but all he could think about was how much of his father's wrath would fall on him.

"I have no one to spare, Sir. Really and truly." Malkai raised his palms. "I'm the only one who'd possibly have a chance of seeing him do something wrong, but even then... Well, Sir, I've learned not to question—"

"Alright!" Terk rolled his eyes. "I get it. But don't you dare let my father see him by himself."

Malkai agreed. Terk shook his head and huffed. The only reason Benjiro had been allowed to live after Father discovered he'd been unknowingly passing secrets on to Lord Enomoto was because Sensei Jeruko had convinced him he could be used to feed false information.

The man had gotten off easy. Terk's mother had as well. She was probably much happier living in exile.

Terk shuddered. He doubted it'd be the same for him. Most likely, he'd suffer the same fate as his brother.

*****

3791:054:09:26. The three-dimensional hologram hovered above the central war room table. Hundreds of symbols representing Emperor Kenji Mizuki's fleet were disbursed throughout his territory.

He frowned. The Toradon dominion had been larger in his grandfather's time. Now the Mizuki house commanded only these four star systems—a mere four populated planets and two habitable moons.

He jabbed at the control, expanding on the Aboru system to take over the holographic table. A red mark pinpointed his current location in the outer asteroid belt. A red line showed the path he'd traveled over the past month. Several color-coded dots and lines connected, indicating all the cargo ships that delivered supplies during that time.

"Explain what this means," he ordered Nezumi regarding the classification system.

The rat-faced general pointed to the legend illuminated on the table. "The blue dots represent ships I've already cleared."

Mizuki nodded. After he'd contacted the cyborgs for help, Nezumi and his team had spent days scrutinizing surveillance videos. Benjiro, who'd unwittingly passed on sensitive information in the past, wasn't in any of the scenes. This meant someone else, probably a worker or one of those damned cargo vessels, leaked intelligence to Fujishin. That traitor likely already heard about the emitter from other outside sources, but he couldn't have known Mizuki's location or the location of the *Fire Breather* without help.

"We should investigate the rest of the ships," Nezumi continued. "I've color coded them based on different factors, with the white ones being the most suspicious."

"I see three whites."

"Yes, Sire. Two of those visited us within the past ten days. We don't have their plotted courses, which makes them prime suspects."

Mizuki straightened. "Alert the authorities. If one of our ships finds them, tell them to begin interrogation. If it's a refueling station or space station, they are to detain them until I send someone."

"Yes, Sire. Shall I do this for all the suspicious ones?"

"Did you receive the projected courses from them all?"

"Yes, Sire."

"How many reached their designated ports on time?"

"Those in orange were over two days late. The ones in yellow haven't arrived yet."

"Which of these ships made port on Jinsekai or Meixing?" Mizuki asked.

Unlike his own ship with access to communication hubs, cargo ships had to be within a few light minutes to transmit messages. This meant they couldn't simply send sensitive information to Mizuki's enemies. They had to use the arc drive to get in radio range first. Them not having instantaneous communication capabilities also meant he'd be unable to verify their projected courses until they checked in at their next destination.

"The ones in green docked near Meixing. None have reached Jinsekai yet."

Mizuki rubbed his chin. Fujishin had been last seen on Jinsekai while Lord Enomoto ruled almost the entire planet of Meixing. The man held substantial power, but he had no authority in space. Swearing fealty to the Mizuki house allowed him to trade throughout Toradon territory. Collusion with Fujishin seemed unlikely, considering how far Jinsekai was from Meixing and how long it took the smaller arc drive engines of cargo ships to make the trip. He didn't rule out the possibility, though.

"Put an alert out for all these ships, but no one is to conduct their own interrogation until they speak with me first."

Nezumi bowed to the appropriate degree. "Yes, Sire." He cleared his throat. "If I may inquire about the other side of our investigation?"

Mizuki gritted his teeth. The muscle by his right eye spasmed. Colonel Jeruko had checked all outgoing transmissions and reported he'd found nothing suspicious. If true, no one aboard the *Dragon* had told Fujishin about the emitter. But could he trust Jeruko?

In times past, Mizuki had trusted him with more than just his life. Jeruko had witnessed the many beatings and humiliations Mizuki suffered from his drunkard father, and he never revealed it to anyone.

Of all the Five Talons, Mizuki once appreciated Jin Jeruko the most.

"I crosschecked a sample of his report, and they match up," Mizuki replied. "I also checked his personal transmissions."

"Begging your pardon, Sire, but there are two people who left this ship recently who might have leaked the information about the emitter."

Washi and Michio—Jeruko's sons and Jori's personal guards.

Something tickled the back of Mizuki's neck. He turned sharply, but no one was there. He resisted the urge to massage the throbbing of his skull. *It's not real. Jori's gone.*

After the boy's betrayal, Mizuki had nearly killed Washi and Michio for not watching him closely enough. Jeruko pleaded for mercy. If not for their lifelong friendship, Mizuki would've denied it. He exiled them instead.

Perhaps he shouldn't have been so lenient. Emotion was a weakness and Mizuki couldn't afford to be weak—not even for the sake of his friends. After all, Fujishin had been his friend the same number of years as Jeruko.

Jeruko had a different personality, though. All the sons of Lord Maru Jeruko strictly adhered to a code of conduct that surpassed most other men. They maintained flawless self-control, were loyal to a fault, consistently exhibited respect, and possessed an integrity worthy of a Shanliang monk.

Mizuki rubbed his chin. One thing he always counted on was Jin Jeruko's refusal to lie.

He tapped the comm placed behind his ear. "Colonel Jeruko, report to the war room."

General Nezumi cleared his throat. "Excuse me, Sire, but will asking him be enough?"

Mizuki shot him a glare. "Careful, General. I've known Jeruko a hell of a lot longer than I've known you."

Nezumi's mouth twisted, but he bowed with respect. "Of course, Sire."

At least I hope I still know Jeruko.

27

6
Exile

3791:054:12:48. Jin Jeruko's mouth fell open. He snapped it shut and replaced his shock with a mask of assurance. "I doubt Washi and Michio would dare contact Fujishin. They are aware of the thin ice they're walking on and wouldn't jeopardize their safety—nor mine, for that matter."

The emperor's eyes subdued but the muscle tic by his temple remained. Not a good sign. A volatile temper lurked beneath the man's tremendous stress.

What happened to the self-assured youth I used to revere?

The great Mizuki dragon in the picture behind the desk seemed to bear down on the emperor rather than champion him. Jeruko's heart ached for him at the same time his gut stirred with worry.

He struggled to maintain a calm stance. If Emperor Mizuki could kill his own sons, anyone could be next. Thank goodness he hadn't executed Washi and Michio as well. His mercy had been a close call. If only Jeruko had intervened before the emperor killed Jori.

"You doubt it, but you don't know for certain?" Emperor Mizuki replied.

"It's true, Sire. I'm not certain. But I'm sure my sons' loyalty to the Mizuki line is much greater than their regard for Fujishin."

General Nezumi stepped forward with a pinched expression. "You told me once that they looked to Fujishin as their uncle."

Jeruko bowed. "True, General. However, Fujishin's betrayal shocked them. It shocked us all. And we renewed our oath to the Empire and disavowed the traitor."

"My son disavowed him as well, yet he still betrayed me," the emperor snapped. "And right under Washi and Michio's noses, no less. Either that or they helped Jori betray me."

Jeruko's heart skipped a beat. His sons weren't the only ones who had participated in the betrayal. He was also culpable. The decision hadn't come easy. Loyalty was his conviction, a quality he'd inherited from his ancestors who had served the Mizuki house from the beginning. However, Jeruko's regard for Jori, a Mizuki prince, was stronger—and the boy's quest for honor had been greater.

Since the emperor didn't ask him outright, Jeruko found a truthful reply. "Jori liked Fujishin well enough once, but he had no reason to collude with him."

Nezumi harrumphed. "He had no reason to collude with the Cooperative either."

"One of those Cooperative officers saved his life," Jeruko said. "He probably felt obligated to save him in return."

The emperor's face darkened. "Emotion is a weakness, and he gets it from you."

Jeruko hung his head. "You're right, Sire. I *have* failed him." *I should've protected him from you.*

The truth of these words wrenched his gut. The horror of that incident haunted him, and he couldn't help but look back on it. Jeruko had questioned the emperor's actions against his youngest son and received an unhinged reply in return. There'd been no room for reasoning, so Jeruko had knelt before him with his eyes downcast.

"He's dead because he helped the Cooperative prisoners escape," Emperor Kenji Mizuki had said on that dreadful day. "He betrayed me!"

Jeruko kept his head down to hide his grief as well as his shame.

"Does that surprise you?" the emperor asked.

Jeruko swallowed the lump in his throat. Lying would not change anything. "No, Your Eminence," he said in a low tone.

Emperor Mizuki rushed forward and kicked him in the jaw. "Explain yourself!" He balled his hands into fists.

Jeruko's muscles quivered as he pushed himself back to the kneeling position. Alarms resounded through his body at the extent of the emperor's madness. He stole a glance at his sons. Washi and Michio remained stiff as they awaited their turn for questioning.

Jeruko bowed lower than usual. "I have seen evidence of the boy's sentiment," he said carefully.

"And you didn't report it?" the emperor roared.

Washi and Michio cast worried looks his way.

"The boy has always been softhearted, your Eminence." Again, Jeruko spoke without hiding behind the cowardice of lies. "I thought I had done my duty as his mentor to talk sense into him. You know how stubborn he could be."

The emperor seemed to accept his half-truth, though fury still stained his features. "Did you see anything that told you he would betray me?"

"No, Your Eminence," he said truthfully. He'd spoken to Jori about his plans, but he never actually *saw* anything.

Emperor Mizuki's expression hardened. "You've failed me, Colonel. You failed me through my sons."

Jeruko bobbed his head. "My most sincere apologies, your Eminence. I never meant for this to happen. I've always had the best interest of the Mizuki empire in mind."

He would have felt a sense of pride for speaking the truth without revealing it, but this wasn't the end. A punishment crackled within the stormy emperor, just waiting for the moment to strike.

He deserved whatever came. Nothing could atone for what he'd done or alleviate the remorse that plagued him. Although he believed that supporting Jori was best for the empire, he didn't mean for things to turn out this way.

"You've always been loyal, Jeruko," the emperor replied in a surprisingly soft tone. "All these years of service, your loyalty has been unwavering."

Jeruko stiffened in hope but didn't respond.

"But," the emperor said and Jeruko waited for the lightning to strike, "I must do something about this gross negligence. My son somehow fooled you and the other guards. He helped our enemies escape and you, the one person who sees him every single day, claim to have known nothing about his intentions. He defied me under my very nose. No. Under your nose. On your watch."

Jeruko held his breath. He wanted to say he understood but couldn't form he words.

"You will all be scourged. Even you, my friend," Emperor Mizuki said with a tinge of warmth. "And the guards who'd been stunned by the enemy during their escape will..."

The emperor's hesitation inspired Jeruko to speak up. "They are loyal, your Eminence. And they've always served you well. Please don't let this one incident, bad as it may be, undo all the good they have done."

The emperor frowned, though it seemed to be more in thought than in anger. "I can't allow this to go unpunished, Jin," he said, the use of Jeruko's given name conveying how close they'd once been. "I would execute anyone else for this."

Jeruko looked up with pleading eyes. "Exile them," he said. "Send them away on some distant mission where they'll prove their loyalty in the face of this oversight."

Emperor Mizuki drummed his fingers on his thigh. Silence endured until his chest heaved with a sigh. "A scourging. Then exile."

Jeruko blew out the breath he'd been holding and bowed in thanks. It had never occurred to him that the emperor would blame Washi and Michio for the Cooperative escaping. He should have known better. The exile of his sons and Jori's death fell on his shoulders. At least Washi and Michio got to live. Jori was gone forever.

Emperor Mizuki grunted, banishing Jeruko's memory and bringing him back to the present. General Nezumi wore a haughty expression, undoubtedly enjoying the scrutiny the emperor put Jeruko under.

"Don't make the same mistake with Terkeshi," the emperor said regarding Jeruko's failure with Jori.

"I won't, Sire," Jeruko replied in a quieter tone. It crushed his heart when Jori had died. It squashed further with the exile of his sons. Now it crumbled to dust with the way the emperor forced so much responsibility onto Terkeshi.

Not for the first time, Jeruko considered how much better off everyone would be if someone assassinated the emperor. He wouldn't do it himself, though. Such an act would bring the ultimate dishonor to his entire family. Perhaps for Terkeshi's sake?

Although Terkeshi had conceded the honor in helping Jori save the enemy, Jori's resulting death wounded him so deeply that he no longer saw it. Much of the young man's hurt came out as destructive energy, threatening to send him down the same temperamental path of his father. Jeruko must do something to steer him away from it.

"Back to the matter at hand," the emperor said. "Contact your sons. Ask them if they've spoken to anyone about the emitter. I want the conversation recorded."

Jeruko bowed. "Yes, Sire."

Nezumi's mouth twisted. "Perhaps we should have them return to us and interrogate them ourselves."

Jeruko clenched his fists behind his back. He'd never liked Nezumi. The man didn't have an ounce of honor. He didn't seek the truth for the emperor's sake. He did it for himself and fed Jeruko to the blackbeasts in the process.

"If that is what you wish, Sire," Jeruko said.

Emperor Mizuki hesitated. "No," he finally replied.

Nezumi's upper lip twitched. Jeruko slowly exhaled and vowed to watch his back around the rat-faced general.

"Contact them and record it." The emperor flicked his hand. "Dismissed."

"Yes, Sire."

Jeruko left. A weight lifted from his shoulders. Washi and Michio wouldn't be foolish enough to let anything slip, and he'd maintained his honor by speaking truthfully, implicating no one.

7
The Cyborgs

3791:065:18:05. A colossal spaceship dominated the bridge's front viewscreen. Kenji Mizuki leaned back in the central chair. He tried to appear composed, but his body remained rigid. Although he'd invited the cyborgs, their bizarre ship with its unfamiliar tech set his teeth on edge.

The pockmarks of the sensor arrays on the vessel's insectile head resembled mites. Thrusters attached to the midsection jutted out like wings, while the ship's abdomen comprised a stunted arc drive. How had the cyborgs traveled here so quickly with such a small engine? And where was the gravity wheel?

"I don't suppose they'd share their spaceflight tech," Nezumi said from the chair on Mizuki's left.

Jeruko, to his right, shifted in his seat. "Perhaps, but at what cost?"

"You worry over nothing," Nezumi replied. "An alliance is reasonable."

"Not if they plan on going against the entire galaxy."

Nezumi harrumphed. "We're warriors. It's our destiny."

"They won't give their tech away for free," Mizuki said. "We can't rely on them too much or we'll find ourselves subjected to their rule."

Nezumi shrugged. "I didn't get the impression that they want to rule us, Sire. They merely wish to spread their ideology."

Jeruko's eyes widened. "You mean their desire for everybody to become machines?"

A sour taste rose from Mizuki's throat. The cyborgs were like religious fanatics, spouting their evolutionary beliefs with zeal— and sometimes force. Although they were as human as everyone else in the known galaxy, they considered themselves superior, if not godlike.

Nezumi's mouth curled. "Would that really be so bad? Imagine no mech suits, just sheer power."

Mizuki's insides recoiled at the thought of his brain and body being augmented with computer chips, metal, and wires. "I'd rather defeat my enemies as a man than a machine."

"And you can, Sire." Nezumi's eyes widened as he bobbed his head. "These people offer so much more than mechanical augmentation. Imagine how germline engineering may improve the prince's skills."

"There's great honor in being legally bred," Jeruko replied with an edge in his tone. "The nobility might question the legitimacy of the Mizuki supremacy when we align with these cyborgs."

Nezumi grunted. "They don't have a say. *He* is the emperor. *He* makes the laws. Let them cry and whine all they want. In the end, our emperor reigns supreme."

Jeruko's brows furrowed while Nezumi's words resonated in Mizuki's skull. What would it be like to rule unchallenged? He could regain the glory of his grandfather and more—powerful lords like Enomoto be damned.

"Caution remains necessary," Mizuki replied. "It's important we get what we want without being indebted."

Nezumi bowed. "Of course, Sire. I'm sure it wouldn't cost too much for germline engineering. If not for the prince, then for yourself. If they can repair the damage done to your genes, you could sire more sons."

Mizuki tapped his chin. The prospect of having an heir worthy of being the next Dragon Emperor had its appeal.

Major Niashi turned from the operations console. "They're in position, your Eminence."

Mizuki acknowledged with a sharp nod. "Connect the skywalk." He rose and faced his advisors with a commanding mien. "Notify me when the hard point connection is complete, then meet me at the platform. Bring my son."

After the men dipped their heads at the appropriate angle, he promptly retired to his office. His son's report left a lot to be desired, which meant it was up to him to figure out how to fix the *Fire Breather* without overly depending on the cyborgs.

Why couldn't it have been Terkeshi to betray me instead of Jori? It still would have been a betrayal, but not as much of a loss.

*****

3791:065:20:49. The floor tremored slightly as the skywalk tube attached. A short hiss followed as the pressure equalized.

Kenji Mizuki waited. While his insides teemed, he projected a forbearing stance with his feet planted at shoulder width and his hands clutched behind his back. Terkeshi, Nezumi, and Jeruko matched his posture with the same stoicism.

"Sire?" Nezumi said. "Are you certain we can trust them not to smuggle spy tech aboard? Should we scan them?"

Mizuki gritted his teeth. If it had been Terkeshi questioning his decision, he would have backhanded him. "We've discussed this already." *To the point where we talked in circles.* The cyborgs' biometrics would set off the scanners, making it difficult to distinguish them from spy tech. And it wasn't like he'd allow his guests to traipse about his ship unescorted.

Nezumi tended to reignite topics that didn't go his way, but at least his disagreement was obvious. Mizuki glanced at Jeruko's relentless, unreadable expression and narrowed his eyes.

After several minutes, the skywalk hatch opened. A pair of cyborgs emerged. One had once given his sons temporary nanites. It was hard to forget his large mechanical eye, harder still to ignore his skin's plastic-like veneer.

Ambrose dipped his head. "Emperor Mizuki," he said in with an unsettling monotone voice. "It is an honorable pleasure to see you again."

Mizuki replied with a perfunctory nod.

"This is my assistant, Brian." Ambrose waved his hand at the chubby, balding man beside him. "He's an aerospace engineer."

Although this skill set was exactly what Mizuki needed, he gave the man an even lesser acknowledgement. This cyborg wasn't as ugly as Ambrose, but the tilt of his nose and the bored look on his face indicated equal arrogance.

Mizuki reintroduced Terkeshi and his advisors, then led them on a wordless trek to the auxiliary docking bay.

The bay door slid open to reveal a span of five lofty docking platforms. The lifeless carcass of the perantium emitter spread in pieces throughout its breadth. Four shokukin worked with desolate slowness, but otherwise the place was as still as a deprivation chamber.

Mizuki stepped inside and took a humorless stance. "This device has been more trouble than it's worth. We've been unable to finish it."

Ambrose's brow folded up and he nodded mechanically. "You want us to fix it."

"And help set it up on the *Fire Breather*."

"I see."

"You should know that the ship incurred damage from our enemies. They may return, but it's nothing we can't handle," Mizuki said with more confidence than he felt.

"Hmm."

Mizuki waited for the man to say more, but the drawn-out silence spurred his impatience. "I'm ready to discuss terms."

Ambrose turned to him with a flat smile. "Certainly. Our price remains the same—an alliance."

"It depends on what this *alliance* entails."

"Approximately one standard year from now, we require six warships and a hundred thousand ground troops to assist with our endeavor to impress enlightenment. We will need this assistance for five years with an option to renew."

"That's too much," Mizuki barked. "It won't cost you even a hundredth of that amount to fix the emitter."

"Monetary compensation shall be provided. All we ask now is your commitment."

Mizuki quelled his uneasiness. It was a lot to give, especially since support and transport ships would also be necessary. However, he could spare these assets if the device worked. Besides, breaking the alliance remained an option. "You will convert the perantium emitter into a weapon and teach us to maintain it. It will be for my personal use only."

Ambrose bowed. "Agreed."

"And you'll repair our warships if they're damaged in battle."

Ambrose inclined his head again.

Jeruko cleared his throat. Mizuki nodded curtly and the man faced the cyborg with a staid bearing. "Will you require our senshi to receive enhancements?"

"No. Our leader understands your reluctance to go against your injunction. He hopes that our ways eventually influence you."

"And who is your leader?" Mizuki asked.

"Why MEGA-Man, of course."

Mizuki's spine tingled. "Who?"

Ambrose smiled again. "MEGA, as in mechanically enhanced and genetically altered."

"Doesn't he have a real name?"

"He has evolved beyond the need for a simple human moniker. You people seem to like the MEGA acronym with your MEGA Injunction and MEGA hunters, so you can simply call him MEGA-Man. He is the ultimate being in the galaxy, after all." Ambrose's veneer complexion brightened.

Chills spread over Mizuki's back and arms. "If he's so remarkable, why do you need us?"

"We have the technology but don't yet have the soldiers." Ambrose held his stupid smile. If he thought it made him look friendly, he was mistaken.

"Aligning myself with you goes against everything the Toradons stand for," Mizuki replied. "Our leaders are bred. Our abilities are natural. Our alliance may cause an uprising."

Ambrose's brows rose with the precision of a machine. "Ah, but you will have a powerful weapon to subdue them."

Mizuki agreed, but it would be easier if he didn't have to put down a rebellion at all.

"Father," Terkeshi whispered. "They feel off."

"This is no trick," Ambrose said, likely having heard the boy with his cybernetic hearing. "We want you as an ally. That is all. It would be an arrangement beneficial to us both. We obtain the aid of the most feared soldiers in the galaxy, and you get a powerful weapon."

"Did he speak the truth?" Mizuki asked, taking advantage of the boy's unique sensing ability.

Terkeshi hesitated. "I think so, Sir."

Useless boy. Mizuki huffed and faced the cyborgs. "How soon can you fix it?"

"We will assess the device and let you know."

"It must be done quickly. Our enemies are mounting."

"Of course. We ask for a small recompense in advance to ensure our alliance."

Chusho. "What do you want?" Mizuki asked.

"Five thousand crates of titanium ore from your Kyunayama mines."

The hairs on the back of Mizuki's neck rose. *Just how many cybernetic freaks do they plan on making?* "That's hardly small."

"Your emitter gets fixed. We get the ore. And we will repay you with some other commodity when we're ready for the terms of our alliance to be fulfilled."

"What sort of commodity?"

"Tech perhaps."

Mizuki liked that part, but not the hit to his bank accounts. He inhaled deeply. The terms were enticing, but the risk was still great. He looked to his advisors, inviting their input.

Terkeshi's brows tilted inward. "Our men will die for *their* cause."

"He's right, Sire," Jeruko added. "We'll be relegated to mercenaries."

Mizuki's upper lip curled. Why did Jeruko keep taking the boy's side? Were they up to something?

"I am authorized to offer an incentive," Ambrose cut in. "I can provide enhancements to five of your soldiers."

Mizuki frowned. "How is that an incentive?"

"Your concern is that we will become so powerful, you cannot stand against us."

Mizuki suppressed a shiver. Had the cyborg read his mind? Could cybernetics do that?

"However," Ambrose continued, "that won't be true if you remain the dominant force in the galaxy with your super-soldiers. Let us do this for you so you can see how much the MEGA Injunction is holding you back."

"And what is the price for *this* incentive?"

"Nothing," Ambrose said. "It is our hope that you will request more enhanced soldiers in the future."

"How do I know you won't use them against me?"

"They will remain your soldiers, your Eminence. We shall, of course, provide full disclosure on the enhancements and how they work to ease your fears."

My fears? Mizuki's gut soured. He wasn't afraid. His prudence merely made him reluctant. But so long as these machine men remained upfront, it would be interesting to see the results.

Jeruko's throat bobbed. "Your Eminence, using cybernetic soldiers may bring dishonor."

Mizuki narrowed his eyes at the man's audacity. He opened his mouth to counter the accusation, but Nezumi beat him to it. "You speak too harshly. There's no dishonor in testing this on five senshi."

Jeruko shook his head. "If the lords get word of it too soon, more will side with Fuji—with that traitor."

"And who would tell them, I wonder?" Nezumi replied.

Jeruko's placid composure slipped into a stormy expression. Mizuki studied him, hoping innocence had sparked his indignation.

Despite the niggling doubts, Mizuki embraced the offer. The prospect of seeing what an already deadly senshi could do with implanted tech intrigued him. "I see no harm in this experiment."

Jeruko bowed lower than usual. "Your eminence, there is an ancient saying. Beware of strangers bearing gifts."

Mizuki ground his teeth. "My enemies grow by the day. I must stop them."

"Yes, Sire. Perhaps forego enhancing our people, for now. We can always reconsider later."

Mizuki weighed the pros and cons. The only potential obstacle was the combined protests of the lords. With the emitter fixed, they wouldn't matter. Plus, getting a preview of cybernetic abilities would prepare him for a future with the cyborgs.

"We will accept this gift," Mizuki finally said.

If Jeruko was disappointed, he hid it well.

Ambrose turned a fake smile to Terkeshi. "If this works out, perhaps your son can be—"

"No," Mizuki snapped. "Not my son. I can get away with enhancing a few warriors, but not my blood." Despite his threat to the boy, he wouldn't give the lords an excuse to turn against him. Terkeshi might not be as good as Jori, but he still had potential.

Terkeshi exhaled noisily. Mizuki gritted his teeth at the boy's unprofessionalism.

"As you wish," Ambrose said with a bow. "Five soldiers, and your emitter in exchange for a formal alliance."

Mizuki gave it a little more thought. He didn't like being in debt, especially not to a potentially powerful race, but they could still be powerful without him. Perhaps he should align with these people before they joined forces with Fujishin or another of his rivals.

"Allies, then," he said, "but my army remains under my ultimate command, even while you use them for your purposes."

Jeruko paled. Nezumi jutted his chin. Terkeshi's shoulders fell, but he quickly pulled them back when he noticed Mizuki eyeing him.

Ambrose bowed. "Of course. We wouldn't want it any other way. My people shall draw up a contract."

Mizuki almost smirked at the idea of a contract. Keeping one's word was a point of honor. But if this deal with the cyborgs didn't work to his advantage, he'd break it in a heartbeat. Nothing would stop him from being the greatest Dragon Emperor in Toradon history.

8
Diminishing Faith

3791:066:04:08. Clack. Clack. Jin Jeruko's bō clashed with the young prince's weapon.

They stepped back and circled one another in the center of Jeruko's private dojo. He looked for a weak point, but Terkeshi's guard remained strong, as did his stance. The youth's dark eyes sparked, and his brow furrowed with intensity.

He's a good warrior. Not great, but better than most.

Terkeshi swung his staff from the left.

Jeruko deflected it easily. "You're telegraphing. Step at the same time you strike, not before."

"I can't hit you if I don't step forward first," Terkeshi replied irritably.

"You can. Just aim in such a way that you can adjust as you move."

Terkeshi growled and attacked again.

Jeruko parried. "Good. If you do that several times in quick succession, then you'll have me."

Terkeshi struck repeatedly, but with too much lag.

"Faster," Jeruko said. "Mushin—no mind. Don't hesitate. Just do it."

Terkeshi's face reddened. The youth had been too sensitive to criticism lately. He'd always had a hot temperament, but it worsened after Jori's death.

"Keep your anger in check, boy. Mushin applies to both your actions and your emotions."

Jeruko doubted his words had any influence. Terkeshi's expression tightened as he advanced. He swung, snapped, thrusted, and feinted with his bō, not once landing a blow. As his temper flared, his moves turned desperate and careless.

An opening came for Jeruko to lay Terkeshi on his back, but he didn't take it. Humiliating the youth wouldn't make him better and would only feed his darkening emotions.

Jeruko sighed with an inward sadness. Although younger, Jori had been Terkeshi's anchor. He'd been the one thing that kept the elder prince from going down their father's dark path. With him gone, Terkeshi was lost to the storm.

Jeruko stepped back and planted the butt of his staff on the floor with a clap. "That's enough for now. We'll resume later."

"Getting winded already, old man?"

Jeruko didn't take the surliness personally. "I may be old, but I can still compete against the best of them, young one."

"Liar. I know your leg is bothering you."

Jeruko resisted the desire to stretch out the ache in his knee left over from a terrible injury that not even the most sophisticated healing nanites could fix. "Not a lie. I *can* hold my own."

"Perhaps you could ask Father if he will let *you* get the enhancements," Terkeshi added.

Jeruko soured. "I am a *true* warrior. I don't need any artificial abilities."

Terkeshi grunted as he plunked his staff in onto the rack.

Jeruko frowned at the mistreatment of his equipment but didn't comment on it. "I take it you don't like the idea either."

"No." Terkeshi crossed his arms and looked away with a scowl. "Those cyborgs are up to something, but Father won't believe me. He doesn't trust me with anything. He treats me like a child yet expects me to do everything as well as an adult."

Jeruko agreed but still found it hard to speak against his old friend. "He's under a lot of stress lately."

Terkeshi huffed. "That's his own fault. He shouldn't take it out on me."

Jeruko put his hand on the youth's shoulder. "I understand, Terke-chan. Don't let his criticisms get to you. You do exceptionally well at your martial skills, better than I was at your age."

Terkeshi's mouth tilted into a dubious expression.

"It's true," Jeruko continued. "Better than even Dokuri had been."

Terkeshi lowered his head. "But not as good as Jori," he mumbled.

Jeruko's heart wrenched. He wanted to offer comfort, but the words caught in his throat. He turned away to hide the wetness filling his eyes. "You should return to your duties. Come back in a few hours for another session."

Terkeshi stomped off. Jeruko reined in the hardest of his emotions, but a deep ache remained. He faced his dojo's central mantle and stepped into commencing form.

The flowing movements of his body as he practiced the tai chi forms usually calmed him. Not this time. Troubled thoughts plagued him.

The emperor's temper had deteriorated since Dokuri died in battle. Montaro, his next son, had matched his older brother's level of cruelty, but nothing close to his martial prowess—and his intellect left much to be desired.

Jeruko's gut tightened. Montaro's murder had shocked him, but Jori's devastated him. He loved that boy as much as his own sons. He'd loved the emperor once, too. No more. He could no longer revere a man who murdered his own children.

He stepped back after performing the Repulse Monkey and staggered. With a sigh rather than a deep relaxing breath, he continued. He should be practicing no-mind, but he couldn't help reflecting on the good person the emperor used to be.

Jeruko was nineteen when he'd entered the Senshi Dragon Academy. He'd kept up with the intense training but made a dangerous enemy of a big man named Buru.

After weeks of tolerating Buru's bullying, Jeruko finally faced him in the practice ring. With measured sidesteps, he remained focused on Buru's bared teeth and clawed hands.

"I'm gonna turn your insides out, little man." Buru's eyes blazed.

Jeruko didn't bother engaging in useless banter. Buru lunged, foolishly telegraphing his moves. Jeruko easily deflected two punches and a crescent kick. Buru followed with more attempts only to have them all foiled by Jeruko's swiftness and dexterity.

"Fight me, coward!" Buru bellowed.

Jeruko reacted defensively, biding his time while Buru wasted his energy on his anger. The large man's actions grew more aggressive, but also sloppier. When he swung wide, Jeruko ducked and jabbed the man in the kidney. He followed with another punch to the gut and a hook to Buru's temple.

Buru's head snapped sideways. Spittle flew from his mouth, and he fell with a thud. A thunder of whoops and hollers broke out from the onlookers, many who had also fallen prey to Buru's bullying.

Buru recovered quickly and charged. Jeruko expected such a childish move. He dodged and smacked the big man in the back of the head. The erupting laughter that followed sent Buru into a blinding rage. Jeruko ignored the numbing pain that spread over his forearms from blocking all the man's strikes.

The big man shot out a side kick. Jeruko grabbed his leg and wrenched it. Buru tumbled with a yell, then jumped to his feet with a roar.

"Enough!" The drill sergeant stepped between them and glared at Buru. "Face it, soldier. You lost."

Buru turned purple as the cords of his neck strained. "This isn't over, little man," he said to Jeruko with a jab of his finger.

He hadn't lied. Jeruko ran into him and his friends in town a few days later.

Buru cracked his knuckles. "I told you it wasn't over."

Jeruko should have tried to break away, but the foolishness of his youth didn't allow him. He stepped into a defensive stance and braced himself.

The three men attacked at once. Jeruko did well at first, but soon lost his ground. One man caught him by the crook of his arm and twisted it behind his back. Kicks and punches hailed down on him. He strived to regain his wits but succumbed to the onslaught.

"Leave off, cowards!" a voice hollered.

Jeruko shook off his disorientation and identified his rescuer. Prince Kenji Mizuki jumped into the fight with a fury that matched Buru's, except faster and harder. With combined skills, Jeruko and the prince expeditiously overwhelmed the three bullies and stood victorious.

Jeruko had swelled with elation. The Mizuki heir fought for the fourth son of a lowly lord. No soldier could ask for a better leader.

Jeruko returned to the present with a deep sigh. Back then, his loyalty had been unyielding. As the years wore on, he found his faith diminishing and his doubts multiplying. Jori's death had dealt a detrimental blow, leaving him with an expanding emptiness and the heavy burden of a wasted existence.

He sank to the floor, his knees hitting the wood of his dojo as he choked out a cry.

If Terkeshi lost his way, Jeruko would too. Without the elder prince, his life of service would mean nothing.

After some time wallowing in his misery, he sucked in a breath and hardened his resolve. He must stay strong—not for the emperor, but for Terkeshi. The young man needed him. And if he was honest with himself, he needed the youth just as much.

9
Lifeless

3791:067:13:44. Terkeshi bolted upright with a gasp. His heart hammered as he labored to make sense of his surroundings.

The light of his small, neat room brightened. His fleecy blanket laid crumpled at his feet. The sight of his desk against the wall with everything in its proper place tempered the pang of his awakening jolt. The whispering whir of a cleaning bot disinfecting the bathroom eased the resounding chaos in his skull.

His breath reduced to a deep pant as his dream flittered away, leaving a ghostly feeling.

Not all of it had been a dream. The memory of Jori's murder infiltrated his sleep nearly every night. Even though he hadn't witnessed it with his eyes, he'd sensed it. The pain of death was like no other sensation. The more familiar the lifeforce of the dying person, the more it crippled and blinded him.

His nightmares filled in the gaps of the parts he hadn't witnessed. His father's maddening fury as he caught Jori helping the prisoners was easy to recreate. So was Jori's brave trepidation. His fearlessness in the face of danger had been one of his many admirable traits, though sometimes courageously foolish.

Terk pictured him standing up to Father with his teeth bared. He imagined him fighting to defend himself. Although Jori was highly skilled, even better than Terk, he was a child. He never had a chance against Father's fury.

Remembering Jori's lifeless body and his father's knife sticking into his heart made Terk wince. That blade practically pierced his own heart. His brother's lifeforce had been snuffed out, just like that. Gone forever.

Terk clenched his blanket and struggled to hold the shock wave of his emotions at bay. A sob escaped his chest. Tears forced their way out of his eyes.

He punched his leg, hoping to distract himself with a more bearable type of pain. It didn't work. He pummeled harder and faster, screaming as he did so.

With a roar, he discharged the expansiveness of his sorrow.

He heaved through clenched teeth. His sadness abated as an internal heat took over. This had been Jori's own fault. He was too weak. He'd allowed his sentiment to override his reason when he helped those prisoners. If only he'd listened to Terk and Sensei Jeruko when they said to let them die. So what if one saved Terk's life when they'd found themselves on a Cooperative vessel? That only made them fools, and everyone knew fools didn't deserve to live. Jori had owed them nothing.

Terk threw off his blankets and stood. Another bot exited its cubby hole. *Chusho.* That meant it was still the middle of his sleep cycle. He wasn't tired, though.

The compact floor cleaner edged along the wall, picking up any debris that might have fallen there since the night before. Its cylindrical shape reminded Terk of a cyborg's head. The thought of all its electronic innards made him grimace. He booted it back. "Cancel."

After the cleaning bot returned to its compartment, Terk placed his music player behind his ear. With a tap, a hard leaden song drowned out his thoughts. He dressed in single-minded determination. As the last Mizuki heir, it was up to him now to be the best warrior possible. It would take a lot of practice, but one way or the other he would surpass Jori. And he would succeed not just because he'd be a better fighter, but because he didn't have his brother's foolish sentiment.

Terk exited his room. Tokagei, his least favorite personal guard, jerked up from a slouch. His larger bottom lip stuck out and he made a sucking noise. "You're up early, my Lord. What's the occasion?"

Terk marched past him, down the corridor. "Your job is to keep guard, not talk. If I want you to know my business, I'll tell you."

If Tokagei had taken offense, he kept it to himself as he trailed behind.

Terk missed Washi and Michio. They never questioned him, whispered about him to others, or told Father whenever he made a mistake. Tokagei, the snitch, couldn't be trusted with much of anything, probably not even his life.

A sourness filled Terk's mouth. Ever since Jori's betrayal and Washi and Michio's exile, his remaining personal guards stuck their noses into everything he did. His only respite was when he trained with Sensei Jeruko. Even then, surveillance cameras kept watch.

Terk came upon the entrance to the auxiliary bay and hesitated. The distinct muted essences of the cyborgs churned his stomach. How did implanting a few electronics dampen their lifeforce? Did it make them only half alive?

He turned off his player, then gritted his teeth and entered. The scene halted him in his tracks. More than the few cyborgs he'd sensed swarmed around the emitter. His jaw fell as he tried to focus on individuals and found many had no sensations—not even the basic essence found in animals.

Terk gulped as the sense of their lifelessness reminded him of his dead brother.

Tokagei cocked his head. "What is it, my Lord? Are they up to something?"

Goosebumps prickled Terk's arms as he noted the silent laborers. One who might have been a woman took measured steps, halted, turned ninety degrees, then advanced to her destination. "Most aren't even human. They're pure machines."

"They look human to me."

Terk frowned. No wonder Father and the others seemed alright with enhancing a few senshi. They didn't feel what he felt.

"You better hope so," Terkeshi replied. "You'll become one soon." Thank goodness Father had selected Tokagei and not him.

Tokagei shrugged. Terk curled his lip. *Fool.*

Only two shokukin assisted the cyborgs. Benjiro knelt over a conduit, his tongue sticking out as he worked. Terk frowned, still not believing this idiot was his uncle. Most rulers, Terk's father included, got rid of incompetent sons. But for whatever reason, Lord Enomoto's father had allowed Benjiro to live.

Terk held back a shiver and walked over to the other shokukin.

Malkai halted his work and bowed deeply. "How my I serve, my Lord?"

"How are things going here?"

Malkai lowered his head, making his shoulders hunch. "I-I think it's going well, my Lord." His eyes darted to the cyborgs working on the emitter.

"What do you think about our guests?"

Malkai hesitated. "They certainly seem to know what they're doing, but..."

"It's alright. Speak your mind."

"They're strange."

"They're MEGAs, mechanically enhanced and genetically altered."

Malkai shifted his feet. "I thought that was illegal."

"It is, and it isn't."

Malkai tilted his head.

"Do you know what the MEGA Injunction is?" Terk asked him.

"It's the law against being enhanced."

"It's more of a guideline that worlds can choose to adopt. Most have, but not all. And it doesn't outlaw enhancements. In general, it prohibits people with enhancements from being in the military or holding positions of power."

"So these cyborgs are from somewhere that hasn't adopted the MEGA Injunction?"

"Yes." Terk didn't know where that was, though. Rumor had it that it was beyond the Parvati star system.

Malkai shuddered. "That means they can do whatever they want to themselves."

The hairs on the back of Terk's neck rose. "Even change into machines."

Malkai's throat bobbed and Terk kept his from doing the same. The longer he watched the cyborgs at work, the more disturbingly rote their actions appeared, and the more his stomach roiled.

The lead cyborg Ambrose paused, then faced him with a detached smile.

A shiver ran down Terk's spine. He left before the churning of his gut hurled something up.

10
Difficult Conversations

3971:095:05:13. Terkeshi stared blankly at the screen of his tablet. Checkmark after checkmark indicated work done—work that would've taken his people weeks to complete.

This was pointless. With the cyborgs here, he was even more useless.

"Sir!"

Terk snapped his attention to the green-eyed man bustling toward him from across the hall. He squared his shoulders and waited.

"Sir," Malkai said, then caught his breath. "You must hurry."

"What is it now?"

"The senshi. They're harassing Benjiro."

Terk soured. "So."

"Sir, they'll put him out of commission for days, maybe weeks if we don't stop this."

Bullies. The stupid senshi were always harassing the workers. Benjiro's idiocy made him an even bigger target, yet Terk couldn't bring himself to care. "Yeah, well, that's nothing new. Besides, we have other workers." He flicked his hand at the nearest cyborg.

"Sir! It's bad. They're really hurting him."

Terk heaved a sigh. "Alright." Even though his senses picked up on the distress, he followed Malkai down the hall.

Benjiro's terror intensified and busted through Terk's indifference. "Chusho!" He pushed passed Malkai and broke into a run. Shokukin darted out of his way. Two senshi did as well, but one giant man decided to be stubborn. Terk didn't stop. He lowered his shoulder and ran into him, jamming his elbow at the same time. "Move next time, chima!" he bellowed as he sped on.

Two turns later and he came upon an open supply closet. One senshi had Benjiro by the back of the neck and the other tweaked his nose, which already oozed blood. "Does this hurt?"

"Benjiro hurt!" the idiot blubbered.

Both men laughed.

"What the hell do you think you're doing?" Terk shouted in his deepest and most commanding tone.

The men turned his way but didn't stop. "Just having a little fun, my Lord."

A fire in Terk's gut exploded. How many times had he and Jori been beaten down by their older brothers all in the name of *fun*?

He couldn't defeat these men in a fight but he could humiliate them. That's what Jori would do. "What big tough men you are, picking on a helpless creature. I see how it is. Having *fun* with someone of your own skill is too tough for you. I've always suspected you two were weak, now you're proving it." He spit at their feet.

Both men reddened. One squared up to him. Terk held his glower. This man was nothing compared to his father, so it was easy.

The man emitted a low growl, then stepped back. "We got better things to do anyway."

"Damn right, you do. I suggest you get to it before I have you demoted to shokukin."

The man shouldered past. Luckily, Terk had expected it and turned aside in time to avoid most of the impact. The other man followed, not daring to meet Terk's eye.

As soon as they left, Terk relaxed. If these senshi had a higher rank, this wouldn't have worked. He turned to Malkai only to find him gone. *Of course.* Terk shook his head. If those men had suspected Malkai had snitched on them, they would've victimized him too.

Terk looked down at Benjiro, who had slumped onto the floor. His busted nose added a sickening squelch to his blubbering. *Pathetic.*

The disparaging thought turned Terk's stomach. It wasn't Benjiro's fault he was the way he was. The constant inbreeding of the nobility with their intent to perpetuate certain traits was bound to backfire once in a while. Besides, the man wasn't useless. And

51

some people had cared about him enough to let him grow into adulthood.

His heart ached at the thought of his mother. Too bad Father hadn't exiled Benjiro too. Then she wouldn't be so alone.

Then I wouldn't be so alone.

*****

3791:069:02:58. As instructed, Jin Jeruko returned to his personal quarters for the appointed meeting with his sons. He settled in the padded office chair and pulled a glass and bottle from his desk drawer. With the lid removed, a smooth, fruity tang wafted to his nostrils. He drew in the aroma before pouring two finger-widths of clear liquid.

The taste bit his tongue, but the lingering sensation spread out in warmth. He leaned back and savored the heat. He wished he could enjoy the upcoming conversation as well. Although it would take place in his own room, it would be far from private.

Jeruko turned his chair around and regarded the stone pagoda statue on his shelf. The surveillance camera dwelled in one of its windows and he shivered at the thought of the emperor's eyes lurking in the dark recess.

Hanging from the ceiling and down to either side of the pagoda were two shodo banners. Jeruko studied the black sweeping lines and curves of the calligraphic symbols. There'd been a time when contemplating them had instilled pride—in himself and in his family.

The old codes of honor thrived in the Jeruko house. His father and brothers never lied, exhibited amazing self-control, and were considered the most loyal family in Toradon.

Jeruko emulated them, appreciating how far he'd come in developing the same principles. But two codes stood out as falling short—justice and compassion. As his years of loyal service wore on, the importance of both had diminished. With the way the emperor was now, they might as well not exist at all.

Is there still honor in loyalty if the one you serve is a brutal tyrant?

Jeruko's composure sagged. Telling himself that the emperor's dishonorable acts were not his own was no longer enough. The lack of equity and compassion weighed on his soul. If only he could ask his father what to do. *Damned surveillance.*

He returned to his deskview screen with a sigh. No new messages, but it was only two minutes past the hour. He forced himself to stop bouncing his foot and waited.

Lord Qing ruled Hisui Island and had the only means to communicate beyond it. As overseer, he not only monitored the local populace, but also policed the inhabitants who'd been banished there. Arranging this meeting for two of his subjects had taken time, and now they were three minutes late.

Jeruko wiped the sweat from his upper lip. As much as he wanted to see Washi and Michio, he prayed they wouldn't say anything to incriminate themselves—or him. If only he'd had a way to warn them.

He pushed his worry aside. Washi and Michio weren't stupid. They undoubtedly knew this conversation would be monitored, even if it took place in Jeruko's quarters. Given the emperor's recent state of mind, though, treachery might be found in the most innocent words.

A new message popped up in the queue. He clicked it and forced himself to be still as the video screen flickered to life. Two young men with the same chevron mustache and patch under their bottom lip appeared. They both had their mother's smile and Jeruko's strong forehead and hairline. But where Washi had the round eyes and dimpled chin of his mother, Michio had the narrow eyes and diamond-shaped face of Jeruko.

"Father!" Michio said with a wide grin that made his cheekbones stick out. His expression lit up with boyish joy.

"Hello, Father." Washi smiled too, but with more reserve than his younger brother.

"Ah, my boys," Jeruko replied with a tone that laid in the middle of their extremes. "It's good to see you again. How are things there?"

"Peaceful," Washi said.

"In other words, boring." Michio rolled his eyes.

Washi gave his brother a side-eye smirk. "We're assigned to a small farming community just south of the city. The people are hardworking and pleasant. The most trouble we've encountered was a drunken tussle during their fall festival."

53

Jeruko nodded in approval. Hisui Island wasn't a terrible place. Lord Qing's estate sat in the center of the island's only city—if less than a hundred square kilometers could be called a city. Jeruko had visited there a few years back. The streets were as clean as the fresh oceanic air. Theft and violence rarely occurred, and the people had appeared happy.

That Washi and Michio were stationed on the outskirts made him feel even better about their situation. Though exiled, they still had a job to do—police the inhabitants and protect them from intruders. Human trespassers were rare. Bears and other predators showed up more frequently but quickly disappeared back into the wilderness when discovered.

"I'm having a difficult time imagining you on a farm," said Jeruko, trying to keep the amusement from his expression as he pictured his sons wrangling chickens.

Washi shrugged. "It's not so ba—"

"Ugh! The pigs." Michio threw his hands in the air. "They're horrible. I've never smelled something so awful in my life."

Jeruko chuckled.

Washi grunted a laugh, then wrinkled his nose. "He's right about that."

Jeruko beamed at his sons' buoyant moods. "Were you permitted to visit your mother?"

"Yes. She is doing well."

"And she's happy," Michio said. "She made us pie with fruit from her own garden."

Jeruko warmed. She always loved gardens. He remembered how rosy her cheeks would get whenever she went outdoors. "Send her my best."

"We will."

And send her my love, he wished he could add. "And Terkeshi's mother, she is adjusting?"

"Her and Mother get along fantastically," Michio replied.

"That's good news." He wanted to tell them he'd pass the word on to Terkeshi, but the emperor would probably see it as a perpetuation of sentiment.

The warmth fled from Jeruko's body as he switched to the unpleasant purpose of this communication. "Have you heard anything about Colonel Fujishin?"

"We don't hear much out here at all," Washi answered with a casual air. "Not even rumors. Lord Qing keeps us on a tight leash and has made sure no one discusses politics with us."

"I assume that means you are also not speaking about politics, or anything to do with the emperor's affairs?"

"We wouldn't dare!" Michio said.

"We know better, Father," Washi added. "Some lesser lords have hinted that they'd be willing to exchange information, but we've firmly expressed our loyalty."

The muscles in Jeruko's upper back knotted. Even a hint of such a discussion could get his boys in trouble. "The emperor will want the names of those lords."

"We've reported them to Lord Qing."

"Good."

"You don't need to worry, Father," Washi said. "We wouldn't do anything to soil our family name, and it's our desire to return to the *Dragon* someday."

All the tension in Jeruko's shoulders fled. His sons embraced the same value of honesty, which meant Jori's death and their resulting exile hadn't tempted them to side with the emperor's adversaries.

Michio leaned in. "Speaking of dragons, how is Prince Terkeshi holding up?"

Sadness surged, but Jeruko kept it from showing on his face. "He is grieving in his own way. Mostly by immersing himself into his training."

"Good lad. I know he has it in him," Michio said.

"How have you been, Father?" Washi asked.

Jeruko put on a fake smile. "I'm doing well."

*****

3791:069:05:31. A rising sense of horror darkened Jin Jeruko's vision as he peered through the plasti-glass. The specialized equipment spread throughout the surgically clean room held the same frigid quality as the cyborg medics. At first glance, it buzzed with disjointed activity. The more he studied it, the more the staff seemed to interweave among the robotics with the exactitude of gestalt intelligence.

Five senshi roused from varying stages of their medical alteration procedures. Yujio smiled as he flexed his new robotic fingers. Tokagei tested the realistic eye-like membrane that either concealed or revealed his mechanical eye. The other three senshi sat perfectly upright and motionless.

Jeruko cringed. *Don't they know they're losing their humanity?* It was one thing to use machines, but another entirely to become one.

Yujio's mouth broadened. He noted Jeruko standing there and raised his cybernetic thumb.

Jeruko frowned. Fine. If the emperor supported this, he must go along with it—but he didn't have to like it.

He studied Yujio's new arm. The metal contraption corded with wires and hydraulics. A bluish light illuminated from within, growing in brightness as though charging up.

Captain Wang's head jerked. The lid of his true eye fluttered simultaneously with the false membrane of his biometric one. His body tweaked oddly, then fell back into convulsions. Robots and cybernetic beings rushed in.

Jeruko left the plasti-glass window and charged into the room. "What's going on?"

Yujio and Tokagei glanced over with a dispassionate expression, then resumed playing with their new parts. The cyborg medics ignored him as they pushed the spastic senshi down to the bed. A robot pressed a hypospray to the man's neck, but nothing changed.

Jeruko grabbed the arm of the closest cyborg. "What the hell is happening?"

"Do not interfere," it replied in a mechanical voice. With an unexpectedly swift motion, it twisted its arm, breaking Jeruko's hold.

As it pivoted with brisk precision, Ambrose approached with a humorless smile. "His body is confused about the new implants. A little calibration will return him to normal."

Jeruko winced. *Whatever normal means.*

Wang stilled. Another robot maneuvered its mechanical arm until it hovered over the man's false eye. A long needle extended downward and plunged into the iris.

Jeruko shivered.

Ambrose put his hand on Jeruko's chest. "He will be alright, I assure you. Please step outside."

As Jeruko backed out, the other two senshi seemed to wake. They turned to him with a deadpan expression that matched the lifelessness of their eyes.

After Jeruko returned to the observation window, Terkeshi stepped beside him.

"My Prince. What do you think of this?"

"It doesn't matter what I think."

"It *does* matter," Jeruko replied, trying not to sound defensive. "Adding your approval may inspire others to ask for enhancements."

Terkeshi's jaw twitched. "You don't need to worry. This is a onetime thing. Father doesn't want to be indebted to these *people*."

"I hope you're right. I would prefer not to rely on these machines in a fight."

"They're still men," Terkeshi replied.

Jeruko shook his head. Was the boy in a contrary mood or was he truly not bothered by this? "For now. I still don't get why the cyborgs are doing this, though. And for free, no less. There must be more to it."

Terkeshi nodded. "I have the same suspicion, but I have nothing to base it on."

"That frightens me even more."

"You'd expect Father's paranoia would make him suspicious too."

"He is, but he's too desperate to heed the dangers they pose."

Terkeshi crossed his arms. "Obsessed, you mean."

Jeruko grunted. The tide of the emperor's mad ambitions swept them all toward the jagged cliffs, yet he was too blind to see it. "We must keep a close eye on them." *Since the emperor won't.*

Terkeshi agreed.

Jeruko gave the young man an appreciative look and slowly breathed out. Maybe Terkeshi wouldn't follow in his father's footsteps after all.

The more Jeruko thought about it, the more he worried. He considered their similar situations. When he'd first met the emperor at the academy, he'd been enamored. Prince Kenji Mizuki had been well mannered with just about everyone. He provided encouragement to those who'd had a tougher time keeping up with the strenuous curriculum. He never ridiculed or abused anyone. And he exhibited a keen sense of self-control.

Jeruko had been so proud the day Prince Mizuki had asked him to serve as his personal guard. However, the job proved more taxing than he'd expected. The demands of his regular duties had been easy compared to the times he'd been forced to stand by and do nothing while Emperor Botan Mizuki went in a drunken rage.

Because of his father, Prince Kenji Mizuki soon fostered the same mood-shifting temperament as Terkeshi held now. One moment he'd express compassion and consideration, and the next he'd lose his temper and rant and rave over some perceived slight.

The more the prince suffered the emperor's abuse, the blacker he became. This cycle repeated itself as Terkeshi endured the same torment. Jeruko prayed the young man wouldn't go down the same boorish and maddening path.

Terkeshi's brow wrinkled. "What? Why are you looking at me like that?"

Jeruko sighed. "I'm just worried about the future."

Terkeshi harrumphed. "If the past is any indication, we're fucked."

The young man's words pierced Jeruko's chest. He faced him with a softened expression. "Don't let your father change you."

"He won't turn me into one of those things."

That wasn't what Jeruko had meant, but the prince turned on his heel and left. Jeruko's heart went with him.

11
MEGA Plans

3791:070:12:15. The adaptor extended from Ambrose's metallic finger. He touched the port and the nanites configured to the proper shape. Seconds later, data streamed from the emitter's CPU and scrolled over Ambrose's vision. It was far too much for even him to take in, so he selected a few of the most important program files and forwarded them to his specialists.

After several minutes, they responded with error notifications. Ambrose froze as his internal processor labored to make sense of them all. The probability that the scientists on Thendi had made all these mistakes calculated at less than five-point-two-three percent. Analysis figured a twenty-one-point-seven-six percent chance the unskilled Toradon workers caused the errors. The most plausible scenario—someone had purposely altered the emitter specifications.

Ambrose eye-clicked through his database and opened the list of everyone who had been working on the device since it came aboard the *Dragon*. It included several Toradons, a handful of Cooperative prisoners, and the emperor's youngest son.

Ambrose accessed another file and pulled up the data his team had taken from the *Dragon*'s computers. According to documentation, nearly all the captured Cooperative officers held a science or engineering degree. He cross-referenced them with Cooperative files.

He blinked. Records didn't match. He checked the file again. Someone must have made alterations. No wonder the emperor had difficulty fixing this device.

He transmitted the information to Brian.

<Ambrose1633A> Compare PE issues with known intellectual skills of workers and calculate who may be responsible for intentional impairment.

Seconds passed.

<Brian29Z16> Data on Prince Jori Mizuki insufficient but the probability outcome indicates he most likely caused intentional impairment.

<Ambrose1633A> Detail probability of all parties, listing top three candidates only.

<Brian29Z16> Prince Jori Mizuki – 43.51%; Chief Sam Simmonds of *Odyssey* – 21.87%; Toradon worker designation Malkai – 16.94%.

Ambrose's eyebrows reflexively shot up. How did a mere ten-year-old child know so much about the emitter technology?

<Ambrose1633A> Primary basis of this analysis?

<Brian29Z16> Content of Prince Jori Mizuki's tablet and control over 71.08% percent of PE activities.

Ambrose cocked his head. Even though investigating the young prince's motivation wasn't necessary, he indulged in his natural human curiosity.

Both the princes had spent time on a Cooperative ship called the *Odyssey*. Comparing the names of the captured Cooperative officers on the *Dragon* with the crew members of that vessel matched six people. *Interesting.*

Did they coerce the youngest prince into helping them escape, or did he do it willingly? Ambrose didn't have enough information to calculate a reliable probability, but taking the likelihood of sabotage into account, he suspected they had somehow corrupted the child against his own family.

Did they corrupt Prince Terkeshi Mizuki as well? He should investigate further. Such knowledge would provide him with ideas on how to convert him.

With a mental nudge, Ambrose moved everything into a special file. MEGA-Man would want to know about this, along with all the other observations about the Toradons. The more information MEGA-Man procured, the better he could forecast events and manipulate them in his favor.

Ambrose indulged in the warm sensation coursing through his body. Getting a foothold in Toradon culture provided a whole new set of variables for analysis. His abilities were vast, but MEGA-Man was god-like with all his knowledge and power. With Ambrose's help, the most remarkable being in humankind would have more information that would enable him to better predict future events—thereby expanding his all-knowing capabilities.

He would have smiled if it wasn't such a human expression. Instead, he used his internal computer to run various diagnostics on the emitter and generate a supply list. He then wired his findings to Brian.

<Ambrose1633A> Create an optimal project timeline for the PE. Account for further analysis of the PE's remaining programs and assume the same percentage of errors.

Brian froze in the middle of his current task. Ambrose admired the man's ability to perform complex analyses so rapidly, but he had a flaw—he couldn't do more than one multiplex problem at once.

After a short while, Brian replied with a proposed timetable. Ambrose assessed it. Fixing this device would take more time than expected, but it should be complete soon enough to please the emperor.

Brian returned to his work. Ambrose uploaded and transferred more program files from the emitter. Hours passed, but he didn't experience the same boredom he'd had before receiving his enhancements. A simple adjustment to his internal controls dulled his perception of time and triggered a release of hormones that made him feel satisfied.

Brian sent a file that interrupted Ambrose's tasks.

<Brian29Z16> The results on the enhanced Toradon soldiers are in. One had a reaction but recovered.

Ambrose reviewed the information.

<Ambrose1633A> Good. All five must operate successfully.
<Brian29Z16> When will they integrate with the Great Commune?
<Ambrose1633A> When the emperor becomes more disposed to having cybernetic soldiers.

Ambrose suppressed the human pride that came with being an integral part of MEGA-Man's plans. Ultimately overturning the galactic agreements that prohibited enhanced humans from attaining positions of power made him giddy. Soon, mankind could evolve.

12
Rivals

3791:071:16:55. The arena resounded with cheers, sending an energizing vibration through Emperor Kenji Mizuki's body. He clasped his hands behind his back to keep the contagious spirit from spoiling his stately mien.

The crowd of warriors in the stands showed no such restraint. Some stood and pumped their fists while shouting. Others sat on the edge of their seats and called out words of encouragement as the opposing teams below fought a mock battle.

His son tossed a flash bomb as his team opened fire. Mizuki almost smiled. Not a single shot landed, but that wasn't the point. Terkeshi directed two of his men to flank the left and another set to the right. While the cover fire spewed forth, the four flankers dodged, ducked, and rolled to the next barricade.

You've got him, boy. Keep it up. Mizuki's chest lightened as General Samuru's team defended themselves with wild desperation. Would his son finally defeat the seasoned warrior?

Senshi Yujio on Samuru's team exposed his cybernetic arm from behind the blockade and fired. His aim appeared off, but the shots found their marks. The vests of Terkeshi's two right flankers flashed red, indicating they'd been hit.

The spectators erupted with a mixture of cheers and jeers. Mizuki's jaw hardened. The idiot boy's strategy didn't account for the opposition's cybernetics. And somehow, the energy blasts could change course midstream. Something about how it drew to its target like metal to a magnet. The science of it made his head hurt.

Use your own enhanced senshi, boy.

But Terkeshi didn't. His attempt to surround his opponent came to naught and he had to pull back. Mizuki's eye twitched as he clenched his teeth. The airiness he'd experienced earlier thickened like smog.

Damn it, boy. Why aren't you using your assets?

Nezumi grunted with a disdainful tone. "This doesn't look good, Sire."

Mizuki pressed his lips together. The man was right. What an embarrassment his son was.

"Is it possible Colonel Jeruko has been too soft on him?" Nezumi continued.

Mizuki didn't reply. A year ago, the training his friend provided to his two youngest sons had impressed him. Jori's potential alone promised an unsurpassed Dragon Warrior.

What had happened? Jeruko's sentiment ruined them, that's what—drove Jori to betray him. Would that same weakness lead to disloyalty from Jeruko as well? Mizuki's blood pressure rose.

It wasn't impossible. Emotion led to such weaknesses. Despite Jeruko's ability to maintain a steady temperament even through the most trying times, he'd retained a tendency for leniency and compassion that exposed his flaws.

Mizuki thought he'd cured him of that sentiment long ago. Apparently, the man had kept it hidden from him and passed it on to Jori and Terkeshi.

A small figure shot from behind a pillar. Its eyes held a hardness that Mizuki equated to stubbornness.

Wait, that's not real. Mizuki blinked until Jori's image disappeared. He regained his composure and focused on the match.

"I'd be happy to take over his training, Sire," Nezumi said.

As Terkeshi struggled to regain control of the battlefield, Mizuki considered Nezumi's offer. The old general had trained Dokuri, after all. Dokuri died in battle, but he'd still won. Terkeshi couldn't even win a mock fight.

The boy signaled to his squad. The men replied by hurling several hovering dorbs and other auto-fire weapons at their opponents. Terkeshi followed by pitching a Lazarus shield. With this dual energy defense, one absorbed enemy fire while the other regenerated in a repeating cycle.

It was a desperate move to regain the field, but General Samuru's men destroyed the auto-fire guns before Terkeshi advanced. The boy fought on with determination, but it wasn't enough. Samuru's cyborgs somehow took out the Lazarus shield, and Samuru himself ended the battle with a shot that made Terkeshi's sim-gear flash. The boy's face turned as red as his vest.

Mizuki maintained his composure, though his insides toiled. Terkeshi was a great disappointment. His defeat had been quicker than the other two teams combined. He certainly didn't have his little brother's skill. Jori would have defeated Samuru, even if he'd lost all his team members.

The cheers of Samuru's success echoed in the arena, creating a spirited noise that should have been for the Dragon Heir.

Samuru marched to Mizuki and bowed at the shallow angle appropriate for his rank.

Mizuki dipped his head. "Well done."

Samuru went into a stiff, at-ease stance. "Thank you, Your Eminence."

"Terkeshi," Mizuki called.

Terkeshi stood at attention. "Yes, Sir?"

Mizuki let his displeasure show. "I expected better."

Terkeshi darkened. "General Samuru has had decades of experience over me."

"*He* isn't my son!" The muscle by Mizuki's eye spasmed.

"Even Dokuri never beat him."

Mizuki growled. "But Jori did. Are you telling me you're no better than a ten-year-old?"

Terkeshi's jaw twitched as though he wanted to say something, but he wisely held his tongue.

"From now on," Mizuki continued, "you will train with General Nezumi every other day."

Terkeshi's eyes darted to the older man. His lips twisted. "Yes, Sir," he replied through his teeth.

Mizuki addressed the spectators. "The astounding display of these cybernetics has given me hope. A new day dawns on the Toradon Nohibito. No more will we sulk in the darkness of space. A reckoning is coming and soon all will bow to the supremacy of the Dragon Empire!"

The grand dojo reverberated with the roar of warriors. Pride swelled in Mizuki's chest.

A beep in his comm interrupted his moment. The distinct sound indicated importance but not urgency. He waited for the cheers to die down, then dismissed the men. The senshi filed out in quick order. Mizuki considered dismissing Terkeshi as well, but the boy was still his son.

He tapped the device taped behind his ear. "Go ahead."

"Your Eminence," the man said. "We've received word that one of the cargo ships you've flagged has taken port at the Kortsu station."

Mizuki tightened his fists and glowered at Terkeshi. "You have one more chance, boy. *Do not* disappoint me again."

Terkeshi paled. Mizuki lifted his chin. *Good, he should be afraid. I won't have a failure as a son.*

13
Mission Prep

3791:072:20:30. Ten flinty-eyed senshi stood shoulder to shoulder with the rigidity of a mountain range. Their black armor accented with metallic barbs matched their ominous expressions. They clasped their RR-5 phaser rifles in port arms position across their broad chests. Pitch black hilts of katana swords protruded from sheaths at their back while tanto daggers were strapped to their thighs.

Terkeshi faced them with a taut stance, hoping his forbidding mien matched theirs. His black battle armor's gold trim and decorative spikes marked him as their leader. The same bladed weapons jutted from his scabbards, but he didn't carry a rifle for this ceremonial display.

His heart thumped hard enough to hurt his eardrums as he put on an air of readiness for his first real battle. The emotion was fruitless since the confrontation was days away. The only purposes the ceremony served were to inspire the men and solidify Terk's role.

Two squads instead of one stood ready to deploy now because another errant ship had shown up at the space station dubbed New Nishiki Market. Terkeshi would lead ten senshi, including two enhanced, to the market while General Samuru would take a larger squad to Kortsu.

Orders were clear. Root out any traitors and make an example of them.

"Present—arms!" Terk commanded.

The warriors simultaneously held their rifles out and shifted them to a vertical position, then stomped their right feet. The solid strike of their boots to the floor boomed throughout the staging area. A spotlight above Terk and his squad brightened, casting the surrounding senshi observers into deeper shadows.

The spectators beat out a slow tempo with their own stationary march as Terk made a show of inspecting his team. He spent two stomps before each man. Stomp one, he glanced at the rifle's settings on the upper and lower receiver. Stomp two, he nodded sharply to the soldier, who replied by returning to port arms position.

Terk struggled to keep from making a face when he reached Yujio. The cables of the man's cybernetic arm twisted like a clew of worms. The central bone core glowed a dull blue, indicating it didn't have full power. More disturbing were the skeletal titanium fingers holding the rifle in an iron grip.

After the second stomp, Terk moved to the next enhanced soldier and suppressed a grimace. Tokagei wore a smug expression, as though he believed he was special. Didn't he know Father chose him to be a cyborg because it made little sense to enhance a warrior that was already great?

Terk completed the sham inspection and planted his feet before them. He gripped his hands behind his back and puffed out his chest. "Our assignment is to secure the Bantam-class ship, *Flying Fish*, docked at the New Nishiki Market. Are you ready?"

"Yes, Sir!" they all boomed at once.

"Right—face!"

The senshi pivoted ninety degrees and stomped in unison.

"Forward—march!"

Cheers broke out among the spectators as the warriors tromped from the staging area. Men whooped and clapped with a resounding ferocity.

"You can do it, Prince Mizuki!" one voice called.

Terk soured. Of course he could. This would be a simple mission. A Bantam-class vessel supported less than a dozen occupants and their systems were easy to hack. Plus, there wouldn't be any real confrontation since the captain was unlikely to refuse a Mizuki boarding team.

Terk had another role besides leading. Asking the ship's crew if they'd passed on sensitive information was at least something he did better than the newly enhanced soldiers. No one else had the ability to sense emotions or determine whether anyone had lied.

The march continued through a wide corridor, then onto a docking platform where a Serpent-class ship awaited. Memories bombarded Terk's thoughts at the sight of the sleek, black vessel. He'd flown one of these some months back. The elation he'd felt at leading an expedition to a distant space station had been spoiled when he crashed the *StarFire* on an enemy planet belonging to the Prontaean Cooperative.

He'd been sure he would die. The details of the blue planet had sharpened as his ship hurled toward it. Mountain ridges rose like grasping claws. Canyons widened like hungry mouths.

"You shouldn't have come," he'd said to Jori seconds before the *StarFire* smashed into the ground.

Terk sighed. That event continued to plague his dreams. They'd survived, but that wasn't the end of the disaster. Being rescued by their enemy hadn't been so bad. They were treated as guests. Jori even made friends with their commander. Problems arose a few months later when Father had captured Cooperative prisoners. Because the commander was one of them, Jori had gone behind Father's back to save them. Now he was dead—all because of his sentiment.

Terk shoved the memory away. He couldn't afford for his own sentiment to impede this mission.

He grabbed a dose of determination and forced it to the forefront of his thoughts.

I am a Mizuki. I will succeed at any cost.

*****

3791:072:21:07. Jin Jeruko's heart swelled as the young prince marched out with his team. During the ceremony, Terkeshi's controlled expression had held just the right amount of hardness expected of a leader. He maintained a robust carriage throughout, one that easily matched the senshi he led.

"Your son has grown strong, Sire."

Emperor Mizuki grunted.

Jeruko regarded the austere man beside him. Was that an agreement or dissent? Probably the latter. The emperor's mood left little room for optimism.

Nezumi's nose twitched. "He should do well with the enhanced senshi by his side."

"If he uses them this time," the emperor replied with a twist of his mouth.

Jeruko bit down to keep from getting defensive. Yes, a leader should figure out how to best use each soldier's individual skills. However, depending on cybernetically enhanced warriors might set a dangerous precedent.

After Samuru marched away with his team, the ceremony ended. The room emptied with strict formality as row after row of soldiers exited the staging area. Jeruko waited with the emperor while Nezumi bowed and excused himself.

The tension in Jeruko's shoulders relaxed. "May I speak to you as your friend, Sire?" he asked, hoping to see a spark of his old comrade now that Nezumi wasn't here to create dissent.

Emperor Mizuki replied with a sharp dip of his head.

Jeruko hesitated, uncertain if the emperor would be open to this discussion. "You remember what it was like when you were his age, how harsh your father's criticisms were."

The emperor's eyes sparked. "My father was a weak fool."

Jeruko bowed. "True, Sire. Your father didn't have your strength or intellect, but his biting words still affected you."

The emperor stiffened. "Why are you bringing this up?" he snapped. "Don't remind me of that drunken chima."

Jeruko paused, considering the best way to phrase his thoughts. "Terkeshi is trying, Sire. Despite some setbacks, I believe he's doing very well for his age. He could use some encouragement."

"Don't be ridiculous. My father may have been an ass, but his words made me work harder."

They did much more than that. "His words sometimes made you reckless, Sire. Remember that time—"

Emperor Mizuki spun to face him, eyes ablaze. "I said, don't remind me!"

Jeruko flinched. "Of course, Sire." He wanted to say more, but the spasm in the emperor's brow hinted at the increased anger boiling beneath the surface.

How can he not see it? The constant criticism the emperor had received made him perpetually angry. The young man who'd helped an insignificant son of a lord was gone.

To see Terkeshi toeing that same line made Jeruko's heart heavy. What would he do if the boy became his father? *Being loyal shouldn't feel dishonorable.*

He glanced at the exit Terkeshi had passed through and wished him a successful mission.

14
Inadequate

3791:081:19:17. Terkeshi fought for air. His heart thudded as the crook of Tokagei's cybernetic arm crushed around his neck. His lungs screamed for oxygen as a building heat saturated his face. He groped for the man's eyes, struck at his arm, trying every trick to get out of the hold.

Tokagei's solid grip remained. A tingling spread to Terk's limbs. Dizziness swirled into a tunnel of blackness. His heartrate pulsated.

Desperation overtook him and he tapped out. As soon as Tokagei let go, he choked in air. His head and face prickled as freshly oxygenated blood rushed in.

Cheers broke out and echoed throughout the small ship. Terk's temper sparked as some men discreetly passed something on to the others. How dare his people bet against him. They should root for *him*, not praising the newly made cyborg.

"Knock it off," he said with a roughness in his throat.

The voices died down, but smiles lurked at the corners of the men's faces.

Terk glowered. "He's no longer a real senshi. His skills are fabricated."

A few men dropped their mirth.

Terk pulled back his shoulders. "Again," he said to Tokagei.

The man smirked and went into a fighting stance. They circled one another in the small, open cabin area of the ship. The other senshi hugged the walls and corners or watched from atop equipment.

Terk considered his options. Sensei Jeruko often advised he should let his opponent make the initial move. Although Terk preferred to attack first, he waited this time.

Tokagei's mocking smile broadened. "Come on, boy."

"That's *my Lord* to you, you cock-eyed freak." *Damn Samuru's favorite.* Terk balled his fists, resolving to best this man lest his enhanced self-importance get out of hand.

"Apologies, my Lord," Tokagei replied with a shrug. "I like a little banter before a match."

Terk frowned. Usually, he could read Tokagei as easily as he read the instruments in the cockpit of a ship. This time was like flying blindfolded. Tokagei's lifeforce had dwindled to a whisper. Should this be happening already? He'd only received a few enhancements.

Tokagei threw a double punch. Terk's questions fled as he deflected them, then responded in kind. The man's cybernetic arm blocked him and sent a twinge along the nerve of his forearm.

He gritted his teeth and swung again. Tokagei parried and jabbed. Terk rebuffed him and counterattacked. He swept a lower kick to the side of Tokagei's knee. The man avoided it with ease. Terk punched him in the jaw.

As Tokagei's smile fell, the corner of Terk's mouth curved up. He held his own better this time, but his forearm where he'd been blocking itched with increased numbness. When he tightened his fist, a sharpness ran up his arm.

Tokagei put on a wicked grin and attacked. Jab. Jab. Uppercut. More punches and swings. Terk blocked them all. He should have been grateful for the lack of feeling in his arm, but his strength waned with every impact.

He growled and let out a slew of counterstrikes, aiming for the head, kidney, and sternum—but only a weak punch to the side landed.

Tokagei barked a laugh and swung. His cybernetic arm smashed into Terk's and followed through into his temple.

Terk's head rang. He maintained his balance and struck back. Tokagei parried and bashed him with his metal fist. Terk's brain rattled, sending him stumbling. Tokagei took advantage and kept at it. Three more blows sent Terk to the floor. Warm blood burst from the side of his eye.

Tokagei retreated a step and laughed. "You need to hit harder."

"Fuck you." Terk struggled to stand. He grasped the corner of some nearby equipment and wiped the blood from his temple. "I don't need a cybernetic arm to win."

"Haven't seen you win anything yet," Tokagei muttered.

Terk fumed. "You're supposed to teach me, chima. Tell me how to defeat you. Surely there's a weakness in that *fake* armor of yours."

Tokagei shrugged. "I don't have weaknesses anymore. To be frank, my Lord, you're either gonna need more skill or get some armor of your own."

Senshi Pachin frowned at the smug cybernetic warrior. "Show some respect! Another year of training and Prince Terkeshi will surpass us."

Tokagei huffed. "I don't mean anything by it. Insults build character."

Terk blocked Pachin's line of sight. Although he appreciated the man's attempt to defend him, he didn't need the help. He glared at Tokagei. "The only reason you can best me is because of your cybernetics. But those haven't made you any smarter. You're still the same dumbass who tried to pick his nose with a metal finger earlier."

Tokagei glanced at the laughing onlookers. His larger bottom lip stuck out as he frowned. "I haven't seen you outsmart anyone, *my Lord*." He bowed mockingly. "Your own little brother was smarter than you. He schemed right under your nose, and you had no—"

Terk punched him, igniting a splatter of blood over his face. The men snickered. Terk fumed, unsure whether they laughed at Tokagei's remark or that he got hit. Either way, there was no excuse for their asinine behavior.

He met the eyes of each one and glowered. He had known all about Jori's plan to save the Cooperative prisoners. Hell, he'd even helped him. They didn't know that, though. *Who has no clue now, stupid chimas?*

"You better watch it, Tokagei," he replied. "I won't always be this young."

He pivoted on his heel and left the cabin in a huff. Quiet laughter lingered behind him. He ground his teeth and ignored them, knowing any reaction would make him look like a whiny child. Someday he could kick their asses and show them once and for all that he wasn't a dragon to be messed with.

"Dismissed," Terkeshi said to the man in the cockpit. He dropped into the pilot's chair and reviewed the instrument panel. Two more hours and they'd be at the space station. He'd lead these doubting chimas on a successful mission and do it better than those stupid cyber senshi ever could.

15
The Flying Fish

3791:081:21:38. Terkeshi's hand twitched over the arc drive deactivation button as his Serpent-class ship neared the edge of the gravity well. As soon as the yellow dot on the screen touched the red boundary line, his hands blurred over the controls. The horizontal bars of the arc gauge decreased at the same time his stomach completed a half-somersault.

He pressed another series of buttons on the instrument panel to slow down the ship. After verifying all systems operational, he tapped the screen to activate the viewport cams. The New Nishiki Market was a flea-sized point of light compared to the glowing red dwarf nearby. He willed it closer, but without the arc drive it would take several hours to reach the station.

While Terkeshi waited for the tedious process of deceleration and approach, scenarios for the space station played out in his head. Would the captain allow them to board, or would he force Terk and his squad to employ infiltration weapons? Once on the ship, would the crew surrender, or would they put up a fight?

A part of him hoped it would be easy. He'd known Captain Tobiuo for more than two years. The man had a good sense of humor, took care of his crew, and was one of the few transport captains who didn't also do business in the human trafficking trade.

If the captain resisted, though, Terk would finally have a real battle under his belt.

He leaned back in his chair and let his daydreams take over. The hours crawled as his mind raced. By the time his console beeped to alert him to the station's proximity, his anxiety had morphed into excitement. He bolted upright and popped his knuckles.

The New Nishiki Market dominated the screen. An immense titanium ring spun around a cylindrical mass as the distant red dwarf illuminated it with a subdued glow. Eight spokes connected the wheel to the hub. The hub contained fuel, water, and tons of machinery. The outer wheel was where all the docking platforms were located while the inner ring housed all the markets.

Terk hailed the station. "Prince Mizuki here, authorization code seven-R-four-Y-seven-U-eight-one."

"Welcome, Honored Prince. How may we assist you?"

"You're holding the *Flying Fish* in port. I need its location, and dock me as close to it as you can."

"Yes, Honored One."

Terk drummed his fingers as he waited. When his terminal pinged, he tapped the message icon. The *Flying Fish* was docked at section C port 18 and he'd land in the same section nine ports down.

He entered the coordinates and maneuvered the helm. "We dock in one hour," he yelled back to the crew. "Get ready."

*****

3791:082:04:41. Terkeshi marched down the middle of the corridor with his squad stomping in unison behind him. He held his chin high and his rifle close. The hustle and yells of the station's populace scattering out of his way assailed his ears. They ducked into shops full of gaudy clothing, greasy mechanical parts, dilapidated computer components, and near-spoiled food.

If he had time for inspecting, he'd probably also find black-market wares—but this wasn't his mission. He couldn't care less anyway. Keeping this station in check was the responsibility of lesser men.

C18 loomed just ahead. Terk's heart kicked into overdrive. He quickened his pace and shouldered his rifle. Once at the keypad, he jabbed in the code the station authorities had provided. The doors remained closed. *What the hell?* He tried again. Nothing. *Chusho!*

His muscles tensed, ready for a fight.

"Sir," Tokagei said. "Don't go so quickly. You're making mistakes."

Terk scowled. "No, I'm not. The station either made an error or lied." He reentered the code with vexed slowness to prove it.

The door swished open. *Oh.* He masked his embarrassment and went inside.

The *Flying Fish* dominated the small bay. The blunt-nosed and unwieldy ship looked nothing like a fish. It bore a closer resemblance to a fat river mammal he'd once seen on Jinsekai. Bulky docking clamps could have been its legs. The two top thrusters could have been its ears.

The side hatch lay open, revealing a cavernous maw. Sealed crates sat in a strict row just outside the ship, curiously perfect.

"Where the hell are they?" Tokagei said. "They're supposed to be on lockdown."

"Captain Tobiuo!" Terk called out, assuming the crew lounged inside.

With a flick of his hand, the senshi squad took positions with their rifles poised. Terk held his crossways, but still prepared to whisk it out if necessary.

A tall, gangly man with dark skin and white hair poked his head out, then ducked back in. "Captain! The Toradons are here!"

Terk tightened his grip on the forestock and pistol grip of his weapon.

A second man with only a little more meat on his bones ambled out. His skin tone was just as dark, but his grey hair darker. The furrows in his forehead smoothed at the sight of Terk. "My Lord," he said deferentially, quickening his pace.

Terk maintained a stony expression as the man knelt before him. "Captain Tobiuo, we are boarding your ship for an inspection."

"Of course, my Lord," the captain said with a worry that smacked Terk's senses. "Did I forget to deliver something?"

"We shall see," Terk replied. He tilted his head at the senshi designated to check the ship's incoming and outgoing messages. Then indicated for the others to begin their search.

As the team split, half to the crates and half to the ship, Tobiuo looked on with a wrinkled forehead. Terk delved his senses deeper into the man. The captain's worry wasn't as apprehensive as he would have expected from someone hiding something. His disquiet seemed normal for a person confronted by the Dragon Prince. Still, he had to be sure.

"Who did you talk to when you were on my ship?" Terk demanded.

Tobiuo startled. "Just Sunsu, the docking master."

Terk sensed truth, but he maintained hard eye-contact. "Did you receive anything from him? A message perhaps?"

The captain wagged his head. "No, my Lord."

"Not even a data transfer device?"

"Nothing. I swear. You give me good business. I would never act as a spy."

The tension in Terk's shoulders lessened as the captain's sincerity permeated his senses. "Did you and Sunsu gossip?"

"We exchanged pleasantries only. He never speaks of anything other than basic trade information."

All Tobiuo's words had been truthful. Terk chewed the inside of his cheek, wondering if he should push harder. Samuru would beat the man into submission to get any secrets out of him, but Terk didn't need to do that. Should he do it anyway for appearance's sake?

He held a glower as his men lined the crew along the wall. "Wait," he said to the captain, then left to face the others.

Some glanced up at him, but most kept their eyes down. One crewman shuffled his feet. Another let out a nervous cough.

Terk gave each man the same penetrating look. "While you were on my ship, did any of you speak with anyone?"

The men shook their heads in earnestness. Terk concentrated on each of their emotions, not finding the slightest hint of falsity about them.

"Did any of you take anything, something with a message perhaps?"

Again, they said no, and again their emotions reflected their sincerity.

"Watch them," Terk said to his men.

He went inside to the *Flying Fish*'s cockpit. "Did you find anything?" he asked Senshi Biskol.

"So far, they're all normal communications, my Lord. I'm still looking."

Terk watched over the man's shoulder. He was about to ask about one message with questionable attributes when Biskol clicked on it.

The voice of Tobiuo and another man conversed for a good fifteen minutes. They gossiped a bit, but nothing about cyborgs or genetically enhanced men.

"It might be in code," Biskol said.

Terk doubted it. Tobiuo was smart in his way, but not smart enough to speak in code.

"Send a copy to my tablet," Terk said.

He left the ship and confronted Tobiuo, who still waited on his knees.

The man's brow furrowed. "What's this about, my Lord?"

Terk opened the message and hit play. After a few sentences, he stopped it. "Who is this you're speaking to?"

The captain emanated bland emotions. "His name's Jeffston. He's another cargo transport captain. We're good friends."

"Did you tell him anything about us, about our ship?"

Tobiuo shook his head. "No, my Lord. Of course not."

"In code?"

Tobiuo's brow furrowed deeper. "No, my Lord. Jeffston knows better than to ask and I know better than to tell."

"What's this?" Tokagei yelled from over by the crates.

Terk turned to see him holding up a canister of blue gas.

Tobiuo answered without concern. "It's pentaduna."

Tokagei snarled. "No one but the emperor should have this stuff!"

The captain paled. "I-It's just a small container. Hardly enough to power a shuttle. Not stolen, either. A senshi traded it to me."

Tokagei stormed forward. "It's contraband!"

Terk stepped in front of him. Tokagei moved to go around and Terk grabbed his metal arm. The cybernetic senshi pushed on. Terk growled and planted himself before him. "Wait! That's an order!"

Tokagei's cybernetic eye flickered and his mouth turned down. The resolve emanating from him sparked unnaturally, making Terk uneasy. Where was this coming from? Did his enhancements go to his head? Or was he being manipulated somehow?

Terk recovered and matched Tokagei's glower. "I said wait."

Tokagei stepped back with a flourish of his fleshy arm. "Fine."

Terk curled his lip. "Try again, chima."

Tokagei jutted his chin. "Yes, Sir," he said with a sour twist of his mouth.

Terk turned to the captain. "Which senshi?"

"Senshi Geun. He serves at Toku station. I-I-I thought the emperor had lifted the ban. I see this stuff everywhere. Folks are always trading it. When it came from a senshi, I thought nothing of it. I swear, I didn't know I—"

Terk stopped him with his hand. The part about him thinking the emperor lifted the ban was a lie but the captain had been honest about everything else. He stepped back and took in all the crew members. Nothing suspicious cropped up in their emotions.

Samuru would have inflicted a physical punishment. That seemed overkill for such a small thing. Besides, Captain Tobiuo did his job better than most. It would be a shame to drive him away.

"Take the canister and move out. We're done here," Terk said to his men. Then to Tobiuo, "You'll be fined on your next visit to our ship."

The captain nodded vigorously.

"You're letting him go, Sir?" Tokagei said in a tone that made Terk grind his teeth.

"I'm not concerning myself with this petty stuff," Terk replied tartly.

"But if he's a smuggler, then he could also be a spy."

Terk halted and squared up to the man. "You may have all these enhancements that make you think you're better than others, but you're still a simple senshi under *my* command. Can you tell when someone is lying?"

"No."

"No, what?" Terk bared his teeth.

Tokagei nearly snarled. "No, my Lord."

"Well, I can. And I'm telling you that these people are not the ones who leaked information."

"But they are smugglers!" Tokagei's face reddened and Terk growled. "My Lord," Tokagei finished.

"All cargo haulers are smugglers."

Tokagei's emotions indicated he wanted to argue, but Terk pressed his lips together and made a slight shake of his head.

81

"It's your call, my Lord."

"Damn right it is. Now let's go!" Terk turned away and headed out. The senshi followed, but not with the same precision and fortitude they'd shown earlier.

Terk fumed. Damn them. Damn Captain Tobiuo, too. And damn himself for leading such an unexceptional mission.

At least it had gone well. He'd used a skill that only he had and determined none had acted as spies, thereby preserving the services of a reliable cargo ship. It wasn't an exceptional victory, but still successful. Something had finally gone his way.

16
Another Failure

3791:092:23:29. Terkeshi exited his ship. His heart skipped a beat as he met Father's stormy features. *Chusho.* The last time his father had bothered to meet him after a mission was when he'd crashed the *StarFire* and gotten captured by the Cooperative. *What the hell is it this time?*

Terk gulped and stood in a stiff at-ease stance. "Father."

The muscle above Father's eye twitched. "You've failed yet again."

Terk startled. "My orders were to discover whether anyone on the *Flying Fish* had been selling our secrets. I confirmed that none did."

"You barely questioned them!"

Terk knitted his brows. "That's all I need to do, Sir. If they were hiding something, I would have sensed it."

Father's eyes remained turbulent. "What about the pentaduna?"

"It was a small canister. We confiscated it."

"He never should have had it to begin with! Yet you let him go without so much as a slap on the hand."

Terk glanced away from Father's glower. "I told him we'd fine him on his next visit."

"Fine him?" Spittle flew from Father's mouth. "He had an illegal power source!"

"So what should I have done? A scourging seems a bit excessive."

"You want to know what you should've done?" Father ripped off the MM tablet from around his wrist and flattened it with a snap. He jabbed the screen, then shoved it at Terk. "Watch this."

Terk hesitantly took it. A video played. A dozen men knelt with their bloody backs exposed. One by one, a senshi flicked a short whip, creating more torn flesh. Bile rose to Terk's mouth, and he swallowed it back down. He'd seen people punished before, but he'd yet learned to harden himself against it.

Every man cried out. At least four of them blubbered and two begged. One fainted. Terk broke out into a cold sweat. The video ended with General Samuru slicing the captain's neck and threatening the first mate with the same punishment if he ever dared to flout the emperor's laws.

"What did they do?" He asked as he handed the tablet back with a trembling hand.

"They contacted a known smuggler—likely passed on our secrets."

Likely? Terk's jaw dropped, and he snapped it closed. "Did he? Did he pass on our secrets?"

"He confessed to many crimes, including selling on the black market."

"That's a petty crime, hardly deserving of this. And you wonder why people betray you."

Father's open palm smacked the side of Terk's face. Terk grunted and blinked the stars from his vision. He straightened, holding his ground but unable to meet Father's eyes.

"Coward." Spittle flew out of Father's lips. "If we let them get away with a single infraction, they'll take more liberties. How many times must I tell you that discipline is the only way to keep people from walking all over you? It's one disappointment after another with you, isn't it?"

Terkeshi studied his feet and wisely kept his mouth shut. *Chusho.* He should have punished Captain Tobiuo.

"You're a long way from being like Dokuri," Father said in a sour tone. "And you definitely don't have Jori's intelligence."

Terk snapped his head up. "I can be better than Dokuri. Just give me time. I'm only fourteen."

"Dokuri was making examples of traitors at the age of twelve! You and your brother's damned sentiment has made you weak and cowardly."

"I am no coward!" Terk replied.

Father struck him again. Terk absorbed the blow and ignored the sting. Hot air puffed in and out of his nostrils.

"Then why didn't you at least punish that man?" Father said through gritted teeth as his eye twitched menacingly.

Terk resisted the urge to rub his jaw. He avoided his father's eyes while trying to think of a response.

Father swept his hand to the door. "You want these men to respect you? You want the cargo captains and lords to respect you? Then you must punish them! Don't let them get away with *anything*. Make an example of them."

Terkeshi looked down in shame. "I will be more strict next time, Father. I promise."

"You had damned well better. Your sentiment will get you killed, boy," Father said. Terk not only saw the threat in his father's piercing eyes, but he also sensed the truth of his words. "Just like your brother."

Blood flushed away from Terk's head, leaving behind a sharp chill. It had been Jori's regard for the commander that made him want to help the enemy prisoners, so his sentiment had led to his demise. If Terk didn't quash his squeamishness soon, he'd end up like him.

17
Great Commune

3791:094:08:35. Kenji Mizuki supervised the melee in the TTAC room below with rapt attention. He sucked in a breath as Senshi Yujio caught Tokagei's arm and twisted him into an expeditious flip. It was a common move, but the result would have been less dramatic if performed by an ordinary man. Tokagei landed on the flat of his back with a wallop that should've driven the air out of him.

Tokagei leapt to his feet and threw a counter strike at Yujio's head. Yujio darted out of reach, making Tokagei swipe through air. Yujio took advantage of the man's diverted energy and struck at the resulting opening. Tokagei moved faster than the pounce of a blackbeast. His cybernetic arm swung back around and blocked Yujio's move.

Mizuki appraised their skills. *The things I could do with soldiers like this!*

Despite his desire to lean closer to the observation window for a better look, he maintained a cool stance. Decades of discipline and control made it easy.

Terkeshi stood beside him, matching the same attentive pose. His expression, however, turned down with seeming anger. At what, Mizuki neither knew nor cared.

"They are magnificent, are they not?" Ambrose said.

Mizuki blinked at having almost forgotten the man was there. "They are. How is it that even their fighting ability has improved?" He understood how their targeting had, but how could they fight better?

"Their cybernetics include a nano-network that runs throughout their entire body," Ambrose replied.

Mizuki frowned in a lack of understanding.

"Does this mean you can control them?" Terkeshi asked.

Mizuki flinched inwardly. *No. It's impossible.* What if it wasn't? What if the cyborgs use his enhanced senshi against him? *Don't be stupid. It's just five soldiers.* But what if the cyborg were collaborating with Fujishin? Or worse, Enomoto? What if his enemies were here right now within his own men—watching? *No. Impossible.* Ambrose had said the brain was too complex. Sure, some aspects of the cybernetics required external intervention, but only a bare minimum.

He scrunched his eyes and pinched his brow until the thoughts settled. "What did you say?" he asked after realizing Ambrose had spoken.

Ambrose's mouth widened, but the smile didn't reflect on the rest of his face. "The answer to your question is no, your Eminence. We can't control them, only make them more efficient. This nano-network is faster than the human nervous system. It saves important data and amplifies muscle memory. The more they practice, the stronger the network becomes and the quicker they react."

Mizuki's brows shot up.

"Consider the power these enhanced soldiers will rain down on your armies," Ambrose added.

The words opened a floodgate of possibilities and Mizuki's suspicions fled. He imagined his grandfather's helmet and sword restored to pristine condition and being worn by a powerful version of Terkeshi. A vast army followed in his wake. Although the metal of their cybernetics blazed like a billion stars, his son burned the brightest of them all.

Of course, this wouldn't happen the way things stood now. Too bad cybernetic enhancements were against the law.

"Your son would greatly benefit from this tech," Ambrose said, as though reading Mizuki's mind.

"No!" Terkeshi snapped.

Mizuki shot a glare at the boy, then turned back to the cyborg. "I can't. A form of the galactic MEGA Injunction applies here as well."

"True." Ambrose nodded. "But when you have strengthened your rule, it will no longer matter."

Mizuki remained stiff, but his insides leapt. He'd already considered and discarded the notion, but the more he saw how much better his senshi performed, the more it appealed to him.

"Father, I can't tell if they're lying about anything." The boy glowered at the cyborg as though making an accusation and daring him to argue. "We don't know what their motives really are. I don't trust them."

Mizuki didn't trust them either, but the empire was at stake. Besides, if he didn't take advantage of these cybernetics, another race would. His Dragon Warriors were unsurpassed, but they paled compared to the new cyber senshi.

"Is the tech detectable?" he asked. "I don't want my son walking around with obvious cybernetic enhancements. He mustn't look like one of these freaks."

Terkeshi's jaw dropped. "Father, you can't seriously consider this."

Mizuki narrowed his eyes. "I can't afford to have a failure as a son."

Ambrose spoke before the boy could argue. "It is not currently detectable."

"Explain."

"It means people will find out eventually," the boy muttered.

Ambrose shrugged. "Once our enemies realize we can camouflage tech, they will discover a way to detect it. You do not need to worry. Our cybernetic technology surpasses even the most advanced races, so we'll easily get ahead once more."

Mizuki nodded. If he enhanced Terkeshi, he had plenty of time to regain his supremacy before anyone found out. "And what will it cost me?"

"This we shall also do for free," Ambrose said.

"That's suspiciously convenient," Terkeshi replied.

The muscles around Mizuki's eye shuddered. Not this again. Not another betrayal.

Ambrose held up his hand. "I understand your suspicions of our gifts, but we are not doing this to be altruistic. We get something in return."

Mizuki frowned. "And what is that?"

"We move closer to revolutionizing humanity. What better way to promote our agenda than to have a powerful leader with enhancements? This MEGA Injunction holds us back. We can be so much more. *You* can be so much more."

"More freakish, you mean," Terkeshi said under his breath. "Don't trust them, Father."

Despite the boy's warning, Ambrose's words resonated. Mizuki's ancestors had struggled with their desire to be superior. Selective breeding was a convoluted endeavor. Finding the right match was challenging. Overcoming the randomness of genetic inheritance compounded the difficulty of creating a superior heir. It didn't matter that Mizuki had all these skills—he had no guarantee his sons would receive them. Terkeshi was proof of that.

Only Jori seemed to have all he had hoped for. Not only did the boy inherit his own abilities, but he had his mother's too. Terkeshi also inherited her ability to read emotions, but Jori had been a pure genius in everything. If only his damned sentiment hadn't turned him into a traitor.

A pang spiked through Mizuki's gut as the ghost of Jori flashed in the corner of his vision. He should have punished the boy in another way. His actions could've been vindicated. He was still a child. Mizuki could've pushed him into being the hard warrior that Dokuri had been.

Now the only legacy he had left was Terkeshi's repeated failures. It was time to end that.

"I will consider your offer."

Terkeshi's forehead wrinkled with desperation. "Father, you can't! I succeeded in the mission. I just need to learn to be firmer. Cybernetics won't change me in that way, but I can work harder to improve myself."

Mizuki pressed his lips together. "How many chances do you think you deserve, boy?"

Terkeshi's shoulders dropped. "Please, don't, Father. I will do better."

Mizuki made up his mind but withheld his reply. No doubt the boy would beg him not to, and he despised begging. Jori had never begged.

Ambrose smiled. Mizuki frowned, wondering whether the man had read his thoughts again. He turned his attention back to the melee and ignored the warning bells going off in his head.

*****

3791:094:09:11. Ambrose's emotions swelled. The feeling was unusual, yet he embraced it. If the emperor followed through and allowed his son to receive enhancements, MEGA-Man's primary objective would be one step closer to fruition.

He excused himself from the performance and headed to his own ship. His steps were lighter as he trotted down the skywalk. A merry tune from his nearly-forgotten childhood popped into his head as he navigated the white halls.

If his behavior seemed odd to the other enlightened ones, they didn't react. Even if they did, he'd tell them he had every right to be happy. Everything was coming together. Just one thing remained—make sure the prince complies willingly.

Ambrose entered his quarters and plugged in. Within moments, MEGA-Man's symbol popped up on the overlay of his vision.

> <Ambrose1633A> Ambrose1633A reporting.
> <*M*> _
> <Ambrose1633A> All dealings with the Dragon Emperor are proceeding as planned. The perantium emitter will take slightly longer than expected, but it shall be done.
> <*M*> Explain delay.
> <Ambrose1633A> We suspect the emperor's youngest son attempted to sabotage it. I am sending you a file explaining further.

Ambrose eye-clicked through his internal drive and sent the documents. He hadn't told the emperor about his young son's actions. It would only complicate matters due to the man's emotional instability. Brian had predicted a seventy-six-point-three-four percent chance Emperor Mizuki would lose his temper and make rash decisions that could affect MEGA-Man's plans.

> <Ambrose1633A> The emperor agreed to five enhanced soldiers. At first, he refused to allow us to do this to his son. However, he has amended his stance. The prince is still against it,

but I have an idea that has a good chance of inspiring him to change his mind.

<*M*> Explain.

Ambrose told him about the prince's upcoming sim battle taking place in space later today and sent detailed information on how he'd programmed a set of nanobots to affect his ship.

<*M*> Excellent. Prince Terkeshi's acceptance is important. What of Emperor Mizuki himself?

<Ambrose1633A> We estimate only a 10.56% chance that he will upgrade.

<*M*> As I predicted. Enhancing the heir is sufficient. Do not press the emperor. We will deal with him later.

<Ambrose1633A> Yes, Great One. I'm sending you the link channels to the five warriors.

He mentally copied the information saved in his files and pasted it into the conversation.

<Ambrose1633A> They are now connected to the Great Commune. You have visual access to their optics. Audio as well. They are not high-ranking soldiers, so it isn't much, but I expect the emperor to agree to allow us to enhance more in the future.

<*M*> Well done.

<Ambrose1633A> I will report again soon.

>Connection terminated.

Ambrose smiled as he took in a savory breath. The information continuously streaming from emperor's enhanced warriors contributed to MEGA-Man's pool of knowledge. Adding the Dragon Heir would provide a more reliable source of intelligence and allow the great man to improve his ability to predict and manipulate the future.

MEGA-Man will soon be a god.

18
Drifting

3791:094:18:21. Terkeshi banked hard, making his insides lurch. His suit tightened around his lower extremities, forcing blood to his brain. His facemask forced air into his lungs, yet his vision still narrowed and the pressure in his head increased at the edge of G-LOC.

The sensations didn't concern him. He knew how much G-force his body could handle. His opponent, however, probably assumed he'd lost consciousness after that high-speed turn. That assumption would cost them. Terk smiled as he sent a half-dozen torpedoes up their ass.

After zooming by the enemy, the proximity alert from his Asp space fighter shut off. He'd cut it close on purpose. The fake missiles displayed dashed yellow lines on the viewer. The red dot of the targeted jet veered off its trajectory, but the weapons still struck their mark.

"Yes!" A broad smile creased Terk's face. This was something he excelled at. No other space fighter matched his skills. Even the cybernetic senshi flying the spacecraft he'd just virtually destroyed was no match. Certainly, Father wouldn't turn him into a cyborg now.

He glanced at the viewer and analyzed the battle. His team had corralled the enemy fighters and the odds were in his favor. "Red Dog, buster to Fire Wing. Two missiles are tailing him."

"On it, Dragon Spawn One."

Terk jinked the ship to avoid a new threat. He depressed the blaster button and destroyed the missile before it reached him. A tight turn put another enemy in his sights. He glanced at their trajectory and speed and estimated where to aim his next shot. Within moments, the projectile was away. Forty-seven seconds later, the rival vessel exploded in a virtual pop on the screen.

Terk's heart raced but his mind remained fiercely focused as the battle exercise neared its end. His fighters had gained an almost two-to-one lead now. It wouldn't be long before he obliterated the enemy.

The engine light blinked rapidly in yellow. Terk's breath hitched as he assessed the gauges. *Chusho!* He thought he'd been monitoring the pressure, but the reactor engines were dangerously hot.

He adjusted the thermal regulars, but the warning remained.

The proximity alert blared, keeping him from implementing further repairs. Terk growled and refocused on the dogfight. An enemy vessel hugged his tail. The AI of his ship automatically destroyed their first three missiles, but one got through.

Terk engaged his blaster once more. However, the missile had its own shielding. The one shot that hit its mark did nothing to stop it. His ship jostled as the simulated blast struck his shield, bringing his defenses down to twenty-four percent.

The emergency alarm amplified, drowning out the proximity alert. The engine light now flashed red and sent Terk's heart into a stomping thud. This couldn't be part of the simulation. He flew a real ship, and these readings were authentic. He flipped switches and jabbed buttons. Nothing worked as his opponents continued firing at him, depleting his shield.

The instrument panel blacked out. Terk's heart leapt to his throat. If this had been an actual battle, the enemy missiles would've destroyed his ship. However, the red engine light still flashed, indicating it just might blow up for real. The heat filling the cabin and penetrating through his suit told him an explosion was imminent.

"My engine's bent and it's not a sim! Dragon Spawn punching out."

He jabbed the eject button. The entire orb of his cockpit blasted out, sending a forceful jerk throughout his body. If he hadn't strapped his head in place and if the auto gel hadn't released around him, his spine would have snapped. Thrusters on the bottom of his chair automatically engaged, hurtling him into space.

His vision narrowed. As unconsciousness from the G-forces closed in, he prayed he wouldn't be thrown into the path of another vessel. Chances were small in this vastness, but his muscles still tensed. He held onto that tension in the lower half of his body and relaxed the upper half to keep blood flowing to his brain.

A shock wave sent him into a spin, telling him his ship had exploded. The proximity alert blared again as shrapnel pelted his pod and jarred him about.

His stomach roiled. He resisted the urge to hurl. His helmet would dispose of the bile, but he couldn't risk a chunk blocking the airflow.

He gulped in air and fought to subdue the nausea. With the pod still spinning, it was near impossible. *Why aren't the stabilizers working?* He focused on the reactivated instrument panel. Trying to move his hand to the thrusters was like attempting to pin a tail on a scurrying jackrabbit while holding a fifty-kilogram weight.

His fingers finally hit the controls, but it took intense concentration to keep them there. He depressed the left side in short bursts. The pod jostled, making him lose his place. Muscles in his arm strained as he inched back onto the console.

The spin on his pod slowed incrementally with each thrust. His peripheral vision steadily returned and the tumbling in his stomach subsided. He took in longer breaths and forced himself to relax. *That was close.*

After the pulsating of his heartbeat dwindled, he regained his bearings and pulled up the viewscreen. The pod had stabilized. He'd drifted thousands of kilometers from the battle, but not too far for retrieval. The homing beacon seemed to work. All other functions operated within parameters except... *Chusho!* Why was his air supply so low?

He reviewed all the stats, including their history, to figure out what happened. The reactor engines had overheated. Instead of devoting all his attention to the other ships, he should have paid more mind to his own. Where did his air go, though? He didn't have the skill to interpret what had gone wrong, especially since the pod reported no damage to the tanks.

Terk tapped the comm button. "Dragon Spawn reporting. I'm alright. But for some reason, my ship is low on air."

No one responded. As the moments passed, Terk verified his distance. It shouldn't take this long for a reply. He repeated his message.

His heartbeat ticked on as time crept by. Did they receive his communication? They should have. He had no indication that communications were out. What the hell was going on?

Terk flinched at the ping of an incoming message.

"Sir," Senshi Edo transmitted, his tone hesitant. "We've been ordered not to retrieve you."

A jolt ran through Terk's body. "What! Why?"

"I don't know, Sir."

Terk's mouth hung agape. Everything seemed to freeze as he absorbed the shock. At first, the incredulity of it kept him from thinking. Then realization sank in. He checked the status of the sim battle and found his team lost shortly after his opponents had taken him out.

His shoulders dropped. Father was pissed because he'd failed—again.

He flicked off the external viewer, not wanting to see the emptiness that surrounded him. However, the confined cockpit smothered him. Would Father leave him out here to die?

He wouldn't.

Yes he would. After all, Father now had the help of the cyborgs unhindered by the MEGA Injunction. They didn't need to enhance Terk. All they needed to do was use their genetic engineering skills to replace him.

Unlike Dokuri, who'd lost his life yet still won the fight, Terk would die in a simulated battle that he'd lost.

He swallowed down the hard lump in his throat. He'd fucked up one too many times. Now he'd perish in a slow and unexceptional death.

His sinuses burned. *Why can't I do anything right?*

19
Wavering Loyalty

3791:094:19:07. An acidic taste rose from Jin Jeruko's stomach as he stared blankly at the bridge viewscreen. The display had long since switched from the sim battle view to standard stats, but the last sight of Terkeshi's escape pod spiraling away had seared into his brain.

While Senshi Edo coordinated the docking of the Asp fighters and Niashi monitored the operations gauges, Jeruko imagined Terkeshi's feelings of abandonment and despair as his pod sped through the void.

Jeruko glanced at Emperor Mizuki's dark, hooded eyes and shivered. *He's lost his mind. These erratic decisions must end.* He searched the bridge crew but found no allies. It was up to him to protest Terkeshi's fate.

One look at General Nezumi in the chair beside the emperor's made him hesitate. The man would undoubtedly respond with a snide remark. He'd say something derisive about Terkeshi or hint at Jeruko's suspected disloyalty, turning the emperor against them both for his own selfish gain.

Why, though? It was pointless. There was no reason to compete among the Talons. Jeruko and Samuru didn't care for one another, but they got along for Emperor Mizuki's sake. Nezumi's conspiring attitude poisoned the emperor's already deteriorating mental state and risked the entire empire.

If things didn't change soon, the last Mizuki heir would die at worst, or be turned into a mindless machine at best. Jeruko had to do something, but what? His options dwindled.

He inhaled deeply to settle his whirling despair. His churning thoughts wouldn't help anyone. He banished them and meditated. Looking inward made him realize he had been clutching the armrests of his own chair, so he willed his muscles to relax.

Several minutes later, he felt more himself. His shoulders had loosened and his mind calmed. He regarded Nezumi and decided the man didn't matter. The only person who did was Terkeshi.

He got up and made rounds to each of the stations, making sure everything was in good order. Senshi Edo kept a live feed of the youth's pod in the corner of his primary display. It would be at least ten hours before it traveled beyond the *Dragon's* sensors, but he couldn't imagine allowing Terkeshi to suffer that entire time.

Jeruko placed his hand on the Edo's shoulder, receiving a worried look in return. He gave the man a nod of assurance and returned to the emperor.

"Sire," he said as he took a respectful at-ease stance, "do you truly intend to leave your only son out there to die?"

Emperor Mizuki's lip curled. Jeruko winced inwardly, wishing he had phrased his words more carefully.

"Why not?" the emperor asked. "The technology to beget more sons lies at my fingertips."

A piercing iciness washed over Jeruko's body, but he kept his face neutral. "That's an option, Sire, but the more we ask from our guests, the more we're required to give."

The emperor darkened.

Nezumi matched his expression. "You keep bringing that up, as if you think he isn't already aware."

Jeruko pretended it was the emperor who had spoken. "My apologies, Sire. I only speak out of concern for the empire."

Nezumi grunted. "One has to wonder whether you still have faith in our leader."

Jeruko pressed his lips together at Nezumi's audacity. At the same time, his gut churned at how dangerous truth of the statement. He wanted to kill the general. The prospect of assassinating the emperor reoccurred to him as well. The empire had a chance through Terkeshi, but not with these two around.

No. Too many consequences. Jeruko tightened his fists behind his back. "I assure you, *General*, that my fealty to the Mizuki house is solid."

Nezumi narrowed his eyes, but the emperor's features softened. Jeruko let out a calming breath, thankful the man trusted him to never speak a lie.

"There's also no guarantee the cyborgs can heal you, Sire," Jeruko said. "And let's assume they are able. What are the chances you'll have another son like Dokuri?" *Or Jori*, he wanted to say but held his tongue.

Jeruko pushed that thought away lest grief overtake him. His stomach roiled as he reflected instead on Dokuri. One time, he'd cut off the digits, then the limbs of a prisoner. He provided medical attention along the way to make sure they lived to the point where all that remained was their bleeding torso and a still-conscious head. It worsened from there. The worst part was that he had forbidden Jeruko to intervene.

Dokuri had made him question his loyalty for the second time in his life. If the emperor had not redeemed himself by rescuing Jeruko after Dokuri had left him for dead on a battlefield, he would not be here now.

The emperor's mouth turned down. "Don't let your sentiment get the best of you, Colonel. I'm just giving the boy the opportunity to reflect on his incompetence."

Jeruko eased out a sigh.

"You may retrieve him, but not until the last moment," the emperor added.

Jeruko bowed low to hide his relief.

"But," Emperor Mizuki said, halting Jeruko's heart, "he will receive cybernetic enhancements. I will not have a failure as a son."

A pang stabbed inside Jeruko's chest. "But—"

The emperor flicked his hand. "No need for concern. The cyborgs assured me the tech won't be detectable."

"That isn't what concerns me, Sire."

"What is it, then?" A flash of anger sparked in the emperor's eyes.

Jeruko treaded with care. "I'm concerned about his loss of humanity."

The emperor's mouth turned down questioningly.

"Have you noticed how these cyborgs never seem to laugh or be angry? Their emotions are flat."

"Emotion is weakness, Colonel. You know that."

"Perhaps, but this is different. They are more machines than men."

"Be at ease, Jeruko," the emperor replied with less severity. "Nothing as drastic as what they did to our soldiers will happen to my son."

"Thank you, Sire, but how can we be sure? We're still struggling to understand the technology on our senshi."

"If it makes you feel better, you may investigate and oversee the procedure."

Jeruko bowed to hide his discomfort. "I have no more understanding of what they're doing than anyone else."

"That's *your* problem. This will be done, though."

Not if I do something about it. This couldn't happen. He must stop this. Some ideas sprouted, but the odds were too great.

"If I may point out another matter that concerns me, Sire?"

The emperor gestured for him to go ahead.

"I'm worried about the false superiority these enhancements give. The abilities of our augmented senshi are artificial. The Mizuki house has been built on real accomplishments. By enhancing the young prince, his deeds will be illegitimate."

Emperor Mizuki darkened.

Once again, Nezumi intervened on his behalf. "How dare you dispute the honor of our sovereign!"

Jeruko's neutral composure vanished with a flash of uncharacteristic anger. "You know that's not what I meant."

Nezumi barked a laugh. "You've done nothing but argue against what's already decided."

"Do not question my loyalty!" Jeruko barked. "All your conniving will not undo all the years I have loyally served—"

"Enough!" The emperor smacked the palm of his hand on the armrest of his chair and bent to Jeruko with dark, hooded brows. "I've made my decision and I will hear no more about it. Is that understood?"

Jeruko winced. "Yes, Sire. Of course."

His heart sank with helplessness. He needed a way to end to this madness. It must be something that wouldn't put either himself or Terkeshi in danger. Risking his own life didn't bother him, but he couldn't leave the young man to deal with this on his own.

First, I must save him from the void. With another bow, he retreated to the operations station to get more information on Terkeshi's status.

*****

3791:094:23:32. The tension in Jin Jeruko's shoulders eased as he caught up to Terkeshi's escape pod. "Terke-chan," he called on a private channel.

"Sensei! You've come!"

The relief in Terkeshi's tone broke through Jeruko's reserved demeanor. "Of course I've come. I wouldn't leave you out here."

"D-does Father know you're helping me?" Terkeshi asked, followed by what sounded like a sniffle.

"Yes. I have his consent."

"I didn't mean to lose. Something happened with the ship. I tried to initiate a fix, but it didn't—"

"It's alright, Terke-chan. I know how well you can fight."

"Father's not happy, is he?"

Jeruko couldn't lie. He grasped for some truth that might ease the boy's worries. Nothing came to mind, though. "I'm sorry. He's losing sight of what's important." First Jori, and now Terkeshi. When would it end?

"I've had a lot of time to think," Terkeshi said. "Father's right. I need these enhancements."

Jeruko's breath caught. "You can't, my Lord. Your father is wrong. Perhaps this isn't your fault. Is it possible someone sabotaged your ship?" His thoughts turned to Nezumi. That conniving chima would stoop that low, but how could he have pulled it off with no one noticing?

He reached Terkeshi's pod and manipulated the controls until he matched his speed and trajectory. "Malkai checked everything over before you left, right?"

"Yes, and I doubt he missed anything."

Jeruko frowned. The young man was right. Malkai had better than average mechanical engineering skills.

"Somebody could have bribed him."

"No," Jeruko replied sharply. "His loyalty is too strong."

"Maybe someone threatened him."

Jeruko aimed the magnetized tow line and fired. It shot out and adhered to Terkeshi's pod. "If that had been the case, he would have confided in me. I saw him just before I left to get you and he didn't indicate anything was amiss."

"What if the cyborgs did something?"

"That's crossed my mind, but how? They've been nowhere near the hangar bay." Jeruko tested the line's connection. The green light on his console told him it held.

Terk made a dejected sound through the comm. "Then it's settled. I'm just a fuck-up."

Jeruko engaged his thrusters to reverse their trajectory. "That is not true. Your father is too hard on you and expects too much."

"He only expects me to be like Dokuri. Face it. I'm not even close to being as good as him."

Jeruko tightened his grip on the controls and towed him back to the *Dragon*. "There was nothing good about Dokuri, boy. Don't *ever* compare yourself to him. You are better by far."

"Bullshit. The only way I'll be better is if I become a cyborg."

Jeruko winced. "This is not the way, Terke-chan."

"What choice do I have, old man?"

Jeruko ignored the boy's disrespect. After all he'd just endured and considering the future horrors to come, he didn't need a disciplinary lesson right now. He needed a friend. "We will figure something out together. I have an idea—"

"What?" Terkeshi barked. "Another half-assed plan that will defy Father and get me killed? No. I must go through with this. I can never be as good as Jori, so this is the only option left."

"Terkeshi…"

"I'm going through with it," Terkeshi grumbled. "Don't try to talk me out of it, either. I'm done being a failure."

The urge to cry swelled, but Jeruko held it back. Terkeshi's hardness frightened him at times. The boy had never been cruel, but would that change if his father kept pushing him? Would becoming a cyborg turn him into both a machine and a monster? Jeruko prayed it wouldn't be so—but praying seemed to do little good as of late.

The young man was right. He had no choices left. Stopping the emperor was no longer an option if Terkeshi resigned to his fate.

He swallowed the lump in his throat and submitted to the inevitable.

20
Healing the Heart

3791:095:07:21. Jin Jeruko walked with leaden steps down the oppressive white corridors of the cyborg ship. He imagined Terkeshi's face in the impassive human machines he came across. A woman with her head shaved to make room for wires and ports passed by with a hiss and creak of her mechanical legs. A large man wore a visor that appeared to be permanently embedded over his eyes. Another man with red-tinted skin didn't have any obvious enhancements, but his unblinking eyes remained forward, and his body moved too perfectly.

Jeruko sighed. Although he prayed for a way to change Terkeshi's fate, his and the emperor's sustained obstinacy zapped his confidence and weighed him down.

Ambrose met him in the hall. Jeruko attempted to retain his outward composure. "Greetings," he said with a dip of his head. "Thank you for agreeing to speak with me."

Ambrose bowed. "Of course. How may I serve the emperor's right-hand man?"

Jeruko frowned at what he suspected was false praise. The emperor used to rely on him, but no longer. He inhaled deeply. "Well, let's start with how no one will detect the tech you plan on putting in the young prince."

Ambrose put on a flat smile. "The components mimic proteins that are already common in our bodies. They don't react to scans, and they create normal wastes so that nothing unusual is found in body fluid tests."

"How can they mimic proteins?"

"Not just mimic. We engineered them from organic proteins, and they work the same way as their natural counterparts, albeit with extra functions."

"I'm not sure I understand," Jeruko said. "Are you saying you are using real human elements to create a machine?"

"The human body is a machine," Ambrose replied.

"I disagree."

"It is the most advanced natural machine in the galaxy—a machine with a soul, if you believe in that sort of thing. The brain is the CPU that controls the body. In fact, machines are often based on what we've learned about our own biological functions. Have we not built them to act like a heart for those with heart defects? And ones that can replace limbs or eyes, or even our digestive systems?"

"But they are machines," Jeruko said, "and machines can be detected by scanners."

"Not our machines," Ambrose said. "We possess the technology to grow an entire heart that looks and acts like a real human heart, but better because it is flawless and will never fail."

"If you can engineer human organs, could you fix the emperor's genetic problem? This way he can sire more children." Jeruko's insides wriggled at the thought of replacing Terkeshi, but this option might buy more time. He'd make a viable plan and convince the young man to leave this terrible place.

Ambrose shook his head. "Growing human organs is one thing. Changing one's genetic code after they are already grown is possible but dangerous. We'd put the emperor's life at risk."

That doesn't sound so bad. Fixing the emperor's genetic replication problem didn't violate the MEGA Injunction because it would only restore him to his original state. However, he was unlikely to take the risk. "What about cloning him without the genetic deficiency?"

"Yes, that is entirely possible."

Jeruko cringed but considered it. Cloning and genetic modifications were just as illegal as biometric enhancements, though. And suggesting them wouldn't deter the emperor from modifying Terkeshi.

"It would be expensive, however," Ambrose added. "We are not authorized to give more."

Jeruko narrowed his eyes. Why were they providing Terkeshi with enhancements then? They'd already given cybernetics to five senshi. They were undoubtedly up to something, but he didn't have enough information to convince the emperor.

Not yet. "May I see the lab where you grow these proteins? I'd also like a look at the enhanced specimens you intend to put in the prince."

Ambrose bowed. "Of course."

The man pivoted a perfect one hundred and eighty degrees and led the way.

Jeruko reflected on their conversation as he followed. What Ambrose said about growing human organs had stuck in his head. This technology was far beyond what the Toradons were capable of, but only because they were warriors—not doctors or scientists.

Did other civilizations know how to do this? He remembered reading something about the complexity of it. The primary complication was getting all the specialized tissues of organs to work together into a function as efficient as the human body. Surely it couldn't be done.

But what if it could? Jeruko's heart thumped at the possibility.

"I'd like to know more about this ability to grow organs," he said as Ambrose pressed his hand to a biometric keypad. "Can your people truly do such a thing?"

The door swished open, revealing a room that shone with sterility. "Most certainly."

Jeruko shielded his eyes from the brightness and wrinkled his nose at the smell of antiseptic. "All types of human organs?"

"All except the brain," Ambrose replied. "The brain is still beyond our abilities."

"So you can grow a heart?"

Ambrose nodded. "Yes. It's an elaborate process but it can be done."

The heart. Where Jori was stabbed. Jeruko's own heart thudded wildly. The emperor's increased madness had put the boy in danger, so the plan had been for him to escape with the Cooperative prisoners. He'd been killed less than a minute before being transported to the enemy ship. What if the Cooperative had resuscitated him? Surely they had the means to temporarily bypass the heart with machines. But did they have the technology to grow a new one? "Do you know if other cultures can do this, or are your people the only ones?"

"The Prontaean Cooperative has this ability and has shared the knowledge with many others."

Jeruko's body tingled at the prospect. Did the people on the ship Jori had escaped to possess the capability? And if so, would they have used it on him?

This wouldn't change the current course of events, but it would mean everything to Terkeshi if his little brother still lived. Instead of listening to Ambrose as he droned on about enhanced proteins, Jeruko considered how he could contact the Cooperative without the emperor finding out.

21
Nightmare

3791:095:15:32. The moist heat settled in Terkeshi's lungs like a wet blanket. He sweltered as he tromped through the forest. A heaviness hung over him as though he carried a dark raincloud on his back. He practically melted, much the way the trees here did with their drooping branches and despondent leaves.

"Hurry, my Lord," Sensei Jeruko said. "He's here, just up ahead."

Terk pushed a branch out of his path and stumbled after his mentor. The man should have been stumbling too, but he glided along like a boat down a river.

Terk considered asking him how he did that, but he couldn't catch his breath. He forced his feet to move and forged on.

Sensei Jeruko stopped and motioned with his hand, urging Terk forward. "He's alive, my Lord. You'll see." A broad smile uncharacteristically plastered the man's face.

Terk wiped his brow with his forearm and flicked the excess water away with a splatter. He frowned at his mentor's back. *Why isn't he sweating?*

Sensei Jeruko almost floated as he led the way. Branches and bushes moved aside for him.

How is he doing that, damn it?

Everything shifted. One moment he trudged along the forest floor, the next he stood at the edge of a clearing. He knew hours had passed, yet time flowed seamlessly.

Sensei Jeruko pointed with exaggerated enthusiasm. "There, my Lord. He's in there."

Terk cupped his hand over his brow and peered into the distance. A pristinely white building sat isolated in the vast valley, contrasting against the emerald meadow surrounding it. As he walked, the grass turned into vicious patches of briar. Sickly trees slumped much like those of the forest except with rotted fruit instead of leaves.

Terk stepped over the dead limbs and trunks that littered the now rocky ground. He dreaded the distance, but he had to see for himself. Could it really be him? It had to be. Everything that had happened must have just been a mistake—a misunderstanding.

As he trekked onward, time shifted again. Now he stood at the base of a large white door. It had no knobs or handles to open it, nor a keypad or biometric scanner. *How do I get inside?*

A doorbell appeared. With the press of his finger, a reverberating gong shook the ground and punched his eardrums. He put his hands over his ears.

"Sensei! What's going on?"

When he glanced around, however, Sensei Jeruko was nowhere to be seen. *Oh, he must've left.*

The door slid upward, revealing white booted feet. A torso appeared next. When the mechanism rose high enough, Terk found himself facing Ambrose, the cyborg with the roving metal eye.

"Where's my brother?" Terk demanded. "I know he's here."

"He is, young Prince," Ambrose said with his bland smile. "This way, please."

Terk followed him. The man's steps were normal, but the clickety-clack and metallic whirring of his cybernetic components echoed down the hall. The corridor went on endlessly. Long, straight white walls disappeared into a singularity of blinding light.

They walked on, never passing any doors or intersections. Nothing adorned the passageway—no pictures, no viewscreens, not even emergency boxes containing breathing apparatuses or fire peril equipment.

Time shifted. Terk stood before another door. This one was also white, but it had a handle.

Was he supposed to go through? He turned to ask the cyborg, but the man had gone. Didn't he say he had other business to attend to? Terk didn't remember.

He gripped the handle and slid it open, revealing pure darkness.

"Jori? Are you in here?"

The pitch blackness should have made Terk wary, but he was too excited to be frightened.

"Jori?"

A blast of cold air swept past him, making him shiver. *This isn't right.* He turned to leave.

A bright light erupted. Terk shielded his eyes. He blinked rapidly and let them adjust. A blurred figure stood before him.

"Jori?"

The form coalesced. It had Jori's short stature. Terk squinted as it came into focus.

Terk gasped. "Jori! You're al—"

He stopped dead. This wasn't Jori. Not anymore. An optical sensor took the place of his left eye. Instead of an arm, he had a cannon-like weapon.

Terk dropped to his knees. "No! What have they done to you?"

"You did this," a mechanical voice coming from Jori said.

Terk wagged his head. "No, no, no. It can't be. This can't be you."

"It is me. And soon it will be you."

Terk froze as Jori's robotic cannon-arm rose. The blue energy point of light from the muzzle aimed between his eyes.

"No!"

Terk bolted upright with a gasp. His heart pounded wildly in his ears. The dream flittered away, but the cybernetic face of his little brother hovered in his vision.

"Lights!" Terk said to the computer.

With a flash, the room lit up. He took in his surroundings. The area came into focus, revealing his own bedroom. Everything appeared normal. He controlled his breathing until his heart calmed. The sweat on his brow chilled, then evaporated.

It was just a dream—a terrible dream. This comforted him somewhat, but the horror of it still lingered.

Hours ago, when Terk had headed to his quarters for his sleep cycle, Sensei Jeruko intercepted him and said he discovered something about Jori. General Nezumi lurked nearby and kept him from saying more. Terk dared to believe he'd meant Jori was alive. That wasn't possible, though. He'd felt his lifeforce extinguish and found the hilt of the dagger protruding from his heart.

A pang filled Terk's chest. His brother was gone. Gone forever. He wasn't coming back. Not ever. And certainly not as a cyborg. He'd rather Jori be dead than turned into a machine.

Realization struck him and fear replaced his pain. He dropped his head into his palms. Soon, this same head would hold cybernetic tech.

He didn't want this. The very idea of scooping out his human parts and replacing them with machines made his stomach turn. The prospect of losing his humanity hovered over him like a heavy club.

But what choice did he have?

Maybe he could run away.

He almost laughed. Jori had tried to escape this awful place and look where that got him.

No, he must go through with the procedure. It was the only way to improve his skills. He could shed this stupid emotional weakness and finally do something great.

He didn't need these emotions anyway. They hindered him. No longer would the loss of his little brother haunt or cripple him. It was time to put an end to his deficiencies.

He sucked in a breath and hardened his resolve. Soon, he would be worthy of the Mizuki name.

22
Surveillance

3791:095:22:57. A draft from an upper vent chilled the communications room. Hopefully, the beads of sweat forming on Jin Jeruko's brow evaporated before those watching through surveillance picked up on his nervousness.

To keep from feeding the emperor's rising paranoia, he opted not to send this message from his quarters. This public area was the best place to keep from raising anyone's suspicions but the worst place to hide his actions.

Jeruko sat a little taller, blocking as much of his screen from the camera behind him as possible. Placing both hands over the keyboard and moving his fingers quickly, he attempted to disguise the recipient's address. The terminal kept track of all entries, but thanks to Jori, he knew how to delete them without triggering the AI security system.

A prompt popped up, asking whether he wanted to send a video or written message. Jeruko selected text. He then moved the dialog box to the bottom corner where the camera wouldn't see it.

> <J.Jeruko> Colonel Jin Jeruko, aka Sensei Jeruko, here. I sincerely apologize for how your visit ended. I pray all is well and hope the subject is safe in your care. Sources indicate it expired before transit. However, I understand you have procedures to counter such mishaps. Is your agency capable of creating replacement parts? If so, would they allow such a procedure in this particular case? Please respond to 19395H5LBX. I anxiously await your reply.

Jeruko paused before hitting send. A pitter patter in his chest casted a wave of nervous energy through him. He reread the message, making sure it was clear yet vague enough in case anyone else discovered it. This was the best he could do, so he sent it off.

No turning back now. A part of him remained uneasy but he breathed a sigh, thankful it had been done. Now to wait on the edge of a precipice until either he got caught or received a reply.

Jeruko created another message, this one innocuous. Afterward, he discreetly entered a backdoor to the system that Jori had set up, then removed all evidence of the traitorous communiqué. If anyone reviewed the surveillance footage, they'd assume he'd only sent the sanctioned one.

He left his station with finality and exited the room. A passing senshi prompted a new concern. This was an ordinary warrior, but how much longer before the emperor wanted armies of cyber senshi? The break from tradition and honor wasn't the only thing that concerned him.

What would it mean for the poorer levels of society if cybernetics were allowed? In Toradon, being born from the lowest caste was hard enough. Those people lived the most difficult lives, subject to the dominance and cruelty of every higher caste. If the upper classes became mindless machines, would that make the others even more dispensable?

A machine doesn't consider the quality of life of its subjects. It doesn't care about the welfare of children. Nor does it account for the chance that one of these lowly people might be worth more than fodder for the mines.

Jeruko passed a shokukin and dipped his head in appreciation. Something that always troubled him about serving the emperor was a detached disregard for the value of the workers—as if they could function without them.

Worse, if cybernetics took over, humanity would be lost. No more mothers doting on their children or fathers praising their sons. No more joyous celebrations or elated feelings of accomplishment. Love and happiness would cease to exist, leaving everything to be assessed by an unfeeling algorithm.

Jeruko shivered.

The corridor ended in a T. Jeruko took the left and nearly ran into Samuru and Nezumi. "My apologies, Generals."

Samuru shrugged. "No apology necessary, Colonel."

"Coming from the communications room, I presume?" Nezumi's eyes narrowed to slits as he put on a fake smile.

Jeruko tensed but maintained an outward calm. "Yes." He owed them no explanation.

Nezumi's head tilted to the side. "Why do it from there rather than in your own quarters?"

Because I know you're plotting against me, you fiend. "I felt it prudent."

"Ah. As wise as ever, Colonel. Well, I'll leave you to your duties, then. I'm sure you have much to do."

As Jeruko moved on, Nezumi's whispers to Samuru pricked his ears. *Damn him.* It was bad enough the rat-faced chima whispered in the emperor's ear. Now he involved another Talon.

He prayed Samuru wouldn't get pulled into these games. Although the man lacked great intellect, he recognized the counterproductive nature of internal dissent.

Jeruko forced himself to stop worrying. Even if Nezumi snooped into his communications, he'd find nothing incriminating. Conniving though he was, he didn't have a way to retrieve an encrypted message deleted from the system.

Before long, Jeruko found himself in the common dojo where the five enhanced senshi sparred. Rather than practice himself, he observed the new ways they moved.

He couldn't pinpoint what made their fight appear automated. Perhaps their attacks and defenses were too flawless, or their eyes remained too fixed on their opponents. Maybe their silence was too strict.

Jeruko tilted his ear in their direction. Neither exchanged the usual banter that accompanied most other competitions.

"They're good, aren't they?"

Jeruko startled at Terkeshi's arrival but regained his composure. "I've seen simulations with more character. They can't even hit one another. It's no longer about which one has more skill, but which one has the superior programming."

"They're still human," Terkeshi replied, yet Jeruko doubted the sincerity of his words.

"Are they? Will you be?" Jeruko lowered his voice, knowing surveillance was everywhere. "Don't submit to this, my Lord. You're better than this."

Terkeshi grunted. "That's not what Father says."

Your Father is wrong. He dared not say it out loud, lest he reveal his increasing misgivings about the current sovereignty. "Being better isn't just about being able to fight or kill. It's about caring for your people. All your people, not merely the ones who support your desire for wealth and power."

"You're talking about sentiment," Terkeshi said as an admonition, though he matched Jeruko's quiet tone.

"Emotion is not a weakness, my Lord. It's the one thing that makes you a man rather than a mindless machine."

"Emotion is death. Just ask Jori."

"There's a chance he might be alive," Jeruko whispered.

Terkeshi blinked, but his expression quickly twisted into disbelief. "Impossible. You cling to false hopes, old man. Face it. He's dead because of his sentiment."

"Your brother had the right of it."

"He was a traitor," Terkeshi said between clenched teeth.

Jeruko forced his voice into a quieter timbre. "His decision to help the prisoners held more value than the honor of everyone on this ship combined."

"What good was his honor if it got him killed?"

A pang struck Jeruko's chest. He opened his mouth to retort but his words stuck in his throat. He grasped for a hope too small to hold. Jori had died to save the prisoners. If it were possible to go back and let the enemies die instead, he do it. But where would that have left Jori if his father had murdered the people he'd come to care about?

Alive but worse off, that's where. "What good is a life without honor?"

Jeruko allowed a pained expression to show through, but Terkeshi wouldn't meet his eyes. The youth's countenance remained ungiving.

"Don't let your father change you, my Lord. I beg you." Jeruko shifted his feet as though trying to balance on the edge of an abyss. He'd come to terms with betraying the emperor by going behind his back because he still supported the son. But what would he do if the son became his father—or worse—a machine?

*****

3791:095:23:42. Terkeshi clenched his fists. Sensei Jeruko's words made sense, but how could he belittle Jori's death so easily? He might as well have said he deserved to be killed because of his honor.

What was honor anyway? Sensei Jeruko spouted idealistic phrases, but they didn't match Terk's reality. Of course it was about fighting and killing. What else was a senshi good for?

But he knew what his mentor would say—fight and kill for a worthy cause, not because your father tells you to. But isn't obedience a part of honor? Even if it means becoming a cyborg?

"Sire," Sensei Jeruko whispered, "I know it's unlikely, but what if the Cooperative had a way to save your brother's life?"

Terk stiffened as he recalled his nightmare. "Don't be ridiculous. I felt him die."

"The technology to grow new organs exists."

A spike of hope jabbed him but cut through, leaving only a wound behind. "The Cooperative would never do that."

"The commander seemed like a good man."

"Him, yes. Not the rest."

"But what if—"

"Don't speak to me of this!" He wanted his brother to be alive more than anyone, but Sensei Jeruko had nothing to base his belief on. Hoping for the impossible only dragged out his grief. In a quieter voice, he added, "Face it. Jori is gone."

Sensei Jeruko kept his expression neutral, but his body seemed to deflate. Terk ground his teeth. *Well, that's what he gets for clinging to sentiment.*

He focused on the cybernetic warriors in the ring. They'd become more machine-like lately. Tokagei attacked with the swiftness of a blackbeast while Yujio defended with the doggedness of a horned prey protecting its young. Without word or signal, the men switched roles with Tokagei taking the defense.

This was why they called hand-to-hand combat a martial *art*. Their moves mesmerized him. Every forceful strike sent Terk's heart beating faster. He could have their strength and dexterity.

It wouldn't cost his humanity. He wouldn't let it. Besides, Father had said his implants would be different. He'd retain all his exterior physical traits. No metal, no wires. It would still be him when he looked in the mirror.

The cyborgs halted by some unarticulated signal. They turned to him in unison with an identical stance.

"My Lord," Tokagei said in an abnormally flat tone. "Did you enjoy the show?"

Terk's blood drained from his face. "How did you do that? How did you know to stop like that?"

"We finished," Yujio replied.

Terk swallowed. "You can communicate silently?"

They didn't react at first. Perhaps they conversed again. Then they moved their heads up and down concurrently.

The hair on Terk's arms rose. He glanced over to Sensei Jeruko, only to find the man had gone. "Ambrose didn't say you could do this."

"There are a lot of things we can do now," Tokagei said.

"You like these abilities more than your humanity?"

"We are better than human."

Terk resisted the urge to fidget. "You didn't earn this."

"No, but these enhancements are the destiny of all humans."

Terk shivered. "All?"

Tokagei shrugged. "Well, not all. Just the best ones."

"You were never the best. We chose you because you're merely mediocre."

For the first time since Terk had been watching them, Tokagei emitted a flash of emotion. "I was a senshi. And now I'm an even greater senshi. Greater than you."

Terk's hackles pricked. "Watch your mouth! I earned my abilities while yours are a sham."

"Your abilities are—"

"Silence, fool!" Terk said before the man's smugness got him killed. "I still outrank you. Soon I'll outmatch you, too."

Tokagei dipped his head in mock respect.

Terk let it pass, not wanting to look like a fool by throwing a tantrum. It didn't matter anyway. In just a few more hours, he would be their superior in every aspect.

23
The Procedure

3791:096:07:14. Terkeshi leaned onto the bed and slid into a seated position. He wet the inside of his mouth and pulled up the sleeve of his medical gown. A cybernetic medic tied a tourniquet around his upper arm, sending an odd twinge prickling down the limb.

This bald medic who might have been a woman, investigated his forearm, then rubbed it with a cold fluid. She held his wrist with icy metallic fingers that made him tremble.

He turned away to quell the disconcerting sensation of seeing the cyborg but not feeling her lifeforce. "*I understand your concern,*" Ambrose had said. "*But this lack of lifeforce, as you call it, only occurs in those with electronic components added to their brains.*" Ambrose emitted more of a lifeforce than most, but Terk still couldn't tell if he had spoken the truth.

The explanation that Terk's enhancements were made from organic material eased his concerns but didn't eliminate them. A nervous energy coursed through him as the needle slid into a vein. The medic taped the IV in place, then removed the tourniquet. His arm tingled as the flow of blood resumed.

She opened the IV line. Frigidness spread from his forearm in a dissipating wave.

"How long will this surgery take?" his father asked.

"Five hours, twenty-four minutes," the medic replied as she verified the IV drip.

Father frowned but didn't comment on her exactness.

Terk cleared his throat. "What will you do to me?"

"The nanites in this bag will—"

Terk flinched. "There are nanites in that?"

"Yes."

Terk faced his father with a furrowed brow. "Did you know about this?"

"What did you think would happen, boy?"

"I thought they were just implanting a cybernetic eye."

Father looked at him as though he were daft. "You need a CPU to operate it."

"The CPU isn't part of the optics?"

Father flicked his hand to the medic. "Explain this to him."

"These organically engineered nanites will coalesce in the optical lobe and create a synthetic neurotransmitter to your eye."

Terk pressed his palm to his chest to subdue his racing heart. "You're fucking with my brain!"

The cyborg cocked her head, but he sensed no confusion from her. "This is how it is done."

"Father! I changed my mind. I don't want to be like them." He pulled at the IV.

The medic grabbed his wrist. "I would not do that if I were you."

"It's too late, boy," Father said. For once, the anger left his face. However, Terk didn't like the satisfied smug that replaced it.

He struggled to pry the cyborg's metal fingers from his arm, but they wouldn't budge. "I can do better without this. Don't let them do this to me. I will be as forceful as Dokuri and as smart as Jori."

"Remain calm, or there could be complications," the medic said in a detached tone.

His breaths shallowed. Faintness buzzed behind his eyes. "What do you mean *complications*?"

The cyborg opened her mouth to speak but Father interrupted. "Don't answer that." He glared at Terk. "Calm down, boy. Don't fuck this up, too."

Terk suppressed a whimper. "It wasn't my fault my ship exploded."

"Who else's fault would it be? The shokukin examined the ship before you took off. Are you telling me they missed something?"

Terk clamped his mouth closed. He didn't want to shift the blame onto them. He considered blaming the cyborgs, but pointing fingers made him look pathetic and desperate. Father would never buy it.

He could fight it, but that was pointless. Father's arms and neck corded with power. The muscle over his eye jerked, making him appear more menacing than usual.

Terk brought up his recent revelation instead. "Did you know our cyber senshi can communicate with one another silently?"

A troubled look crossed his father's face, but it disappeared quickly. It even left his emotions, like a swift wind had blown it away. "I wouldn't concern yourself. When you're enhanced, you'll have the same capability."

A chill went down Terk's spine. "It's not natural. They're turning me into a machine."

His father leaned in. The bronze flecks in his eyes sparked. "At least you'll finally measure up to Dokuri."

Terk's face burned. "He was full grown. You haven't even given me a chance—"

"I've given you several chances!"

Terk swallowed. He should stand up to him and tell him he wouldn't do it. That's what Jori would've done. The little brat's stubbornness had outmatched Father's demands many times.

Terk opened his mouth to voice his refusal, but nothing came out. Fighting him would be foolish.

His father pulled back and spoke in a less heated tone. "You have no idea what we're up against. Worlds beyond ours are advancing in technology every day. My ships and my weapons are becoming obsolete. My father lost much of our territories, and I don't have the resources to recoup them."

Terk shied from the intensity of Father's distress.

"I will not let the Mizuki line end with failure," Father continued. "Since you can't live up to the name on your own, you'll lead a new generation of warriors instead."

Terk swallowed. Every attempt he'd made to prove himself had failed. He grasped for other reasons but only pulled up the same old arguments. "Why doesn't it bother you that the cyborgs are giving us these things in exchange for some distant promise? They must want something in return—something they're not telling you."

"I've got it handled, boy. Unlike you, I don't flounder through life without a plan. So they want our men to fight for their cause someday. I see nothing wrong with that. We are warriors, after all. Fighting is what we do."

"But we're doing it for them, not ourselves."

"We *are* doing this for ourselves. We will have the most powerful army in the galaxy."

Terk searched his thoughts. His father made sense. The cyborgs enhanced their warriors to gain soldiers, but they still belonged to Father. "But at what cost? We'll be machines, not men."

"Don't be a fool, boy. We will always be men."

"This feels like cheating," Terkeshi replied in desperation.

His father huffed. "It wouldn't be necessary to cheat if Dokuri were alive."

Terk dropped his chin. He'd run out of arguments. "I understand, Sir."

"Good. Now get on with it."

The cybernetic medic connected another IV bag. Terk sweated despite the new wave of coldness washing through his body. His eyelids drooped. She pushed against his chest, trying to make him lie down. He considered resisting, but the desire flittered away as his brain fogged.

Was this what it felt like to lose his humanity?

*****

3791:096:09:23. Kenji Mizuki held his chin high as he stood before the viewing window and observed the surgery. Terkeshi lay flat and unmoving on a white-sheeted bed. The pathetic fear that had filled his face only moments before was gone, replaced by a blank expression that he should wear more often.

Emotion is weakness, boy. Why haven't you learned that yet?

It had been one failure after another with him. Getting captured by the Cooperative—incompetent. Being blind to his little brother's sentiment for the prisoners—oblivious. Letting that cargo captain go without so much as a switching—cowardly. The training incident had been the last straw, exposing all his faults and proving he was incapable of doing better.

Sure, Terkeshi didn't have Jori's squeamishness, but he was a far cry from Dokuri—and too damned sentimental to be a true warrior.

Mizuki never should have let either him or Jori stay with their mother for so long. Her weak nature had obviously infected them—Jori to the point of betrayal.

Damn her, damn that boy, and damn Terkeshi.

He clenched his jaw—the spasm jerked hard enough to make him wink. A shadow lurked in the corner of his vision, but he had no patience for Jori's accusations. The dead had no right to keep pestering him.

A towering robotic machine approached Terkeshi's bed. Mizuki craned his neck, looking for the two cyborgs who were supposed to do the surgery. *There they are.* They sat at a console with blank expressions. A cable ran from the back of their heads and plugged into the computer.

Another robot joined the one by Terkeshi. Each machine extended three mechanical arms over the unconscious boy's eye.

Are the cyborgs operating through the robots, then? Mizuki wasn't sure how he felt about his son being operated on by machinery. Then again, Ambrose had said they'd do most of this operation at a nanoscale. The machines were steadier and more precise than a human.

Tiny clamps at the end of each appendage grasped Terkeshi's eyelids and pulled them open. A robotic arm from the ceiling drew down. This one looked like a giant multi-tool pocketknife. The first implement to slide out was a pair of scissors. The arm advanced until the scissors reached a corner of the boy's eyelid and snipped.

Mizuki winced. He mentally shook himself. Terkeshi needed this. How else could the boy effectively continue the Mizuki line? Without enhancements, he'd be just like any other senshi. Nothing special. Nothing to make him stand out.

The scissors cut a thin film from around the boy's eyeball. Mizuki forced himself to keep watching. It was stupid to be squeamish about such things.

A brassy repetitive clack resounded from behind him. He frowned as a man with four mechanical arms passed by. His robotic feet smacked onto the hard floor, creating a grating metallic sound. Nearly his entire face had been replaced with synthetic parts.

Mizuki quelled the horror attempting to rise within. Who would do this to themselves? Perhaps Terkeshi had been right. These people were more machines than men.

He shook off his unease and resumed his observation. After all, it was for the best.

This had better work.

24
Saboteurs

3791:096:12:02. Kenji Mizuki scowled at the man-machine on his deskview screen. Although what Terkeshi had said about the cyber senshi having secret conversations hadn't bothered him in that moment, he'd had a lot of time to dwell on it. How dare this creature hide things from him. What other hidden abilities were implanted in the senshi?

Ambrose planted a flat smile on his veneer face. "Your Eminence, they have numerous functionalities. We outlined them all in the manual."

"Including the ability to have secret communications?"

"They are not secret from you, Sire. You can access them through the interface program."

"Show me."

After Ambrose directed him to a reports page, the twitching in Mizuki's eye subsided. How had he missed it? It was all right here—video, audio, and messaged dialog. All showing the time and where they'd taken place.

They're watching everything. Mizuki tensed. His nostrils flared as the implications hurtled through his thoughts. "Are they spies?"

"They are your spies," Ambrose answered.

"But you can access this too."

"Only until we are sure all their cybernetics are operating properly."

They're lying. They're using these men to spy on me. Mizuki glanced around the room. A shadow darted on the edge of his peripheral vision. He gritted his teeth, knowing it wasn't real—just Jori's ghost haunting his imagination.

"You have all the control, your Eminence," Ambrose continued.

Mizuki rubbed his temple. Even if the cyborgs lied, it didn't matter right now. Once he had the emitter fixed, he wouldn't need them. And if he found out they were using the cyber senshi to spy on him, he'd eliminate them all.

He ended the communication and huffed. Forget about them. He had more important matters to deal with.

Mizuki made a note to assign someone to listen to the communications, then resumed his work. Despite his attempt to concentrate on the financial report, his grandfather's helmet mocked him. The lesson his old sensei had imparted with its story kept intruding on his thoughts. He imagined his teacher shaking his finger as he had spoken. *"Don't rely on technology to win you the battle. Rely on your own strength."*

A sour taste rose in Mizuki's mouth. This second-guessing must stop. *What's done is done.* Terkeshi's path was an honorable one, for he'd be the first Mizuki leader of his kind. He'd help usher in a new era and ensure the Dragon hegemony.

Mizuki's comm beeped. He answered more eagerly than intended. "What is it?"

"Sire," an operations officer from the bridge said. "We've received an alert that a fire has broken out in the auxiliary bay."

Mizuki jumped to his feet. If something happened to the perantium emitter, this would all be for naught. "What caused it?"

"We don't know yet. We've contacted the cyborgs and they say it's under control."

Mizuki was about to open the communications section of his console to contact Ambrose when a priority message icon flashed on his screen.

He jabbed it as he plopped back down into his chair. "What the hell happened?" he asked the cyborg who appeared.

"A minor accident, your Eminence. Nothing more." Ambrose replied.

"Explain *minor*."

"A capacitor shorted. Do not concern yourself. We can easily replace it."

Mizuki flared his nostrils. "I was told there was a fire."

"Not a fire, only a bit of smoke."

A little of Mizuki's tension released. "How did it happen?"

Ambrose hesitated. "It seems someone had redirected several circuits."

"Redirected? As in moved them into incorrect positions?"

"Something like that, yes."

"So sabotage." Mizuki balled his fists.

"Not to worry. It will take less than a half hour to fix."

"Was it sabotage?"

"We are uncertain, your Eminence."

Mizuki growled. "Your best guess, damn it!"

Ambrose put on a flat smile. "It could have been sabotage or ignorance."

Mizuki narrowed his eyes. "Who was the last one to work on it?"

"Prince Jori."

Mizuki struck his desk with a fist. "It's sabotage, you idiot!"

"Not necessarily. Someone so young could have done it in error."

"You don't know what he was capable of. Just because he didn't have enhancements doesn't mean he wasn't intelligent enough to do this on purpose."

Ambrose bowed. "We have no means to find out, your Eminence. However, I wouldn't concern yourself. It is being rectified."

The door chimed. He huffed and ended the call with Ambrose. "What is it *now*?"

"Sire," Nezumi said through the comm. "I have an urgent matter to report."

"If it's regarding the accident in the auxiliary bay, I'm already aware."

"No, Sire." Nezumi paused. "It's about Colonel Jeruko."

Mizuki grimaced at the way the general whispered. "This had better be important. I don't have time for your scheming."

"I'll let you decide, your Eminence," Nezumi replied in a tone that seemed unfazed by the accusation.

Mizuki rolled his eyes. "Enter."

The door swished open, and the rat-faced man entered with a smug expression. He took a deferential stance with his feet at shoulder width and his hand clasped behind his back. "Your Eminence. I suspect Colonel Jeruko is trying to corrupt your son."

125

Mizuki's eye twitched. "What did he do? And you'd better be careful, man. I don't want some flimsy charge made just so you can make yourself look good."

If the allegation offended Nezumi, he didn't show it. "I have a video of him whispering to the boy. The microphone picked up some words."

"Send it to me. I will decide what he's up to."

"Yes, Sire."

Nezumi tapped the MM tablet on his wrist and the message icon blinked on Mizuki's deskview. When he opened it, the recording took up the full screen.

"You may want to turn it up, Sire," Nezumi said.

Mizuki gave him a side-eye leer but turned up the volume. Terkeshi and Jeruko stood side-by-side in matching attentive poses. Their attention seemed to be on the sparring match between the cybernetic senshi.

"They're good, aren't they?" Terkeshi said.

"I've seen simulations with more character," Jeruko replied. "They can't even hit one another. It's no longer about which one has more skill, but which one has the superior programming."

Mizuki blinked. He'd never thought about it this way. Perhaps the enhancements Terkeshi had received wouldn't be enough.

"They're still human," Terkeshi said in a defensive tone that Mizuki was all too familiar with.

Jeruko replied, but the only word Mizuki made out was *don't*. He paused the recording and replayed it. He still heard little, but an s-word followed *don't*.

Rather than replay again, he continued the video.

"That's not what Father says," Terkeshi responded.

"Being better isn't just about being able to fight or kill," Jeruko responded in a low tone. "It's about caring for your people. All your people, not merely the ones who support your desire for wealth and power."

Mizuki's lips curled. What the hell was the man saying? That the job of ruling was solely for selfish needs? Hardly. No one understood the difficulty of his position. He wasn't some wealthy lord indulging in women and luxuries. He worked hard to manage his people and maintain his empire, giving every ounce of energy he had.

However, Jeruko's words weren't traitorous—merely inconsiderate.

"You're talking about sentiment," Terkeshi said.

Mizuki grunted. *Good reply, boy.*

Jeruko's brow turned down. "Emotion is not a weakness, my Lord. It's the one thing that makes you a man rather than a mindless machine."

What blasphemy is this?

"Emotion is death. Just ask Jori."

The side of Mizuki's mouth curled up. *You tell him, boy.*

It didn't seem Jeruko had a response to his comment, yet something caused Terkeshi to bare his teeth. What set him off? Mizuki replayed it.

Sounds like mumbling played through, but he couldn't tell for sure. *Chusho.* After a few more attempts, he let the video play through.

It seemed they had stopped speaking, but then a shadow crossed Jeruko's bearing. "What good is a life without honor?"

Although Mizuki agreed with him, he suspected there was more he hadn't heard. If only the recording had picked up their entire discussion.

Jeruko's face twisted into what could've been anguish while Terkeshi held a scowl. Was the boy angry with him? If so, why?

"Don't let your father change you, my Lord. I beg you," Jeruko said.

A heat ignited in Mizuki's chest. How dare he tell that boy to go against his wishes. *That fucking traitor.*

All the muscles in his body went taut. "Arrest him," he told Nezumi through clenched teeth.

25
Cyber Prince

3791:098:16:44. Terkeshi enabled the infrared feature, turning the surrounding men into red blobs.

"Lights out!" he commanded the computer. Except for the heat signatures, the TTAC room darkened.

A fiery figure came at him. Terk blocked the man's blow and sent him to the ground with a twist and a turn. Another cyber senshi attacked. He dodged the swing of an arm but something else struck his temple hard enough to jerk his head and tweak a muscle in his neck.

"Use the night vision feature," Ambrose said through a comm inside Terk's head.

Terk shook off the swelling unease that came every time he used this communication method.

"You can't see their special features with infrared," Ambrose added.

Special features? Terk twisted his mouth. More like special cheaters.

And now he was a cheater, too.

He mentally engaged the night vision feature in time to dodge another swing of Tokagei's cybernetic arm. More punches and jabs assailed him. Terk blocked and parried in a frenzy. If he didn't know any better, he'd say Tokagei was trying to kill him.

With a wordless signal, Terk shifted into offense mode. His breath quickened. His body burned from exertion. His stamina had always been above average, so how did Tokagei seem more refreshed? The cyber senshi blocked, parried, and dodged with more ease than he'd ever managed as a mere man.

Terk pressed on, his moves seemingly taking form of their own accord. Mushin, no mind, was the ideal way to fight, but this wasn't natural. He'd never fought so well in his life. What the hell?

Did the cyborgs infuse nanites all throughout him, too? If so, how? It was just supposed to be his eye.

Perhaps he'd merely found his confidence. With a conscious effort, he focused more on planning his next move. A feint followed by another, then a jab. Tokagei fell for it. Terk's fist smashed into his nose. Blood spurted, but the man fought on without pause.

Terk shifted to the defensive position. Left block. Upper block. Dodge. Sweat dripped from his forehead as he strained to keep up.

Tokagei swung with his mechanical arm. Terk raised his forearm to intercept but fatigue made him sluggish. A dizzying blow to the side of his head sent him sprawling.

"Chusho!" he said with a winded breath.

He rolled to his hands and knees. "Lights!"

The room illuminated, blinding him. He squinted his eyes and mentally turned off night vision. After blinking and reorientating himself, he discovered his blood puddled on the floor beneath him. He touched a hot stickiness gushing from a gash on his temple.

He forced himself to his feet. More blood spurted and a wave of dizziness washed over him. Someone gripped his arm, keeping him steady. Terk's vision returned, and he found Ambrose at his side. With a jerk, he broke the man's hold.

Tokagei stood before them in a stiff at-ease position. His face was devoid of emotion while blood oozed from his flattened nose.

"You're taking this well," Terk said.

"Why wouldn't I be?" Tokagei replied in a monotone voice.

"He can't feel it," Ambrose said, somehow knowing the real question.

Terk startled. "What do you mean, he can't feel it?"

"He's been infused with adrenaline."

"My adrenaline is flowing too, but I still perceive pain." Then Terk realized all that Ambrose had said. "Infused?"

"His enhancements are connected to his glands. They can produce more of the hormones necessary for certain tasks."

Terk's jaw dropped. "It gives him drugs?" Any form of stimulant that altered the human state frightened him. He'd taken a stimulant in the past and enjoyed it at the time, but it made him do things he never would have done normally. He'd lost control, and that had terrified him.

"It enhances his own systems," Ambrose said with his stupid flat smile. "When his body secretes certain hormones, like adrenaline, his enhanced network intensifies it and keeps it going."

Terk broke out into a cold sweat. "You will do this to me too?"

"Not to worry, young Prince. You shall soon realize the benefits and be grateful."

"You didn't answer my question."

"This function will evolve, but not to the same extent and not in the same way."

Terk's heart sent a burst of hot blood through his body. "Does my father know of this?"

"Certainly."

A faint sensation of truthfulness came from the man, but Terk didn't understand it. Why would his father go along with this?

"Pretty soon, my Lord," Tokagei said, "you will be as good as me."

The cyber senshi spoke with no emotion. The taunting behavior he had exhibited in the past was gone. Only a cold truth remained.

Terk shivered. *Sensei Jeruko was right.* They'd lost their humanity. How long until he lost his? "This is madness."

He glanced around the common dojo, hoping to see a familiar face. Sensei Jeruko would understand and share his dismay. This was more than either of them had bargained for.

But Sensei Jeruko still hadn't come. Terk had expected him to be the first person he saw when he awoke. Nope. Only machines surrounded him. He had stretched out his senses to find his mentor. A faint lifeforce trickled in, but still too far away for him to tell much. It wasn't until he left the cyborg ship and returned to the *Dragon* a day later that he'd determined his mentor tarried somewhere in the lower levels of the ship.

Several hours had passed since then and Sensei Jeruko remained there. What sort of task had Father given him?

Terk swallowed. Maybe Sensei Jeruko didn't want to see him anymore now that he was a machine.

"This is progress, young Prince. Put yourself at ease," Ambrose said, turning Terk's thoughts into disgust.

He tucked his revulsion away. He'd already figured out Ambrose could read him, so he brought up a mental wall the way his mother had taught him.

"What else can this do?" he asked as he pointed at his eye.

"Check the menu."

Terk mentally opened it. A list overlaid his normal eyesight. Infrared, chemical detection, energy waves, night vision, even adrenaline surge. His jaw dropped at all the options.

He almost missed the last item. "What does the HELP option do?"

"If one of your features ever stops functioning, go to the HELP section and call us. We'll fix it."

"What if it happens after you've gone?"

"Not a problem. We can still fix it."

A shiver ran down Terk's spine. "Remotely?"

"Of course, Prince Mizuki," Ambrose said in a way that told Terkeshi he should have known this already. "How else can we assist you if your new cybernetics malfunction?"

Chusho! I knew it! The implications spun in Terk's head, faster and faster, until a dizziness struck.

Ambrose patted Terk's arm. "Don't be alarmed. All machines break down from time to time, but it doesn't mean you break down. You will never hurt because of it. The worst that'll happen is certain features stop operating."

"I didn't sign up for this," Terk said. "You withheld information from us."

"This was all in the document I sent you and your father."

Terk clenched his fists. With all his duties, he'd only had time to skim the thousands of pages. *Stupid, stupid, stupid!* What had he done?

This was madness. He must tell Sensei Jeruko since his father wasn't likely to care—unless his mentor no longer cared either.

26
Interrogation

3791:098:17:30. Jin Jeruko sat cross-legged on the floor. This position made his bad knee ache, but he ignored it. Concentrating on his breathing generally eased his worries and cleared his mind. Not this time.

He gave up and opened his eyes to the dismal, grey-walled room. Someone had scratched *death awaits* in big letters on the wall before him. A devilish creature had been drawn below it. Other beasts and words marked the walls. The varying grime indicated that a different prisoner may have done each at a different time.

Echoes of the emperor's long-dead enemies should unsettle him. He was likely to be next, after all. However, all he could think about was Terkeshi.

Two days had passed since Jeruko was arrested. Did Terkeshi make it through surgery? If so, what had they done to him? Was he still human?

Who would guide him now, since Jeruko would either be exiled or executed?

Jeruko's eyes burned with regret. If only he had the daring to assassinate the emperor, honor be damned.

But no. Losing his honor wouldn't have been the only consequence. Killing the emperor might've saved Terkeshi from becoming a cyborg, but the difficulty he'd face when taking his father's place at such a young age would instigate trouble—trouble that might steer him away from compassion the way it had with the emperor.

Before becoming the emperor, Prince Kenji Mizuki had looked out for the lower classes. He made sure they were treated fairly and even protected them against overly cruel lords.

One particular act of benevolence had bolstered Jeruko's loyalty, but it also changed the emperor's outlook. As Jeruko sat in his cell, he reflected on that day…

A high-pitched signal commed in Jeruko's ear. He retreated from the battle while the next squad rushed into the fray. Once at a safe distance, he shouldered his phaser rifle. He huffed, doubling over with his hands on his knees. A tingling sensation swept in as his adrenaline dissipated. The cramping of his muscles amplified. A ten-minute break wouldn't be enough, but the failing assault allowed no more.

Sweat dripped from his brow and stung his eyes. He cursed his body armor's cooling system for not doing its job. It was hardly surprising, though. The midday heat of Laohu Dunes could rival that of a live volcano.

Jeruko removed his helmet, instantly regretting the sand that stuck to his skin. He wiped his face with the crook of his arm and scanned the battle line. Swarms of Dragon Warriors clashed with the Tiger Knights of Tora. Billows of orange dust obscured their feet and shrouded their uniforms. The sun's rays lashed out at them all like a yellow viper, sometimes taking down soldiers via heat strokes rather than weapons. The Toran fortress stretched beyond reach, shimmering in a fiery mirage.

This should have been a simple infiltration, but as usual, the emperor's tactics left much to be desired.

"Jeruko!" Prince Kenji Mizuki called into his comm. "Over here."

Jeruko glanced about, unable to tell which warrior was him.

"To your right."

Jeruko found the prince waving and jogged over. "Yes, Sir."

The prince stood with two other senshi. They looked alike with the dust covering their uniforms, until they removed their helmets. Prince Mizuki's sharp features contrasted with Fujishin's round face and Lord Thao's perfectly sculpted looks. Fujishin's light hair set him apart from the black hair of his friends. Where Prince Mizuki kept his short, Lord Thao's flowed into gentle waves.

"Those civilians are trying to reach safety," the prince said, his dark brows drawing inward as he pointed. "I need you and everyone else back in the fight to create a corridor and cover them."

"Will do, Sir." Jeruko donned his helmet.

The next half hour sweltered on as they protected the Toran citizens. Women with babes in their arms and children at their heels ran by with the swiftness of a ship fleeing pirates. Camels galloped past, pulling carts of goods and passengers. Those lucky enough to have motorized vehicles sped through, spewing sand in their wake.

"Dragon Warriors, to me! Charge the fortress!" came a slurred voice through the comm.

Jeruko quickly assessed the situation. The Tiger Knights retreated, but why? They had dominated the field only moments before.

"Father must be drunk again," Prince Mizuki said in their private channel.

"The enemy is luring him in, Sir," Jeruko replied.

"Agreed. Chusho," the prince grumbled. He switched to the command channel. "Father! It's a trap. Don't fall for it."

"I got them right where I want them, boy!"

The prince flipped back to the private channel and growled. "Chusho! Looks like we're going to have to save his stupid ass again."

"Sir, wait." Jeruko pointed at the new cluster of civilians headed their way. "There's more people coming, and I think they're injured."

Prince Mizuki followed Jeruko's finger. "Chusho." His head whipped to where the Dragon Warriors chased the knights to the fortress, then back to the fleeing group. "Fuck it. Help the citizens."

"Sir," Lord Thao replied. "We must obey the emperor."

"Our first duty is to our people," the prince said.

"But if it's a trap, he'll need us."

"If it's a trap, we'll all get caught in it."

The prince hurried to the people. Jeruko and Fujishin followed without hesitation while Lord Thao remained with his hands on his hips. After a moment, he shook his head and came as well.

Fujishin took the bawling infant from a woman with weary eyes so she could help the old man with the gash in his thigh. Jeruko hooked his arm under the man's other shoulder while

Prince Mizuki helped an old woman and Lord Thao grabbed the hand of the young boy.

As Fujishin dashed ahead, Lord Thao pulled the child after him. Jeruko and the prince moved at a slower pace. The old woman shuffled along, but Prince Mizuki didn't force her to rush the way Lord Thao did with the boy.

Although they'd left the battle behind, the commotion stayed with them. Shouts and screams echoed off the dunes while seismic bombardment sent shudders through the ground and vibrated up their legs.

"The emperor's hit!" the general shouted through the comm. "Ring formation. Get him out of here!"

Jeruko froze in the intense desert heat. "Chusho."

Prince Mizuki only frowned. "I told that chima it was a trap."

"Sir, we've still got to go help him," Jeruko said.

Fujishin and Lord Thao already headed that way. While Jeruko eased away from the old man, Prince Mizuki patted the old woman's hand and bid her well. Then he and Jeruko raced to the scene.

They arrived too late. Not only was the battle lost, but the emperor—and many Dragon Warriors—had perished. Although Jeruko considered the prince's actions honorable, several lords accused him of killing his own father.

Prince Kenji Mizuki's reply was that he merely left his father to suffer the consequences of his own stupidity. As much as that statement made sense, those lords had resented him for it and turned against him. As new emperor, he was forced to make a lot of tough decisions—ones that contributed to the hardening of his heart.

A tear rolled down Jeruko's cheek. If only he'd seen it coming and made different choices. As it stood now, his entire life had been a waste. He'd achieved nothing. The emperor's compassion was gone, Jori was dead, and now Terkeshi might as well be. The young man didn't stand a chance against his father. Nor would he fare well if his father was eliminated.

A swish cut through the deathly silence. Jeruko snapped out of his brooding as footsteps from down the corridor reverberated through the cell block.

135

He swept away the wetness on his face and stood, ignoring the twinge in his knee. He clasped his hands behind his back and took an attentive stance.

He'd been hoping the emperor would come but wasn't prepared for the fury that dominated the man's features. Purple veins pulsed over his temples. His eyes seemed pools of pure blackness. And the twitch covered more of his face, revealing that the madness had darkened his temper further.

At least Nezumi wasn't with him. Samuru stood at his left while the cyborg Ambrose waited at his right with a ridiculous smile pasted on his plastic-like face.

Jeruko bowed to the emperor lower than his rank required. "Your Eminence."

"Don't pretend subservience with me, traitor." Spittle flew from the emperor's mouth.

Jeruko's heart skipped a beat. Had he discovered his message to the Cooperative commander? He hid his guilt and furrowed his brow. "What have I done, Sire?"

"You know damn good and well what you've done."

Jeruko resisted the urge to swallow. "Sire, I swear all my actions have been in the service of the Mizuki Empire."

The emperor narrowed his eyes. Jeruko maintained a straight face. He had told the truth, after all.

"Telling my son not to get enhanced after I specifically ordered them is what you call service?"

So that's what this is about. The surveillance had picked up his conversation with Terkeshi. This had nothing to do with the Cooperative commander. Jeruko hid his relief. "You assigned me to look after the boy's well-being, Sire."

"That doesn't mean contradicting me!"

Jeruko bowed. "My apologies, Sire. I admit, I took my directive too far." He chose his next words with care. "I didn't intend to signify he should openly defy you. I had hoped he'd debate the matter with you and convince you not to go through with it."

"You've done nothing but fill his head with nonsense!" The emperor jabbed his finger. "All his failings are on you—including this reoccurring problem with sentiment."

Jeruko's heart lurched. The notion that he'd failed Terkeshi weighed like iron. Yet he hadn't failed the boy in the way the emperor said. "I also admit that I haven't entirely conquered my sentiment, Sire. I undoubtedly passed my weakness onto him." *Even though Terke-chan's sentiment is what makes him noble.* "But he's hardly a failure. It's true that recent events haven't been in his favor, but I sincerely believe he has much promise—if only we'd give him a chance."

"I've given him too many chances already," the emperor replied, albeit with less heat in his tone.

"Sire, I beg of you to remember how old you and I were when we met. You were an exceptional warrior, but your son is almost five years younger than you were then. I don't know what you were like when you were his age, but surely that timeframe made a vast difference in your skill."

"I didn't have his squeamishness."

"Nor is he squeamish. His decision not to punish the cargo captain was due to prudence."

Emperor Mizuki's brows drew in. "Prudent how?"

Jeruko lightened at the emperor's seeming willingness to listen. "Cargo captains are untrustworthy by nature. Captain Tobiuo is not as bad as some. He has not betrayed our secrets. Selling an item that means little to us but could mean the difference between survival and death to his crew is a small price for his silence."

"I pay him well enough," the emperor mumbled.

Jeruko ignored the comment. That the twitching in the emperor's eye had subsided indicated he'd made headway.

Jeruko lowered to his knees, despite the ache of his bad leg. "Your eminence, I have made mistakes. I will atone for them however you wish, but please don't let my failures taint your view of my loyalty. I swear to you with everything in my soul that I am entirely devoted to the Mizuki house."

The emperor narrowed his eyes. Jeruko dared not reveal his nervousness. Although his words were true, he'd meant them solely for Terkeshi.

"He's telling the truth," the cybernetic man beside the emperor said.

Jeruko glanced at Ambrose. Terkeshi had once mentioned that some cyborgs might have a reading ability. However, this was the first evidence Jeruko had seen. Thank goodness he'd kept his words true.

The emperor scrutinized him a little longer. When he spoke, his tone softened but still held an edge. "Very well. I release you. But Nezumi will take over as his mentor."

Jeruko's heart sank. The boy couldn't possibly flourish under Nezumi's ministrations. The desire to kill this mad man rose again. If only he could be sure to succeed. Terkeshi needed him now more than ever.

"Yes, Sire." Jeruko kowtowed as low as he dared without naming himself a slave. A slave he was, though—a man swept up into the whims of his masters with little chance of paving his own destiny.

He took this path for Terkeshi's sake, and it made his servility worthwhile.

27
High

3791:098:19:23. The specs on the screen blurred. Terkeshi forced his mind back to the present and reviewed the information.

He handed the tablet to Malkai. "It looks good."

"We're just waiting for one more part, my Lord. Then we can move the emitter to the *Fire Breather*."

Terk nodded absently. He should be happy that the perantium device neared completion. After all, Father had hinted that he might command the *Fire Breather* after all.

The prospect of taking charge of an entire ship wasn't what distracted him, though. Something else niggled at him. He glanced over his shoulder, but no one was there. Only the back wall of the auxiliary bay loomed behind him. He imagined himself a sika deer hearing underbrush crackle but not seeing the blackbeast lurking nearby.

This is ridiculous. The cyborgs wouldn't watch him through his eye. This was too boring. Even if they did, it didn't differ from being watched by the surveillance cameras Father had everywhere.

He mentally shook off his unease and focused on work.

The cyborgs finalized their tasks in the hushed auxiliary bay. A few shokukin worked among them, mainly on menial labor. Terk did a walkthrough. After the trouble with a small fire, Father tasked him with utilizing his sensing ability to make sure no one felt suspicious.

He held his head high as he did his inspection. Although his cybernetic eye had great capabilities, he took satisfaction in using his natural-born sixth sense.

The lifeforces of most cyborgs were faint, making his task harder. Some emitted almost no emotion. Terk scrutinized a man with half his head encased in metal. He couldn't tell if the cyborg did anything suspicious, but perhaps looking over his shoulder acted as a deterrent.

He sighed and moved on, soon reaching someone with a strong, albeit atypical, lifeforce. As usual, Benjiro's tongue stuck out from the side of his mouth as he worked. Although his eyes seemed almost vacant, Terk sensed the intensity of his focus. The simpleton could barely put on his own clothes, yet he easily kept up with these damned robots.

Terk watched the straggly bearded man with mixed feelings. He'd never given Benjiro much thought in the past, other than to wonder whether the idiot really had as much engineering skill as claimed. Finding out Benjiro was his uncle changed things. Terk still felt no kinship toward him but pitied him more.

Despite Benjiro's noble blood, he was treated as a slave. Terk ground his teeth. Lord Enomoto had somehow managed to get his idiot brother placed on this ship, then used him to gather intel. What sort of person would do this to their own brother, especially to one who didn't have the mental capacity to defend himself?

Malkai peered over the idiot's shoulder, then clapped him on the back. "Great job, Ben! I didn't think we'd ever be able to figure this out."

"Benjiro do good," Terk's uncle replied. He didn't smile, but a sense of satisfaction emanated from him.

Terk looked on with envy. Even the simpleton had people who cared about him. Terk had no one, not even his lifelong mentor.

He suppressed the pang in his gut and approached the two men. "Malkai."

The shokukin's head snapped up and a zap of worry emanated from him. "Yes, Sir?"

Terk bit down, telling himself the man's anxiety came from being called upon by a superior and not soldier-turned-cyborg. "How often do people harass him?"

"Benjiro?" Malkai shrugged. "No more than the rest of us, I suppose. We keep him busy and out of sight most of the time."

"Who's we?"

"The engineering crew."

"Including..." Terk paused, trying to remember the man's name. "Including the maintenance major?"

"Especially him. He's the one who gets in trouble if we screw up. Ben here has saved us more than once."

Terk released a pained sigh. He was glad the idiot had people to care for him but hated the reminder that no one here had his own back.

"So we take care of him like family," Malkai added with a broad smile.

Family. The word stung.

A door to the bay swished open, revealing the one person he'd thought he could count on—Sensei Jeruko—the man who'd abandoned him.

He left the workers, his hurt brewing into a storm as he confronted his old mentor. "Where the hell have you been?"

Sensei Jeruko halted. His eyes bulged. He tried to speak, but Terk didn't give him a chance. His fists clenched in an anger fueled by hurt. "I've been wanting to talk to you but was told you were *too busy*. You don't want to bother with your student now that he's a machine, right?"

Sensei Jeruko's brows drew together. "You mean you don't know?"

"All I know is I woke up from surgery and you weren't there. You've been avoiding me."

Regret emanated from the man's emotions. "No, my Lord. That's not it at all. I was arrested."

Shock doused Terk's anger. "What? Why?"

"The surveillance picked up our conversation. Your father thought I betrayed him when I asked you not to go through with the surgery."

Oh. Terk's emotions shifted. "Will he punish you?"

"No. He pardoned me."

Terk blew out noisily. "No one told me. I assumed you were angry with me."

Sensei Jeruko cast his eyes down. "No, my Lord. Never."

"Good, because I need to talk to you." He had so much to say but wasn't sure where to start. It seemed inappropriate to unload on his mentor after the man had just escaped punishment. And whining about his new abilities was pointless. Still, it would be nice to vent.

Best to cut straight to the most unsettling part of all of this. "Did you know the cyborgs can access us remotely?"

Sensei Jeruko's emotions spiked but he remained composed. "You've spoken to your father about this?"

"He should already be aware. It's in the document they provided," Terk replied with a scowl.

"Perhaps you should mention it and make sure." Sensei Jeruko's brow furrowed up and he made a slight tilt of his head as though indicating something.

Terk sensed the man's wariness and nodded in understanding. The last thing he wanted was for his mentor to be arrested again— or worse, killed the way Jori had been.

"You're right. Well, I'm glad you're out. I'm tired of training with Nezumi." His lip curled.

"My apologies, my Lord. Your father has ordered that Nezumi take over your education."

Heat rushed to Terk's face. "What? I don't want that rat-faced chima to be my instructor." Sensei Jeruko had been his master since… Well, since forever. What would he do without him?

"We must comply."

"Fuck that."

"I cannot disobey, my Lord." Sensei Jeruko's gloominess mingled with his own.

"I can. It's you or no one."

"I must advise against it."

"I know. Be at peace." Terk put his arm on his shoulder. "I will figure it out."

Sensei Jeruko dipped his head, then took his leave. Terk stood there for a while longer as the implications of this new loss surged inside him.

First, the exile of his mother, then Jori's death. Now Sensei Jeruko had been taken away too. He crossed his arms and searched the crowded room, noting how alone he truly was.

*****

3791:098:22:41. Terkeshi finished his work and pointedly headed the direction opposite of Nezumi's personal dojo. *Fuck that rat-faced chima.* Father would be pissed, but he didn't care.

He visited the common dojo instead. General Samuru led a group workout in the central area. About two dozen senshi copied his moves with earsplitting kiais. A pair of senshi wrestled in a ring in the back corner while a handful of warriors lifted weights in the central rear section.

Terk meandered to the opposite end where the cyber senshi practiced. A series of clops resounded as Tokagei and Captain Wang sparred with wooden swords.

He studied their movements. Their strikes fired off faster than a Gatling gun, yet they'd barely broken a sweat. When a red flashing dot popped up in the top right corner of Terk's vision, he mentally activated it.

<Tokagei> Do you wish to spar, my Lord?

Goosebumps formed on Terk's arms at how the man responded while continuing to fight. Despite how much it resembled a comm, communicating this way still unnerved him.

<Prince Terkeshi> When you're ready.

The cyber senshi continued with unwavering fervor. Why they didn't perspire piqued his curiosity. He initiated the features of his cybernetic eye and selected infrared. The typical shade of red overlaid the fighters, indicating normal heat signatures.

He shifted through the other optical options. Most provided no useful information. Then he discovered the answer. These men didn't just have cybernetic eyes or arms. They had other machines in them that helped regulate their body temperature.

Terk's skin crawled. He hoped he didn't have these features.

An unusual emotion caught his attention. He searched for the source and found Yujio slumped against the wall. Drool dripped from one corner of his mouth. Although his eyes were open, he seemed to stare at nothing.

Terk sent him a wireless message. When he didn't respond, he contacted Tokagei.

<Terkeshi> What's wrong with Yujio?
<Tokagei> He has activated a dose of morphine.

143

"What?" Terk said aloud. "He can drug himself?"

<Tokagei> Yes.

"Why? And speak out loud, damn it."

The two fighters halted and faced him with blank expressions.

"It allows us to continue fighting if we get injured," Captain Wang replied.

Terk crossed his arms. "That doesn't explain why he's using it. Was he hurt?"

"No."

Terk threw up his hands. "Then why the hell is he using it?"

"Unknown."

Terk marched over to the drug-addled man and knelt before him. "Yujio!" No response. Terk slapped his cheek. "Yujio! Look at me!"

The cyber senshi's eyes opened to slits. "My Lord?"

"Why did you drug yourself?"

"Pleasure."

Heat ignited Terk's face. Using drugs in this fashion was forbidden. Although some senshi partook in narcotics from time to time, they never did it so openly. Was this because of his cybernetics? His emotions must be so dulled that he did whatever he could to feel something.

"Take him to a cell," he ordered Tokagei. "I'll deal with him later."

He stormed from the dojo. *Madness! Everything is falling into madness.*

He entered the conveyor and considered where to go. Should he tell Father first or give Ambrose a good tongue lashing?

Father's attitude lately made up his mind.

28
Remote Control

3791:098:23:19. The skywalk resounded with the stomp of Terkeshi's boots. He clenched and unclenched his fists as he approached the entrance to the cyborg ship. Cool air struck his face but sizzled off from his fury.

The hatch opened without him having to announce himself. Either their security system was offline, or they saw him coming. Probably the latter. Those chimas kept track of his every move. He was one of them now, after all.

He exited the skywalk docking platform and found Ambrose's assistant in the hall—or the man had found him. "Welcome, young Prince." He approached with his usual detached smile. "You are expected."

Terk frowned. "Where's Ambrose?"

"He is busy. I am here to assist you."

So they have been watching me. Terk gritted his teeth and flared his nostrils. "What in the hell did you do to Senshi Yujio?"

The cyborg tilted his head. "I do not understand the issue. You are already aware of his augmentation."

Terk pointed back to his ship. "He drugged himself just for the fun of it! Instead of working, he is getting high. Why did you make it so they could do that? What purpose does this serve?"

"My apologies, young Prince. This feature was not meant for recreational use. It is only for severe injuries. This allows them to mask the pain while they continue their mission."

"I want that ability out of them. Right now! I don't need a bunch of doped up warriors."

The cyborg's head bobbed. "Of course. Of course. This way."

Terk made a face as the cyborg led him further into their ship. The trek was a maze of halls, yet this man, Bran or Brain or Brian or something, meandered through without pause. His pace was surprisingly brisk, considering his fleshy leg didn't move as smoothly as his mechanical one.

Brian entered an empty computer room. He faced a terminal, pulled a wire from the side of it and plugged it into the back of his head.

Terk shivered. Files popped up on the screen. The cyborg must have been doing it internally because the documents opened and scrolled down without him touching anything.

The monitor blacked out and the cyborg turned to him. "It is disabled. Your men can no longer access this feature."

Terk's jaw dropped. "You disabled it from here?"

The cyborg nodded. "It's a simple thing. Now he must request our permission first."

The implications of what the man had done zapped Terk like a jolt of electricity. "You can control my men whenever you want? I thought you could only do it when asked."

The cyborg shifted his feet. "You are aware we have remote access. How else will we monitor their—"

"You are monitoring them, too?" Terk clenched his fists. He knew someone had been spying on him. "Who in the hell are you to spy on us? You have no right!"

The cyborg remained unnaturally calm. "My apologies. We got the impression that you understood the process. Please understand that our connection is necessary to ensure your soldiers operate properly."

"No! This is unacceptable." Terk jabbed his finger at the man's chest. "I will not have you watching my people or manipulating them!"

The cyborg stepped back. "It is only to monitor—"

"I don't care! Does my father know of this?"

"Yes, young—"

"I guarantee he does not! There is no way he'd tolerate you controlling our men whenever you feel like it. And you certainly won't control me."

"I assure you, we only use it to maintain enhancements. Tech can be—"

Terk wrapped his fists around the man's collar. "Don't you dare ever access me or spy through my eyes without my permission. Do you understand?"

The cyborg's human eye bulged. Sweat formed on his brow. Although Terk barely read his emotions, he was glad these machines still had the sense to be afraid.

"Yes, young Prince," the cyborg replied.

Terk released him and shoved him back. "Good. Because if I ever find out you're here..." He tapped his head. "I'll come for you and make you pay."

"We don't mean you any—"

Terk didn't let the man finish. He cleared out with his thoughts whirling in a storming rage. He'd known all along that these freaks had been up to something. Did anyone believe him? No. They'd been so mesmerized by what cybernetics offered, they failed to consider the consequences.

Father had to listen now. He just had to.

29
Mad Dragon

3791:099:00:11. Terkeshi exited the conveyor to the command deck and halted. His senses told him Father wasn't here. He forced his chaotic thoughts to a simmer and focused his ability.

Within moments, a gust of Father's mood struck him—black, as usual. He heaved a sigh and returned to the elevator. Bothering him in his personal dojo wasn't the best idea, but Terk's restlessness wouldn't let him wait. Besides, Father needed to be informed.

"Deck six, aft," he said to the computer.

The conveyor jerked into motion. He massaged his closed eyes. Both felt the same, but he imagined vibrations from the cybernetic one as it transmitted his thoughts to those creepy man-machines.

If they discovered what was on his mind, would they intervene? Would he just drop suddenly, too drugged to tell Father anything?

The conveyor lurched to a stop. Its double doors swished open. Terk set his worries aside and marched out. Senshi steered clear, even the ones who bordered on disrespect. Was it because they saw his anger? Or had his new cybernetics made them more wary?

When he reached his father's dojo, he filled his chest and pressed the comm. His heart hammered as he waited. Would Father listen now? Would he finally do something about the cyborgs? Probably not. He still needed the perantium emitter completed.

Maybe he'd order the cybernetics to be removed. Was it even possible to take them out when they'd been so entrenched?

The door opened. Father stood bare chested and glowered at him, his eye twitching menacingly. "This had better be important."

"Father, my apologies for the interruption, but I just discovered—"

"Spit it out, boy!"

"Are you aware the cyborgs can remotely control our men?"

Father's mood plunged further. "Explain."

"Yujio accessed an embedded narcotic that's only supposed to be used if he's injured."

Father's brow deepened. "Was he hurt?"

"No, Sir. He did it to get high. I confronted the cyborgs about it, and they turned this function off by remote control."

"Then the problem is resolved. So why are you bothering me?"

Terk froze. This was not the reaction he'd expected. "The cyborgs can access our men and activate or deactivate their abilities. What if they decide to make them stop working? Or worse, use them to attack us?"

"Nonsense." Father pinched the bridge of his nose. "This is only so they can work out any issues before they leave."

Terk sensed Father's confliction of fear and ambition. "Is that what they told you? How do you know they're telling the truth?"

His father flicked his hand. "They're not controlling them. They are monitoring them."

"Monitoring sounds like spying."

Suspicion surged from Father's emotions. "This is temporary," he seemed to say to himself while shaking his head. "They will relinquish control soon. And if they don't, I'll kill them—the senshi, the cyborgs, all of them. No one will ever betray me again."

Terk swallowed as Father's madness spiraled, but he pushed on. "Did you know they can still remotely access our men even when they're far away?"

"Impossible! They can't send signals that quickly without a communication hub."

"They have technology we don't. And Ambrose said—"

"This is not your concern, boy! I'm monitoring everything."

Terk balled his fists. "I want this taken out of me!"

Father bared his teeth. "Too late."

"No! I won't allow them to control me."

"Damn it, boy! I told you, they will give me control."

Terk's entire body tensed. The idea of Father controlling his cybernetics made his insides writhe. "No. I refuse to allow it."

"There's nothing you can do to stop it. What's done is done. This is our path now—the path to glory!"

The path to madness. Terk jutted his chin. "I'll run away."

Father barked a laugh. "Where would you go? If what you say is true, all I need to do is give them the word and they'll continue your transformation with a simple command."

Simple command? Iciness spread throughout Terk's body. "What do you mean?"

"Fool, boy. Your nanites can replicate and create new functions."

Terk wagged his head. "No. I don't want you to control me."

Father's dark eyes hardened. "Do better and I won't have to."

Terk swallowed. He assumed he'd undergo more surgery. However, if all it took was Father giving a command, he was doomed. This couldn't be happening. He should've known it would come to this. The signs had been there all along. Why had he allowed himself to be pressured? If only he'd said no from the start.

The enormity of it made him dizzy. The room spun. His mouth dried. "Chusho," he whispered.

He didn't remember leaving. Nor did he recall entering his quarters. As he lay on his bed, his thoughts spiraled like a spec of space debris falling into an event horizon.

*****

3791:099:00:35. Ambrose frowned. The expression wasn't synthetic. He was among his own people, after all. But he couldn't help it. The video feed of the young prince speaking to the emperor troubled him.

> <Ambrose1633A> You shouldn't have let him see
>   you do that.
> <Brian29Z16> I assumed he knew.

Ambrose blinked as he replayed events. The error had been his own. It had never occurred to him to share the particulars of this task with his counterpart. Brian's functions were different. He didn't have the same depth of psychological understanding, so there'd been no reason to explain the differences between handling the emperor versus the prince. The former's paranoia meant spending more time providing details, making assurances, and feeding his ego. The prince, though suspicious, had too much control over his faculties to be so easily manipulated.

After an analysis, he had decided it was best to omit certain aspects. Giving Prince Mizuki a different document should have helped. Yet more than once, his inquiries meant Ambrose had to make updates.

> <Ambrose1633A> Emperor Mizuki did, but Prince
> Mizuki did not. This might be a problem.
> <Brian29Z16> What do we do?

Ambrose considered his options. The prince needed to embrace his new abilities throughout the transition process or errors could occur. At the same time, the emperor must be so impressed, he'd want more enhanced soldiers.

> <Ambrose1633A> I will handle it. Send the prince
> to me whenever he has questions. I will monitor
> the situation so that we do nothing else to raise
> his suspicions.

Brian acknowledged him with an intercommunication ping, then resumed his work. Ambrose flicked back to his own task. The long-range sensor readings from his ship indicated other vessels headed this way. They were Rhinian, the same type the emperor had said might attack.

Since the Toradon ships couldn't look that far into space, the emperor wouldn't see them coming for another two days. However, since the Rhinians also didn't have the capability, alerting the emperor would give him the opportunity to conduct a surprise attack instead of the other way around.

Ambrose smiled despite himself. This would help him further gain the emperor's trust and allow the prince to discover his new capabilities.

30
Dragon vs. Crocodile

3791:101:13:56. Kenji Mizuki gripped the armrests of his chair and leaned forward. "Get rid of that destroyer!"

The *Black Gharial*, one of four Rhinian destroyers accompanying the *Shadow Croc* battleship, had just lost all its shields. It flashed as an orange dot on the *Dragon* bridge's viewscreen. A translucent circle surrounded it, showing the possible areas traversed during evasive maneuvers.

Idiots. That beastly ship couldn't avoid the energy cannon's light-speed velocity. Hell, it wouldn't even see them coming. It was doomed, proof that crocodiles were no match for a dragon.

Mizuki glowered at the screen as yellow dashed lines representing the cannons spewed from the red dot of the *Dragon* and the blue one of the cyborg's vessel. With their ships no longer connected by the skywalk, they'd spread out to optimize weapon coverage. If they played it smart, it should be enough to protect the *Fire Breather*.

He scrutinized the green dots of the enemy vessels and the information displayed beside them. The *Croc*'s shields persisted at about eighty percent. Of the remaining destroyers, the *Sarcosuchus* had the lowest defenses, a mere twenty-five percent. It would be easiest to take out, but the *Night Mugger* was the most dangerous. Its projected trajectory would get it closest to the *Fire Breather*. Mizuki couldn't afford to lose the ship that would soon house the perantium emitter.

"Focus on the *Night Mugger*," he ordered General Samuru.

"Yes, Sire."

As additional firepower left the *Dragon*, the orange dot of the *Gharial* burst into a larger white one, indicating it'd been struck by energy cannons.

The bridge crew let out a brief cheer while Mizuki remained stoic. *Good riddance.* The rest would soon follow. Fujishin's plan would fail.

"Our port shields are at seventy-seven percent," Major Niashi called out.

Mizuki ground his teeth. "Ambrose!" he said through the comm. "You told me your weapons are more powerful than ours."

"They are, your Eminence," the cyborg transmitted.

"Then why are the *Croc*'s shields still so high?"

"As I said, our weapons work differently. They're getting past their defenses and inflicting damage your sensors can't pick up."

Mizuki growled. Why didn't the man tell him this beforehand? "Send me their stats."

Within moments, additional details on the enemy ships appeared on the viewscreen.

Mizuki blinked. *Did the cyborgs just hack my system?* He'd expected them to reply via the comm, not make changes to his computer.

Those chima took too many liberties, but he had no time to dwell on it. A quick review indicated more than half the *Croc*'s energy cannons were inoperable.

"Whatever you're doing," Mizuki said to Ambrose, "do it to the *Night Mugger*."

"Certainly," Ambrose replied.

As Mizuki evaluated his next move, a vibration ran through his chair.

"Sire!" Niashi called out. "A missile got past and destroyed one of our cannons."

Chusho! Shields protected against energy weapons while the ship's AI targeting system handled projectiles. Apparently, it'd missed one.

His chair trembled again. "What's happening?"

Niashi tapped away at his console. Two other bridge crew members did the same.

"Another missile got in," Niashi replied.

Mizuki's calm battle focus scattered. He leaned on his elbow and bit his thumbnail. "What the hell is wrong with our systems?"

"Not sure, Sire. They appear to be operating fine."

Chusho! Perhaps the enemy had a new type of stealth missile.

"They're using Gemini missiles," Ambrose's voice crackled through the comm.

Mizuki had never heard of them. "How do we detect and stop them?"

"We will do it," Ambrose transmitted, "and destroy the ones we can."

Mizuki frowned, partly because the cyborgs hadn't informed him of yet another technology, and partly at himself for chomping on his nail like some juvenile. He yanked his hand from his mouth and focused on the viewscreen.

The *Night Mugger* turned from green to a flashing orange. Mizuki slammed his fist. "Destroy it now!"

He bounced his knee as the yellow dashes surged toward their target. He found his thumbnail between his teeth again but didn't pull it away. The dashed lines crawled as Mizuki's heart palpitated. They would strike the *Mugger* in two seconds.

One. Two.

His weapons struck the *Mugger*, but it remained a flashing orange. It would take another thirty seconds for information on its status to reach his sensors—and longer after that to determine whether the ship had fired off a shot at the defenseless *Fire Breather*.

"Sire," Niashi said, nearly breaking Mizuki's attention from the screen. "All our shields have fallen below sixty percent."

The *Mugger*'s icon blared white. Mizuki pulled back. *Got it!*

The bridge crew didn't cheer this time. They probably awaited his response.

Niashi's words had registered, but nothing could be done about it. The fact that all shield strengths were about the same indicated his men had done their job by evenly distributing strength or presenting different faces of the ship.

He opened his mouth to order focused firepower on the *Croc*, but another enemy destroyer unexpectedly flashed white.

"We destroyed the *Sarcosuchus*," Ambrose broadcasted.

Mizuki didn't remember its icon turning from green to orange. "How?"

"Our weapons," Ambrose replied.

What the hell are they using?

Within moments, the last remaining destroyer followed suit. Mizuki's jaw dropped. He must have these weapons. To hell with the price.

"Concentrate all firepower on the *Croc*," he ordered. "I want their shields down, but don't destroy the ship."

"Are you certain, your Eminence?" Ambrose asked.

Mizuki flexed his fingers. "Yes, damn it! I'm certain." Fujishin might be there, and he wanted that chima alive.

"They're turning around, Sire," a bridge officer called out.

"After them!"

A series of tugging sensations indicated the ship had adjusted course and picked up speed. The dots on the viewscreen showed the cyborg vessel also giving chase.

"Ambrose," he transmitted. "Protect the *Fire Breather*."

Although the cyborgs had sworn the enemy only brought five ships, Mizuki wouldn't take any chances. Rhinians were crafty. Besides, the *Croc*'s shields were now down to forty-eight percent—six percent lower than his own. He could handle this.

The *Dragon* didn't just have stronger defenses. It was faster and had more firepower. As the red dot on the viewscreen approached the green one, yellow dashed lines connected them as Samuru fired the energy cannons.

Mizuki clutched the armrest of his chair to keep from biting his thumb.

"Shields at thirty-eight percent," Niashi said. "The enemy is at forty-one."

Mizuki held down his anxiety. Information from the *Croc* was several seconds old, so their shields were likely less than that. "Put it on the screen."

A rectangle in the top right corner appeared. Mizuki bent forward, his elbow on his knee again, but he pointedly kept his fist under his chin.

The *Dragon*'s shields dropped to thirty-three percent, the enemy's to thirty-five. Twenty-seven to twenty-six. Twenty to thirteen. Eighteen to seven.

"Their shields are down."

Mizuki sat up. "Stop firing. Release the Asps, then pull out of range!"

"Squad one, away," the major of the Asp space fighter division replied through the comm.

"Take out all their weapons. Sidewinders," he transmitted to Terkeshi, who led the two Sidewinder-class infiltration ships kept in the *Dragon*'s primary docking bay. "Are you ready?"

"Yes, Sir."

"Good, now go. Our shields are low so cover me until their defenses are destroyed."

"Will do, Sir."

Mizuki released the arms of his chair and leaned back. His part was over. The rest was up to his hopefully more competent son.

31
Infiltration

3791:101:21:52. A slight jerk quavered through the cockpit chair as the Sidewinder's grappling arm peeled away the last section of the *Shadow Croc*'s inner hull. Terkeshi manipulated the ship's thrusters, countering the force. With this task complete, he puffed out a breath and wiped his sweaty palm down his thigh.

He did it. Although he'd performed many simulated infiltrations in the past, he hadn't succeeded enough times to get his score above ninety percent. The complicated process demanded a little engineering knowledge and a lot of patience.

Several specialized tools were needed, including a giant crowbar, vacuum-rated torches, and explosives. Plus, twice as many gauges required monitoring.

Having a cybernetic eye to calculate the arm's movements certainly had its advantages.

"Firing missiles," he said to the cyber senshi in the copilot seat.

Captain Wang didn't verbally respond. As his cybernetics systematically checked all the cockpit controls, his normal eye remained fixed. Terkeshi shivered at the man's now complete lack of emotions and nearly indistinct lifeforce.

Terk fired into the enemy vessel. None of the *Croc*'s turrets worked any longer, but the occupants inside undoubtedly had weapons.

The external cameras transmitted a blaring white screen, indicating his missiles had exploded. He flicked the viewscreen back to info mode and waited until all heat and radiation levels had dissipated.

The indicator changed from red to green.

"Get ready to go in," he said into the comm to the warriors in the cabin. "Are the artillery bots prepped?"

"Yes, Sir," Senshi Rushiro replied.

"Send them in."

A light on the console indicated Rushiro had opened the exterior door of an airlock. Terk clicked on the camera from that section of his ship. One by one, five bots assisted by mini thruster packs headed to *Croc*'s opening. As they entered, he switched to the bot cameras, seeing no sign of the enemy. They undoubtedly knew what was happening, and likely had unpleasant surprises waiting.

After the robots settled, Terk commed Rushiro. "Proceed with recon."

"Yes, Sir."

Although the bots used different sensors to see, headlamps on their domes illuminated the area. Terk studied the feeds as Rushiro and the other senshi remotely controlled their movements.

The interior of the ship looked much like their own, with unadorned walls and plain titanium floors. Only the marks left by the blasts of the missiles was different.

The corridor they'd entered curved in either direction, crossed with many intersections. Thank goodness the specs on this vessel were correct and that Terk had penetrated the right spot. Multiple corridors might allow the enemy to attack from various points, but it would also provide keep Terk and his team with more than one way out.

The bots spread out, covering several meters. Still no sign of the enemy, which wasn't surprising considering the work of the missiles.

"Clear, Sir," Rushiro said.

"Alright, let's go."

Terk rose, donning his helmet and gloves while heading to the cabin. Rushiro and four other senshi remained at consoles along the wall to continue operations of the artillery bots. The remaining dozen warriors, two of them cybernetic, put on their helmets. The headgear was black like the enviro-suits, making the warriors difficult to see since much of the enemy ship no longer had power.

Each man bore bladed weapons and RR-5 rifles. In addition, a thick black baton hung from each utility belt. Terk pulled out his own close-quarters weapon. With a press of a button, the baton extended into a shield. Although cumbersome in battle, it would serve well if the energy shield protecting his body shorted from enemy attacks.

With a flick of a switch, the shield folded back into a baton. He dropped it in the loop on his belt and held out his hands. Tokagei handed him a phaser rifle. He gave it a quick but thorough inspection, then shouldered the weapon.

"Let's go," he said as he flipped his visor closed.

Air from his suit vents swept coolness over him, making him shiver. He breathed deep, hoping to quell the jagged current of his nervousness.

Time to show Father I'm a Dragon Warrior.

*****

3791:101:23:14. Kenji Mizuki rested his chin on his palm as he monitored the engagement on the deskview screen in his office. The distant flashes from artillery bot firepower played through the feed from Terkeshi's cybernetic eye. The breathing and rustling of restless movement dominated the internal mics as the boy and his team waited for the robotic vanguard to clear another hallway.

Mizuki willed the situation to hurry while also hoping Terkeshi would take the time to do things right.

Chusho. He should have let Samuru lead rather than act as second. Allowing the boy to conduct this mission was a mistake. It was too soon, and his augmentations paled compared to those of the other cyber senshi.

Mizuki clicked to another tab. The list of Terkeshi's current enhancements remained short. Besides the initial package, only one other function had developed. He'd initially requested the cyborgs to hold off, but what happened with Yujio had given him an idea.

When the time came, would he need to activate it? And if he did, would it be enough? He hoped so. That boy needed all the help he could get.

So far, the operation had gone smoothly. The Sidewinder-class ships under the boy's command successfully blocked the line of sight from the *Croc*, preserving the *Dragon*'s shields. Then while Samuru's Sidewinder broke into the rear of the *Croc*, Terkeshi utilized his Sidewinder's specialized armaments to do the same up

159

front. Neither party had found resistance upon entering the ship and breaching the interior.

This ease wouldn't last. The Rhinians would undoubtedly put up a fight to keep from being captured or killed. Whether Terkeshi could defeat them remained questionable. After all, he'd never had much success in military exercises before. He sorely lacked both Jori's skills and his determination. Maybe his enhancements meant he'd do better now.

His youngest son's shadow threatened to come out of hiding again. Mizuki refused to acknowledge it and stared at his grandfather's sword instead. *Glory is within reach.*

A bright light flared on the screen. Mizuki flicked back to the video feed where the occupants of the *Croc* had destroyed the bots.

No big loss there. Taking heat was another purpose of those machines.

"Get ready," Terkeshi said. "My sensors pick up more than a dozen soldiers ahead."

Mizuki blinked the dryness from his eyes and concentrated on the screen.

You better get it right this time, boy.

32
Genocide

3791:101:23:55. Sweat trickled from Terkeshi's forehead. The resulting itchiness interfered with his concentration, but he couldn't afford to remove his helmet. Although he and his team had penetrated the ship's interior where air remained, the enemy still governed the ventilation system from the bridge. One press of a button and the air quality could turn deadly.

Their control would end soon enough.

Terk hunkered behind a corner with his men, grateful the artificial gravity continued to operate. Jori had said fighting in zero gravity offered more options, but he thought it made things too complicated.

The emergency lockdown hatch closed with a hiss and a thump, enclosing them within the command section. Artillery bots had already cleared this area—getting destroyed in the process. Their carcasses smoldered. A twisted metal chunk still glowed red, then withered out in a swirl of smoke.

He peeked around the corner, scanning for hidden dangers. His visor found two explosive devices in the main corridor. A couple more flashed in a red overlay of his cybernetic vision.

Damn, this eye has some amazing features. No way his simple helmet would have detected those camouflaged ones.

He relayed the information to the cyber senshi. Tokagei and Yujio acknowledged with a silent ping.

Terk focused his sixth sense. Distinguishing his men from the enemy was easy, but too many of the latter in such proximity made it difficult for him to count their numbers. About twenty covered the bridge entrance. Several more protected the inside.

With an eye-click through his helmet's interface, two fairyfly drones flew down the hallway. Their feeds played at the top of his visor, showing another corridor crossing in front of the bridge.

The feed flashed, indicating the enemy fired at the tiny machines. The drones drifted unscathed around the corners, revealing desperate but determined soldiers.

"Sixteen crocs, eight on either side," Terk commed.

"We're outnumbered," Pachin said.

"They're outmatched," Terk replied, hoping to keep the optimism high. "They no longer have a frontline shield."

"Stupid mercs. Using ramshackle weapons," a senshi scoffed.

Terk considered the enemy's still-functioning body shields and four remaining stealth bombs. The next course of action seemed straightforward, so he signaled four fingers followed by a clawed hand. Yujio tossed out hefty palm-sized spheres while the other senshi laid down cover fire.

The balls unfolded into spider-like creatures and scuttled down the hall. These bomb bots swiftly sniffed out their targets and disabled the weapons.

"Frag and clear." Terk and his team advanced, keeping the Lazarus shield in front.

The enemy crocs returned fire. Cracks, pops, and zaps created a racket both heard and felt. The muffs in Terk's helmet automatically dulled the sound.

One by one, the lifeforces of the enemy snuffed out. When Tokagei's cybernetic arm cannon blasted another mercenary in the chest, the pain of this man's death stabbed through Terk's sensing ability.

Terk spurned the ill sensations. *Don't be stupid.* Their demise shouldn't bother him. After all, they were the ones who'd started it. They deserved to die, and he should be proud to defeat his enemies. Besides, he faced soldiers, not old men, women, or children.

If Dokuri did it, so can I.

Terk's cybernetic eye caught sight of another mercenary holding a porcupine bomb. *Chusho!* The Lazarus shield might not stop super-heated projectiles.

He aimed at the soldier, his eye and rifle syncing on the target, and fired a rapid quadruple blast. The first three disabled the man's body shield. The fourth struck him in the heart, sending the pang of his diminishing lifeforce into Terk's senses.

He ignored it and looked for another quarry. As the Lazarus shield moved beyond the intersection, he discharged a series of blasts, all hitting their mark.

The rest of the mercenary soldiers fell in short order. Terk released a long exhale. Three confirmed kills, the same number as the cyber senshi. Father would be proud.

That wasn't so hard. What the hell had he been worried about? They'd extinguished the enemies' lifeforces too quickly to leave any lasting effect on his sensing ability. He could finish this, no problem.

As he and his men hugged either side of the bridge door, Yujio manipulated his cybernetic arm. A small implement extended from beside his blaster. With a quick flick, the cover of the door's keypad popped off. Another feature morphed from Yujio's arm. Seconds later, the door cracked open.

A defensive weapon might go off when the doors opened all the way, but the enemy probably wouldn't use anything too powerful. After all, the backlash would affect those inside on the bridge the most. Terk made a snap decision and opted to depend on the Lazarus shield to protect him and his team.

"Switch to stun," he said. "We want them alive."

He signaled for the cyber senshi to proceed. Yujio and Tokagei put their metal fingers between the doors and widened the opening.

"Go!" Terk called into the comm.

He and his men jumped in. A clap and thunder punched Terk's eardrums as a firestorm shot out. His suit attempted to compensate for the searing heat, sending icy tendrils that burned almost as much. The gust of fevered air hurled him backward. His arms flailed until he crashed to the floor. Blackness covered his vision while a colorless spark flashed through his brain.

A racket erupted around him as the enemy took advantage of his team's disorientation. Three lifeforces from his own people screamed into his senses as their bodies fought for survival.

The pain of their deaths crippled him. He couldn't move. What had he done? He should've known the crocs would risk a more powerful weapon that would overwhelm his shield. *Chusho!*

A thick smoke replaced the heat. Coughing resounded from inside, indicating the enemy lacked self-contained enviro-suits.

163

Eager to redeem his blunder, he rolled to his feet with a grunt. "Yujio! Flash bomb it."

He would have ordered grenades and porcupine bombs, but instructions from Father were clear. Overtake the bridge, apprehend the leaders, capture Fujishin alive.

Yujio threw in a handful of small devices. Terk ducked beside the doorway and shielded his eyes. Pops sounded and blazing lights ignited, making the darkness behind his visor flare red.

He leapt forward. "Go! Go! Go!"

With a press of the trigger, a rapid stun-beam spewed across the room. His senshi followed suit and several crocs fell. A few returned fire. The body shield icon in Terk's visor turned yellow, then orange.

His cybernetic eye automatically targeted an enemy aiming at him from behind a workstation. He fired and received a blast in exchange. A red light flashed.

"My shield is down!" Terk dived behind the central bridge chair.

Three other senshi announced the same thing. One cut off mid-sentence, his lifeforce disintegrating to nothingness as he dropped to the floor.

Chusho! Not Bolin! That made four good warriors lost under his command today.

He poked his head out and looked for more crocs. His cybernetic eye found only unconscious ones. The silence of the bridge confirmed the fight was over.

"Confirm stun!" Terk called into the comm.

Senshi darted past him. He broke from his cover and joined their investigation of the downed mercenaries.

"Clear!" several senshi announced.

"Find Fujishin!" Terk ordered.

He knelt and lifted an enemy's visor. Not Fujishin. He checked more. None were the betrayer. Father had been so sure the man would be here, leading the attack.

"Prince Mizuki," Tokagei transmitted. "Colonel Fujishin is on the comm."

Terk joined him at the communications console and removed his helmet. His heart skipped a beat at the light-haired man on the screen. "Is this live?"

"Yes, Sir," Tokagei replied. "He must be close by."

Fujishin smiled and dipped his head. "Hello, Prince Terkeshi Mizuki. I'm nowhere near there, unfortunately for you. You've done a good job taking out the Rhinian mercenaries. Colonel Jeruko has taught you well."

"If you're not here, then how are we speaking in real-time? You shouldn't have access to our communication hub."

"Your cyborg friends aren't the only ones who have instantaneous communication capabilities."

"Impossible. There's no one else in the galaxy with such technology."

"You're wrong about that, young Prince. You're wrong about a lot of things."

Terk scowled. "Like what?"

Fujishin shrugged. "Your father. Don't you see the monster he's become? Our culture is a giant monstrosity and it's all his fault. He was supposed to improve it, but all he's done is make it worse. He must be stopped."

Terk should have disagreed, but the desire to defend his father didn't come. "Is that why you betrayed him?"

"It is. I'm sorry you and your brother are caught up in this. I'd hate for something to happen to you."

"Jori's dead," Terk snapped.

Fujishin's jaw dropped. "How?"

Sourness rose to Terk's throat. *Father killed him.* In a way, Fujishin was also to blame. His betrayal had caused Father's madness. Without it, Father might never have entertained the cyborgs long enough to find out about the perantium emitter. Terk and Jori never would have ended up in Cooperative hands, Cooperative soldiers wouldn't have been taken prisoner in return, and Jori never would have felt he needed to save a Cooperative officer.

Terk clenched his fists. "It all started with your betrayal, you chima. How could you? After everything Father has done for you?"

Fujishin harrumphed. "Done for me? You mean how he guilted me into murdering our own people? Lord Shiu certainly deserved to die for his betrayal, but your father ordered the slaughter of not just his family but also his entire household." Fujishin's face reddened. "Nearly twenty of those were children."

An iciness flushed down Terk's spine.

"And he wonders why I turned against him," Fujishin continued. "Fucking monster."

Father's voice resounded through Terk's comm. "Those lives are on Lord Shiu! Boy, tell that son of a red-faced monkey that he and his friends will die for his betrayal as well."

Terk swallowed. "Father says Lord Shiu is to blame for that."

Fujishin made a face. "Bullshit. Shiu wasn't the bad guy, and neither am I. Your father is. *He* ordered the murder of innocent people. To set an example for anyone else who considered betraying him, he said. But we could have let them live. The method of Shiu's death alone was enough to send a powerful message. Do you know what your father had done to him?"

Terk's stomach turned. He knew. The others got off easy in comparison.

"Ask that chima where he is," Father ordered. "And where did he get the communication tech?"

Terk pressed his lips together. *Why don't you ask him yourself?* It wasn't like Fujishin would answer, but he asked anyway. "Where are you? Father has questions."

Fujishin belted a laugh. "I bet he does. Tell him he'll see me around soon enough."

Father ranted and cursed, making Terk's eardrums throb. He accessed his visor and muted the communication.

"You'd be wise to separate yourself from him as well, young Prince," Fujishin added, "before he makes you do something you regret."

The viewscreen blacked out, indicating Fujishin had disconnected.

"Boy!" Father yelled through his cybernetic comm. "Don't you ever cut me off like that again."

Terk flinched. Did Father remote in with him? "Sorry, Sir. I couldn't hear Fujishin."

"Don't listen to that chima's lies. Now gather up these mercenary bastards and bring them to the *Shadow Croc*'s common room."

Terk ordered the senshi to carry the unconscious enemy soldiers. As he headed to the center of the ship, he replayed the conversation with Fujishin in his head. Although he disliked the idea of executing children too, it was stupid to be so squeamish about such things. *Emotion is weakness.*

Besides, obeying orders was part of the senshi code of honor. If Fujishin didn't like doing it, he should have just stopped serving. Instead, he'd started a rebellion—which, ironically, got more innocent people killed.

Fujishin was a hypocrite. A real senshi wouldn't be so prissy about killing. And a real senshi would have obeyed orders without complaint.

Terk halted. Jori had often questioned and disobeyed Father. Did that mean he deserved to die?

No. Jori's death was Fujishin's fault. Maybe partially Sensei Jeruko's fault as well. After all, *his* sentiment had rubbed off on Jori.

The common room door swished open with a gust of air into Terk's face, bringing him back to the moment. He entered to find several of the *Shadow Croc*'s workers kneeling and with their heads hung low. Samuru and his own team stood around them like blocks of granite.

The saliva in Terk's mouth vanished, leaving his tongue as dry as a wad of cloth. During the infiltration process, General Samuru had secured the rear engine rooms while Terk had concentrated on the front. Both had taken prisoners, but Terk didn't like the looks of these. They weren't soldiers, and some were women.

The senshi from Terk's team dragged in the unconscious mercenaries and threw them down beside the workers. Tokagei and Yujio plucked the body shields off them, then used something in their cybernetic arms to zap them awake.

The enemy crocs shook their heads or rubbed away the fogginess. When they realized where they were, their eyes popped. Some whispered curses. One prayed.

The wall of well-armed senshi kept them from doing much else. They were doomed, and they knew it.

"Keep the captain and commander for interrogation," Father said through Terk's cyber comm. "Kill the rest."

"What about the workers?" Terk asked. "We can use them to help us with the emitter."

"We have the cyborgs, idiot. Now kill them, damn it!"

Terk swallowed down the bile rising in his throat. He could do this. This was the enemy. Senshi killed their enemies. They didn't quibble over whether those enemies were soldiers or workers. They did their job without question.

So why the hesitation? He'd just killed some during the infiltration and it wasn't so bad. Hardly any feedback from the pain of death had bothered him.

He hoisted his weapon and waited for the senshi to join him. Seconds ticked by, yet only he took aim. "We have our orders," he said to the men.

"Those are your orders," Samuru replied.

"He wants *me* to kill all these people?"

Samuru flicked his hand at the workers. "You can keep the women for yourself if you want, but they're awfully ugly."

Terk ignored him. Taking spoils had never interested him.

"Boy!" Father called into the comm attached behind his ear. "What the hell are you waiting for? Do it!"

Terk startled, then shot a heavily bearded mercenary. He pulled the trigger again. Another fell. He mindlessly fired until all but the workers were dead. Though they had gone quickly, the repetition of so many lifeforces being terminated still registered in his mind. When he lowered his weapon, his gut churned.

"You're not done yet, boy," Father said. "All of them."

Terk's hands tingled. "But why? They're probably slaves, just like ours. They didn't have any part in this, and we could use them. If not for the emitter, for our own engines. They might have more skill than—"

"Damn it, boy! Don't be a fool. They work for the Rhinians. I won't have them on my ship. Now kill them, you fucking coward!"

Terk took aim, glowering at the first prisoner. Why shouldn't he do it? If he didn't, someone else would. What would Father think of him then? It was about time he did something right.

He clenched his jaw. His finger hovered over the trigger. A prickling heat surged into his veins. His face burned as his temper flared. Still, he hesitated.

Make Father happy, you fool. He snarled. *Do it!* Blue energy burst from his weapon as he plowed down the workers. They cried out as bodies sprawled or fell into heaps. A woman pushed to her feet and attempted to run. Terk shot her in the back. One man pleaded for his life. Terk hit him in the face.

He roared through the slaughter. His anger ate away the pain of their deaths.

The massacre ended. Terk sucked in ragged breaths as the blood lust continued to surge over him. He aimed his rifle at Tokagei, considering taking him out as well.

Why not? That chima had wronged him more than these damned mercenaries. And he was just a cyborg, after all—not even human.

Before he pulled the trigger, he dropped to his knees. Pure exhaustion overtook him. His entire body tingled as his rage fizzled away.

He shook his head, trying to release the fog that had fallen over him. *What the hell happened?* He shouldn't be this tired. But neither should he have been that angry.

Could Father have remotely triggered an adrenaline surge? Or had Terk lost his temper? He chilled as though blasted with liquid nitrogen.

If Father had done it, how? A cybernetic eye was all Terk should've had. Father had hinted there would be more, but so soon? How long before he'd kill with no emotion at all?

Someone clapped him on the shoulder. Terk blinked as the men cheered. Their elation cut at his horror like a flurry of knives. Each one pierced him. He tried to grasp on to their emotions, but they flittered away like flies from a corpse.

So many dead. Even if his father had caused the adrenaline surge, Terk had still lost control. His eyes fell on a worker sprawled on his stomach. He was so young, perhaps only a couple of years older than Terk. A woman lay slumped over the legs of another fallen worker. Her arms bent at awkward angles. Samuru had spoken truly. She was ugly. But her dull blue eyes had probably once sparkled like sapphires.

Terk quivered. His horror dissipated as a swell of fury erupted inside him—this time, it came naturally. "There. Are you happy now, Father?"

169

Dawn Ross

"Hardly," Father replied.

Terk rose to his feet and embraced his anger. Fujishin wasn't the bad guy. Father was.

33
Shattered Faith

3791:102:00:52. Jin Jeruko believed himself to be going into cardiogenic shock as his heart skipped several beats. The emperor constantly criticizing his son was one thing. Overstimulating the adrenals, provoking Terkeshi into murdering all those people was another. The man had gone too far.

Poor Terkeshi. This would send him over the edge, for sure.

"What the hell is he doing?" the emperor said.

Jeruko leaned in, looking over the man's shoulder at the deskview screen. At first, all he noticed was the heap of dead bodies. But the crosshairs overlaying Terkeshi's cyber vision fell over Tokagei. "He's not thinking clearly. His bloodrage is too strong."

"Foolish boy. I wouldn't have had to do this at all if he'd obeyed instead of argued."

"He made a good point, Sire," Jeruko replied.

Nezumi cocked a smile. "Why are you always so sentimental, Colonel?"

Jeruko gritted his teeth. "You mistake me, General. It wasn't long ago that we considered acquiring more skilled workers. Now when some fall into our lap, we eliminate them."

The emperor flicked his hand. "We have help on the emitter. We don't need potential enemies on the ship."

The argument made sense, but not everyone had the stomach for such killing. Not Fujishin and certainly not Terkeshi. In the Golden Age of the Mizuki reign, such things didn't happen. A stronger code of honor pervaded. How had it come to this?

Jeruko refrained from grimacing at the back of the emperor's head as the man selected another feature under Terkeshi's profile. The youth lowered his gun and fell to the floor.

Jeruko clutched his chest. "Is that good for him, to be so strongly drugged over a short period?"

"His works differently. All this does is stimulates a release of hormones."

"That doesn't sound much better, Sire."

"Maybe next time he'll do as he's told."

Jeruko gulped. The emperor was beyond reason. Fujishin was right, he was monster. The massacre of Lord Shiu's family and estate wasn't the first hint of it either. Incidents like it had piled up over the years, yet Jeruko kept turning a blind eye.

Even after Fujishin had drunk himself into a sobbing mess over those murdered children, Jeruko excused the emperor's behavior. He couldn't stand by and do it any longer. Terkeshi deserved better.

He had limited options, and it might already be too late. He clutched his chest and turned away.

"What's the matter, Colonel?" Nezumi said mockingly. "Aren't you proud of the prince for finally becoming a true senshi?"

Committing murder doesn't make one a senshi.

"There. Are you happy now, Father?" Terkeshi broadcasted.

"Hardly," Emperor Mizuki replied.

Goosebumps formed on Jeruko's arms at the emperor's tone. Terkeshi couldn't flourish under this madness. *I must do something before it's too late.*

"Don't worry," Nezumi said to Jeruko. "This will only harden the boy for when he destroys Meixing"

Jeruko's stomach lurched. "Why would we destroy Meixing?"

"Everyone knows Fujishin is colluding with Lord Enomoto," the emperor replied.

"Surely you're not talking about destroying an entire planet, Sire."

"No, but what we do will profoundly impact it."

"Including Hisui Island?" Jeruko asked, forgetting to keep his sentiment to himself.

"Hisui Island will likely suffer tsunamis and earthquakes."

Jeruko's breath hitched. "You can't use the weapon to that extent!"

The emperor turned with a scowl. "What did you think I would use it for?"

"I thought there'd be a lower setting."

"Not one low enough to penetrate his shield defenses."

The blood drained from Jeruko's head, leaving a prickling iciness.

Nezumi smirked. "Your sons and consort are on that island, are they not?"

"Yes, but they have nothing to do with Lord Enomoto *or* Fujishin."

"Emotion is weakness, man," the emperor said to Jeruko. "This will simply finish what I should have done to begin with. Washi and Michio failed me."

A tremor in Jeruko's core threatened to send him to his knees. Arguing for his sons would only solidify the emperor's belief that he was weak. "It's not just that, Sire. This planet is our primary food source. Harming it will disrupt farming and the processing plants."

"It will also diminish Lord Enomoto's wealth, should he be lucky enough to survive. And it's not like we don't have other resources. It's a simple matter of increasing their yields."

"Simple?" Toradon overlords already exploited the populace to the point of callous cruelty.

"I want Enomoto dead! Besides, this will set an example for anyone else who thinks they can stand against me."

Setting an example! It all came back to that. Didn't he realize this level of violence only angered people? Fujishin and Lord Enomoto might not be so bent on opposing him if he'd been the benevolent ruler he once promised to be.

"At least allow my sons to relocate."

The emperor slammed his palm on his desk. "You are weak!"

Jeruko clamped his mouth shut. Though his insides teemed like a swarm of super-enzymes eating waste, he forced an expression of compliance under the emperor's challenging glower.

"Just think, Sire," Nezumi said with a twinkle in his beady eyes, "with Lord Enomoto out of the way, you can ask the cyborgs to fix you so you'll have the ability to sire more sons—or they can simply clone you."

God forbid. Jeruko ground his teeth. He must do something about those damned cyborgs. Getting rid of them would also save Terkeshi from his fate and stop the perantium emitter from being built. So many lives depended on it, including his wife and sons— and Terkeshi's mother.

His shoulders dropped at the enormity of what must be done. Where would he even start?

The thought of assassination resurfaced, turning his insides out. It seemed like the perfect answer to all his problems until he recalled Emperor Kenji Mizuki's struggles. The death of the previous emperor had seemed like such a blessing, but it didn't take long for consequences to arise.

Though several years older than Terkeshi was now, the emperor was still young when his father had died. Many lords sought to take advantage of his inexperience, either by openly rebelling or by manipulating him with their false loyalty and lies.

He might have overcome these difficulties with his honor intact had it not been for the betrayal of Lord Thao. The tall handsome man with his charming smile and charismatic nature had lured the new emperor into a false sense of security.

Jeruko reminisced on one of the best nights of revelry with his friends, which included Lord Thao. After a victorious battle against rebels, the festivities had swept them into a blur of activity. The highlight of the evening came when Emperor Mizuki and Lord Thao locked arms and sang a battle song with raucous gusto, slurring most of the words into nonsense.

Jeruko laughed so hard, his stomach hurt. He spilled his drink and wiped the tears from his eyes. Samuru and Fujishin cried with the same mirth.

When the song ended, Lord Thao kissed the emperor's forehead. "I love you, my friend. May this joyous night never end!"

Lord Thao's loyalty had seemed so certain back then. Jeruko still remembered the sincerity of his handsome features as he'd spoken those words. But two months later, the depth of his deception came to light.

"Where is he?" Emperor Mizuki had said on that fateful day. He stood before the bridge viewscreen with his hands wrapped in a knot behind his back. The space battle raged with the *Dragon* warship barely able to hold the enemies off.

Jeruko studied the signals on his console screen. Neither the long-range nor the short-range sensors detected Lord Thao's ships. They should have been here by now. The emperor had meticulously planned this battle. His strategy was solid, but it depended on those vessels showing up at the right time and the right place.

That window had passed and still no Thao.

"Have you been able to reach him?" the emperor asked.

"No, Sire," the operations officer replied. "I've reached out to our other allies as well. No one knows what happened to him."

"Chusho." Emperor Mizuki plopped onto the command chair. "What the hell is going on?"

Jeruko turned to the emperor with a wrinkled brow. "Perhaps the enemy ambushed him."

"They couldn't have known he was coming, damn it. I made sure everyone thought I sent him to the Midori sector."

"Maybe someone leaked his actual location," Samuru said, not looking up from his work at the tactical station.

The emperor darkened. "Just keep firing. We must hold them off until he arrives."

Jeruko swallowed, then returned to his screen. Still no sign of Lord Thao. Although two enemy vessels were out of the fight, so was one of the emperor's support ships. Plus, the *Dragon*'s shields had fallen to less than forty percent. If Lord Thao didn't arrive soon, they'd all be in serious trouble.

Something blinked at the corner of Jeruko's screen. Was that a ship? He leaned forward and stared at the spot. Another blink.

He held his breath. A green dot appeared. "A ship!"

The emperor leapt from his chair. "Identify!"

Jeruko tapped his console. "It's coming from the wrong direction. I'm redirecting the sensors."

Emperor Mizuki paced.

"Two more ships," Jeruko called out.

"It must be Lord Thao," the emperor replied.

Information popped up on Jeruko's console. "Yes, it's them!"

The emperor blew out a breath. "Open a channel."

"I've been trying, Sire," the communications officer said. "They're not responding."

"Chusho!"

The battle between the *Dragon* and his allies against the five remaining enemy ships continued with ferocity as Lord Thao approached. He came nearer to the *Dragon* when he should've come in from behind the enemy, but at least he came.

Still, the lord sent no communications. Emperor Mizuki returned to his seat and leaned forward with his elbows on his knees. He bit his thumbnail between barking orders.

Samuru crippled two more enemy vessels, but not enough to stop them from firing their weapons. The emperor lost another allied vessel and the *Dragon*'s shields dropped below thirty percent.

"Communication coming in, Sire!"

"I have a surprise for you, Emperor Mizuki," Lord Thao's voice said sweetly through the comm.

The bridge officers cheered. The emperor wiped the sweat from his face. "Thao! Where have you been? What happened? Did—"

The *Dragon* lurched.

"He's firing at us!" the communications officer called out.

The emperor strapped himself into his chair as more weapon strikes rattled the ship. "What the fuck!"

"I've had enough of the Mizuki reign," Lord Thao said. "We all have."

"Fire on that chima!" Emperor Mizuki roared.

Jeruko fast-forwarded through the rest of the memory. The *Dragon* had barely escaped that battle. The emperor was forced to wage a war that lasted over five years. He finally captured Lord Thao. Jeruko didn't question the brutality of the lord's execution. Nor did he question it when the emperor slaughtered Thao's entire household, including his children.

The memory made Jeruko shiver now. He hated what the emperor had done, but believed it was necessary at the time. The emperor's actions sent the rebels fleeing like kicked dogs. The war had ended, but so did Emperor Mizuki's compassion.

This incident had spurred the emperor to marry Lord Enomoto's sister in hopes of siring sons with an ability to see people's true natures. It also turned on a spigot that splattered suspicions into every corner.

Jeruko put the echoes of the past away and rubbed his temple. Terkeshi was too young to take on the mantle of emperor. The lords would eat him alive. At the same time, he couldn't thrive so long as the emperor was around to abuse and poison him. Emperor Kenji Mizuki had once been Jeruko's dearest friend, but he must be stopped. If only he could figure out a way.

34
Regret

3791:102:20:10. An internal heat burned within Terkeshi as he stood with feet planted and his hands squeezing into fists at his back. A line of attentive men assembled behind him as Father's voice boomed throughout the bay.

"We lost four Dragon Warriors in this battle." His dark eyes pierced Terk's. "The parting of these men will be sorely felt..."

Terk worked his jaw and glowered. Father returned the look, emanating only displeasure. *The duplicitous chima feels nothing for those lost men.*

"But our victory belongs to them as much as it does you," Father continued. "Your skill and bravery easily outmatched those cowardly Rhinian assailants. We won the day, and we acquired a new ship. For this, you shall be greatly rewarded. One of you will take command of it. Some of you may serve on it."

How will they do that with no workers to fix it? An image of all those people he murdered flashed through his thoughts and sent a painful spike into his chest.

"*All* of you," Father paused and glanced at each of the men, "will enjoy a celebration in the lounge."

The men didn't emit a sound and Terk doubted they did more than blink, but he could practically hear their emotions cheering. Their jubilation did nothing to touch the turmoil swirling inside him, though. How could he be happy after what he'd done?

Terk bit down, making his jaw twinge. He barely heard his father dismiss the men. His eyes remained fixed on the chima as the senshi filed out.

"Well, boy?" Father snapped. "What the hell are you waiting for?"

Terk's nostrils flared. "I'm in no mood to celebrate."

"Don't be such a child."

"You did something to me, didn't you?"

"All I did was give you a push."

Terk swallowed. He'd hesitated, but he still would've done it. It wasn't like he'd had much choice in the matter.

No, that's not true. He could have chosen to disobey. If Father hadn't intervened somehow, would he have? He wanted to say yes, but now he'd never know.

Terk set his doubts aside and glowered. "I told you I didn't want you to remote control me."

"If you had done better, I wouldn't have."

Terk hardened his fists. "I succeeded!"

Father's lip curled into a snarl. "You lost four men."

The back of Terk's throat ached. "How was I supposed to know they'd use something that powerful in an enclosed space? Besides, they outnumbered us. We're lucky that's all we lost."

"Your brother never would have lost so many. You're incompetent. Not even cybernetic enhancements have helped you."

Terk's face flushed with heat. "I took over that ship," he muttered.

"With the cybernetics I invested in, the casualties should be *zero.* And let's not forget that you disobeyed me."

Terk huffed. "I was about to do it! You didn't give me a chance!"

Father leaned in, his bulky form towering like an angry bear. "You've had too many damned chances!"

Terk flinched. He turned away to hide the hot liquid building in his eyes.

"General Samuru will captain the *Fire Breather.* The last thing I need is for you to hesitate during a battle."

"The battle was over."

"That's no excuse." Father straightened. "Despite your failure, you will go to the lounge and celebrate. It's bad enough they see you as incompetent. Don't let them know what a sentimental fool you are, too."

Terk stormed away, ignoring Father's grumbling about his disrespect for leaving without being dismissed. *Let him be angry.* What did it matter? One more blunder on top of the heaps of others didn't matter. Besides, he'd turn into a full-fledged machine soon anyway. These stupid emotions would no longer plague him. Maybe then he'd be worth something.

He swiped the wetness from his eyes as he left the bay. *Don't be such a child.*

He stepped inside the conveyor. "Lounge."

As the car moved, he took in a deep breath and struggled to bury the emotions that buffeted against him like the winds of Arashi. The conveyor stopped. Terk pushed his way out before the doors fully opened. He bumped shoulders with a senshi as he stormed past.

"Watch it!" he said over his shoulder before the man dared utter a curse.

He entered the crowded lounge where dozens of senshi ate, drank, and laughed. Smoke tickled his nose. The sickly, sweet smell turned his stomach. *How can anyone deliberately inhale that stuff?*

Nevertheless, Senshi Kelar seemed to enjoy it. As he sucked on a fat hamaki, his half-lidded eyes rolled with ecstasy. That was no ordinary hamaki.

Kelar held it out. "You want one, my Lord?"

Terk pulled back with a face. "No." Although the idea of smothering his emotions had its appeal, he hated how that stuff made him act like a fool. He needed no help there.

"Koshu," he ordered from the attendant at the bar as he took a stool. Aged sake was as far as he'd go to dull his feelings.

The uproarious laughter and exaggerated stories grated Terk's ears. He pulled his music player from his pocket and taped it behind his ear. A few taps found music with superstrat guitars, reactables, and loud, fast drums.

The attendant brought his sake. Terk rested his head in his palm and stared down into it. The memory of those people resurfaced. Father had manipulated him, but the truth was he would've done it anyway. So why did he hesitate? So stupid.

He downed his drink in one gulp and focused on the burning that followed.

It wasn't his fault they were dead. Father guilted him into it, like he had with Fujishin. *I should have just done it and not argued.*

He'd exited the room almost immediately after that slaughter. And even though he no longer sensed the pain of their deaths, the sensations plagued him. They hadn't subsided until after he threw up in the hall.

A flush filled his cheeks, either from the alcohol or the memory. Although no one had seen him heave up his guts, he couldn't hide the orange bile on the floor. Kelar had noticed and poked fun, further entrenching his humiliation.

Why does this bother me so much? This wasn't his first kill, yet killing made him sick every time.

"Another, my Lord?" the bar attendant's voice cut in, making Terk's music automatically turn down.

Terk responded with a frown. The man smiled. "You look like you need more." Without waiting for approval, he poured another drink and set it between Terk's arms.

Terk eyed it until someone slapped him on the shoulder.

"Drink up, my Lord," Rushiro said with a grin. "You won us a glorious victory!"

Terk took a sip but didn't return the man's enthusiasm. The rare compliment should have given him pride, but his mind was elsewhere. The dead faces of the workers, all centered on the woman's dull blue eyes, kept penetrating his thoughts. He'd never executed a woman before.

His gut roiled and he almost heaved. He tossed back the rest of his drink and forced everything down. *Stop this!* So what if he'd taken her life. His eldest brother had killed many people, men and women, and it never bothered him.

Dokuri hadn't just killed. He'd been a bloodthirsty maniac. Terk recalled a time when his brother returned from battle with his black uniform slicked with blood. An iron tang wafted from him. Worse, he radiated a dark lust that had made Jori cry.

A piercing sensation trickled into Terk's senses, giving him a headache. People were being tortured somewhere on this ship—most likely the captain and commander of the *Shadow Croc*. He massaged his temples, but an external torment continued to pound into him. He tried to block it, to no avail.

Terk tapped his player, but the distraction didn't work. The hellacious emotions endured like invasive fungi. He scrunched his eyes and cradled his head in his hands. *Chusho.* This shouldn't

181

bother him. They're the enemy. *Aren't they?* After all, they had been the ones to attack.

Another clap on the back snapped him upright.

"My Lord," Kelar said with a stoned smile. "I bought you a drink."

Terk opened his mouth to tell him he didn't want it, but the man set it before him and returned to the festivities. Terk clenched his teeth and stared down into the clear liquid, inspecting his reflection.

Chusho. He looked just like Dokuri. Hell, he might as well be Dokuri at this point.

He swept the glass off the table. Liquor and glass splattered on the floor. A few glances darted his way, but no one seemed to care. The only significant reaction came from the cleaning bots.

He didn't want to be a terrible brute like Dokuri. Why his father wanted someone like that as a son was beyond him. But that was what he had to be if he didn't wish to be controlled.

Fine. So be it, but I'm not letting you control me anymore. When he turned the music louder, an idea occurred to him. What if he covered his eye and blocked the sound? It wouldn't stop anyone from controlling him through his cybernetics, but it would keep Father and the cyborgs out of his head.

35
Interrogating Crocs

3791:102:22:47. A tang of piss made Kenji Mizuki's nostrils twitch. The captain of the *Shadow Croc* hung by his arms. The tips of his bare feet touched the tainted puddle on the floor. Despite still being alive, the man's head drooped lifelessly. Fresh blood ran down his nose while the older stuff coagulated over his busted lip.

Nezumi inspected a knife no longer than the palm of his hand. Its edge gleamed with sharpness. "Since brute force isn't working, how about we try something more delicate?"

The captain captive coughed. "I'll die before giving up my sponsor."

Nezumi cocked his head. "Oh, I won't kill you."

Mizuki suppressed a shiver. He glanced sideways at the colonel beside him. Jeruko remained silent and expressionless. Mizuki doubted he was so calm on the inside.

Nezumi ran the tip of the blade across the left side of the man's chest. The captain gritted his teeth, releasing only a slight whimper. Another cut created a hook at one end. The prisoner barely blinked.

Nezumi smiled. "That wasn't so bad, was it?"

The captain's brow wrinkled.

Nezumi's grin widened. "You know I'm not done yet, don't you? You're right. I'm not. This is just the beginning. The next step is to peel away your skin."

Mizuki worked his jaw. "Get on with it, man."

Nezumi bowed. "My apologies, your Eminence. This is delicately excruciating work, but you will get the results you want, I assure you."

Mizuki huffed.

Nezumi resumed his task. He dug the tip of his blade into the corner and pried the skin up. The dull side of the knife slid under

183

the flap. He held it and tugged. The captain's whine increased in intensity as the flesh peeled away, a millimeter at a time. Blood trickled first, then streamed.

The captain cried out. Tears ran from the corners of his eyes.

"I've barely started," Nezumi said in a calm tone. "Are you sure you have nothing to say? You know the body has nearly twenty thousand square centimeters of skin, don't you?"

The man sobbed.

"I hear the inner thigh is particularly painful, but not as painful as the member further up."

Mizuki winced inwardly while also admiring the look of horror that Nezumi's words had elicited from the prisoner.

"Why don't we just start there?" he asked.

Nezumi yanked the man's skin in a swift motion. If a rip sounded, the captain's howl drowned it out. The small patch splattered, then oozed. The prisoner's chest heaved as he failed to manage the pain.

"It's worth a try, Sire," Nezumi replied. "I had rather hoped to do more here first, but I think this man is beginning to understand."

As Nezumi removed the buckle from the man's pants, Jeruko shifted his feet. Mizuki's gut swirled. He understood the colonel's discomfort. At least he didn't ask to be dismissed as he often did on other occasions.

The captain blubbered. "No, no. I beg you. I'll tell you whatever you want, but please stop."

Nezumi pulled back with a frown, leaving the front of the man's pants undone. "So soon? I haven't even cut you yet. What sort of warrior are you?"

Mizuki scowled. "Don't give him a reason to change his mind." To the prisoner, he said, "Who paid you to attack me?"

The captain's throat bobbed. "I don't know exactly, but—"

"Cut him," Mizuki said.

"No! Listen, please. It was a lord from Meixing, but I didn't see him, and no one told me his name."

Mizuki sucked in a sharp breath and held it behind clenched teeth. It had to be Lord Enomoto. Since Fujishin had been the one who'd spoken to Terkeshi, that meant both his rivals were working together.

"I believe he's only telling us what we want to hear, Sire," Jeruko said. "His ship's records indicate the last time he'd been to Meixing was almost twelve months ago."

Mizuki narrowed his eyes. The colonel made a good point, but he couldn't help wondering whether this was an attempt to protect Lord Enomoto.

"Only one way to find out." Nezumi tugged at the captain's pants. "There's an area here that is particularly sensitive to pain."

The prisoner scooted back as far as his manacles allowed. "No! You're right! We haven't been to Meixing. The man we met told us he'd come from there. I swear it. Please!"

"We can have Terkeshi verify the truth," Jeruko said.

Nezumi straightened. "Why? This is so much more fun."

Mizuki raised a lip at the man and replied to Jeruko. "The boy is celebrating with the men. Besides, it's unnecessary. I'm certain Lord Enomoto is behind this."

A strained expression crossed Jeruko's features. "Sire, this might be a setup. Although Fujishin is undoubtedly involved, he could have laid false information."

Mizuki scoffed. "To what end?"

"To get us to fight on two fronts." Jeruko's eyes looked almost feverish. "It's probably his backup plan if the Rhinians failed. If our emitter gets fixed, the only way he can save himself is if our attention is divided."

"Is this your assumption because you don't want your consort and sons to die?"

"I speak this because we should consider it as a tactical possibility." Jeruko made a small bow. "Although, Sire, I admit I fear for my sons. I also worry for Terkeshi because his mother is there as well."

"Pah!" Mizuki flicked his hand. "Sentiment. You both must *stop* this nonsense."

"Do you not miss your own deceased sons?"

Mizuki's lip rose at the boldness of Jeruko's question. Sure he missed them, but not like some weeping woman. He mourned them because of the state it left the Mizuki house in.

I shouldn't have killed Jori. He held his glower until the memory of his youngest son disappeared.

"Are you alright, Sire?" Jeruko asked.

"Yes, damn it!" *Why did he ask me that?* Perhaps he'd been muttering. "Quit asking stupid questions," he said, hoping to cover up his momentary lapse.

Jeruko bowed. "Regarding Prince Terkeshi, he's still young," he continued. "He hasn't learned yet to manage his emotions."

Mizuki growled. "He will soon enough."

He turned back to Nezumi and the captain, but Jeruko just wouldn't leave it alone.

"Perhaps, Sire, you'd permit me to have them all moved elsewhere."

"We'll discuss this later," Mizuki said through his teeth. "This man's discomfort is obviously affecting your sentiment. Why don't you go find something else to do?"

Jeruko bowed. "Certainly, Sire."

"Oh, and Colonel."

Jeruko halted before the door. "Yes, Sire?"

"You will say nothing to the boy about my plans for Meixing. Understood?"

Jeruko nodded. "Yes, Sire."

After he left, Mizuki returned to the task at hand. The prisoner's eyebrows raised. Mizuki frowned, realizing the unprofessionalism of having this discussion in front of him.

"Kill him."

"Certainly, Sire," Nezumi replied. "But shouldn't I continue for a while to be sure of the information?"

Mizuki consented.

"And perhaps you should have your son complete the final deed."

Mizuki chewed the inside of his lip. Terkeshi must get over his squeamishness. "Very well. Do what you must but don't kill him. And if he divulges anything more, report it immediately."

Nezumi bowed. "Of course, Sire. I am your most loyal subject."

The saliva in Mizuki's mouth soured. No doubt the sly sycophant meant to highlight Jeruko's failings. Yes, the colonel wasn't perfect, but the cyborgs had verified his loyalty after the arrest. Still, he'd keep an eye on him.

36
Shirking Duty

3791:103:18:22. Brooding electronic music droned in Terkeshi's ear. Each chord sent a discordant twang through his body. He slouched at a corner workstation in the communal workroom where the dim lighting complemented his mood. An ache lurked behind his eyes. Sleep had evaded him last night. The alcohol had brought on drowsiness, but fear of nightmares had made him restless.

He sighed, then scrolled through at the list of mundane tasks on the screen before him. All were moderately important, so he selected the one that would require the least amount of thought.

They'd confiscated a lot of junk from the *Shadow Croc*. The notes and images compiled by shokukin and robots included over a thousand items. Clothing, knickknacks, and random garbage from the occupants' quarters were automatically designated for the recycling facility in the *Dragon*'s lower decks. He assigned shokukin to inspect tools and parts. Foodstuffs went to the main supply pantry for further sorting.

The assortment of armaments piqued Terk's interest. The crocs had everything from ranged weapons to explosives, phasers, firearms, knives and swords, and other close combat weapons. They even had a decent selection of stealth equipment—lead-lined cases to hide their contents, stealthware suits for sneaking about, and a few nanite masks to help criminals defeat facial recognition technology.

Senshi usually disdained this kind of stuff. A real warrior didn't need to behave like devious pirates. However, there was something about these things that captured Terk's imagination. After all, if the cyborgs could be sneaky and underhanded, why not use whatever tools necessary to counter them?

A small apparatus tagged as a disruptor also caught Terk's attention. The tiny black gadget should be discreet enough to attach to his music player. He marked it for his own personal use. If he was lucky, it would disrupt any visual and audio devices in its vicinity. If that included those in his cybernetic implant, then he could thwart Father and the cyborgs from spying on him.

He assigned the remaining spy tech to a storage room and moved on to the next group of items. The senshi involved in the infiltration of the *Shadow Croc* would get to select an item from the close combat weapons. He tagged the rest for inspection. Some ranged weapons and explosives would likely pass, then replenish the *Dragon*'s stockpile. Most firearms and phasers would be of such inferior quality that they'd be sent to Father's fleet of low-ranking troop ships.

Someone tapped his shoulder. Terk touched his music player to put it in the auto volume-adjust mode and turned to see a face that made his mouth twist with sourness.

"My Lord," General Nezumi said with an unpleasant curl to his own features. "You're due for a training session."

Terk growled. "I'm not training with you, General, so forget it."

"Your father gave you specific orders."

Terk sneered. "So go tell on me, snitch. It's not like Father doesn't already think I shirk my duties."

"My Lord," Nezumi said in a less demanding tone, "I'm only trying to help you improve."

"I'll train with the cyber senshi, then."

"There are skills that only I can teach you. Ones that made Prince Dokuri a most fearsome warrior."

Terk's stomach tumbled. "I can fight well enough. I'll leave the nasty interrogation techniques to you."

Nezumi huffed out a breath. "There's more to it than interrogation. You must learn to strike fear into the hearts of your enemies."

Terk grit his teeth. "I'm not training with you, damn it. Now go away."

Nezumi narrowed his eyes but nodded sharply and left.

Terk suppressed a shiver and returned to his work. Once he sorted the bulk of the items, he opened the surveillance section.

After selecting a specific deck, he located three cameras outside Sensei Jeruko's personal dojo and one inside. Clicking the interior one revealed his mentor flowing through tai chi forms. This meant he had either just started or neared the end of his session. If Terk hurried, he could catch him.

Using a trick Jori had shown him, he made several cameras in that area go offline. To negate suspicion, he fabricated maintenance logs and gave them a low priority to ensure they wouldn't get repaired for a few hours.

With a grunt, he sat back and crossed his arms. Fuck that rat-faced general. Sensei Jeruko was his trainer.

37
Wisdom from Sensei

3791:103:22:36. The bokkens smacked against one another in a resonating rhythm. Jin Jeruko advanced. His wooden sword cut down at an angle and halted at the edge of Terkeshi's cross-guard. He flicked his wrist, turning the weapon and swinging it to the youth's other side.

Clack.

Thrust and slice. Parry and block. Hack and slash. Clack-clack.

Back and forth the two went, taking turns at offense and defense. Jeruko's breathing remained even and only a fine layer of perspiration coated his skin. Terkeshi, however, didn't fare so well. The redness of his face glistened like a polished apple as his sweat poured. He bared his teeth like an angry blackbeast and growled at intervals.

Terkeshi's moves became sloppy. Jeruko swung, stopping short of smacking the young man's side.

"Mushin, my Lord," he said.

Terkeshi snarled and swiped his bokken in an upward arc. Jeruko turned his wrist and blocked. The clash of the wooden swords jarred his arm with its ferocity. If not for the tremendous burden the youth carried, he would have reprimanded him.

He called a halt instead. Terkeshi stepped back. His chest heaved as he wiped a layer of sweat from his brow.

"You're distracted," Jeruko said. "Mushin doesn't just mean you should fight without thinking about your next move. It means not thinking about anything. No mind."

Terkeshi hurled the wooden sword to the floor. "I know, damn it!"

Jeruko sighed. "I saw what took place on the enemy ship. It shouldn't have happened the way it did."

Terkeshi looked away with a glower. "Yeah, I should have just killed them instead of making excuses like a coward."

Jeruko glanced about his dojo, wondering if Terkeshi had adequately disabled the surveillance cameras. He chose his next words carefully. "Choosing not to kill doesn't make you a coward."

Terkeshi darkened. "I didn't *have* a choice."

Jeruko swallowed. "No, you didn't. You're not to blame."

"I *am* to blame. I didn't do what I was told. Now instead of feeling pride, I feel..." His mouth twisted as though he'd eaten something bitter. "Used."

"Killing innocent people shouldn't give you pride," Jeruko said in a hushed volume. "I understand what you're feeling and I'm sorry—"

Terkeshi's eyes burned with hate. "I don't need your damned sympathy! All it's done is make me weak."

"You're not weak, Terke-chan."

"I *am* weak! I can't let go of my sentiment like Dokuri, and I can't stand up in the face of punishment like Jori." Terkeshi's expression twisted.

Jeruko's throat hardened into a painful lump. "It's true that you're neither of them. But you're stronger than everyone gives you credit for. Let me help you."

"I don't need your help. You helped Jori, remember? And look where it left him."

Jeruko winced. "Be careful what you say, boy," he whispered with a slight head tilt to a corner that could have held a camera and mic.

Terkeshi ignored him. "At least Jori's dead. I must live as this monster. Since I can't match Jori, I might as well take after Dokuri."

A pain spiked Jeruko's chest. "You don't want to be like him. He was a great killer. Nothing more."

Terkeshi's lip curled. "Better than me, obviously."

"You only know a small part of what he was really like."

Terkeshi crossed his arms. "You've mentioned this before, so tell me more."

Jeruko filled his lungs. Should he say? Perhaps the emperor didn't watch the surveillance, but there was no guarantee the

Dawn Ross

disruptor Terkeshi wore worked. "My apologies, but it's not my place."

"Nobody knows I'm here, remember? I evaded my personal guards." Terkeshi pointed to the small electronic device behind his ear. "And this makes it so no one can see or hear me."

"Are you sure it works?"

"Yes, I'm sure, damn it! You think I want those chima spying on me? Now tell me how awful Dokuri was."

Jeruko pushed past his unease and told him about the emperor's supposed favorite offspring. "When Dokuri came of age, I served as one of his officers. Even in his youth, his cruelty was evident. I reported my concern to your father, but he seemed indifferent. Although he would order torture from time to time, taking part in it himself nauseated him. He hated this weakness and believed Dokuri's propensity for it made him stronger. Because of this encouragement, your brother's brutality worsened."

Jeruko looked at his feet. That time in his life had been the most difficult. The emperor had done things to make him uneasy about serving him. But the first time he'd truly questioned his loyalty was the day Dokuri had inflicted unspeakable torture on an innocent girl.

She had been the young daughter of a rebelling lord. He could still see her face—her smooth skin, bright eyes, and wondrous expression.

He rubbed his brow as the memory replayed in his mind. She'd just turned fourteen, she said. Unlike most women this age, she was still a maiden. Her father had sheltered her to the point that she saw all people as good-hearted souls. When Jeruko and his squad found her, she smiled and welcomed them. She thought they came to save her from the violence happening outside.

The orders hadn't included harming the lord's family, so Jeruko had told her to run away as fast as she could. Unfortunately, Dokuri caught her.

"There was this girl about your age." Jeruko hung his head and covered his mouth, trying to regain his composure. "Your brother was merciless. She had cuts and bruises everywhere. He broke her arms and legs in multiple places, and..." His stomach lurched. "He cut off her tongue and gouged out her eyes."

Jeruko didn't share that she was still alive when he'd discovered what Dokuri had done. He berated the young prince and received only a shrug in reply. Jeruko blamed himself for her suffering. If only he had intervened or sent her a different direction for escape. Even killing her himself would have been better. At least she would have died quickly and painlessly.

Terkeshi turned away, his brow furrowed. "And you still served him?"

Reluctantly. "For a little while longer. Dokuri left me for dead in another battle. Your father rescued me and gave me a different assignment."

Terkeshi made a dismissive noise. "I can't see him doing something so sentimental."

"It began a new chapter in my life. One that renewed my faith and desire to serve."

Terkeshi's brow furrowed.

"My knee was irreparable," Jeruko continued. "I was crippled, so I became your teacher instead. I'm proud to serve you, my Lord."

"Even though I'm a machine now?"

"You are still you. You did a fine job in battle." He lowered his voice. "Until your father made you kill those people. That wasn't you."

"How can you continue to serve him after what he's done?"

"I am loyal to you," he whispered.

"Not my father?" Terkeshi muttered.

"Your father was a good man once."

Terkeshi huffed. "I find that hard to believe."

"It's true. His consideration for others inspired me to swear my oath to him. But he changed. His father had been as harsh on him as he is on you now. And one day he decided sentiment was a weakness and tried to purge me of it."

"How?"

Jeruko hesitated. He stepped forward and leaned in. "He took my wife from me."

"Washi and Michio's mother?"

Jeruko gave a sharp nod. "I loved her too much, he said. So he exiled her. He told me if I was strong, I wouldn't let it bother me. I believed in him so much back then that I forgave him. I almost turned away after what Dokuri had done, but he saved me. Then he assigned me to you. You are a fine young man, Terke-chan, despite what your father says. Please don't become like Dokuri."

Terkeshi pointed to his cybernetic eye. "I may not have a choice. It's only a matter of time before they realize what I've done and make me remove the disruptor."

Jeruko slumped his shoulders as an invisible weight pressed on him. "I'm sorry I failed you."

Terkeshi's eyes watered.

Jeruko's did as well. "And I'm sorry I failed Jori."

"It's your fault he's gone," Terkeshi mumbled.

"I know."

Terkeshi's face turned red. His eyes darkened and the muscles in his neck corded. Jeruko stepped back from his sudden fury.

"Your pathetic weakness has tainted me," Terkeshi said with vehemence. "You knew what my father was, and you still served him. Thanks to you, Jori is dead. You practically stabbed him yourself. And you're no help to me either. You just *let* him turn me into this."

A tear ran down Jeruko's cheek. He swallowed the extra saliva that had built up in his mouth. "I'm so sorry, Terke-chan."

"Fuck you."

Jeruko's knees buckled as Terkeshi stormed off. He clutched his chest as a swelling agony pierced his soul. *I am truly sorry, Terke-chan.*

*****

3791:103:23:28. Ambrose almost cocked a smile at the young prince's rudimentary attempt to defeat the implant. With a click, he easily fixed the distortion created by the device.

As the trivial conversation ensued, he worked on two other projects intended for MEGA-Man. The more information on the Toradons, the better.

"How can you continue to serve him after what he's done?" the voice of Terkeshi broadcasted.

"I am loyal to you," Colonel Jeruko whispered.

So that's how he defeated our lie detector. The colonel just might be more of a problem than predicted. Ambrose added this tidbit into the report to MEGA-Man.

"Please don't become like Dokuri," Colonel Jeruko transmitted.

At the same moment, the live stream of Terkeshi's brain activity indicated agreement with the man's words. With a mental nudge, Ambrose accessed the prince's controls and executed a function under STIMULATONS. He raised it by a single point, then incrementally increased it until the young man made his expletive. *Perfect.*

After the prince left, he reduced the intensity but didn't turn it off. Stopping it completely would give away what he'd done. Perhaps he should keep it at this level until the prince's transformation was complete.

Ambrose halted his other tasks and analyzed the prospect. It could make Terkeshi more impulsive than usual. Based on his personality profile, however, his behavior should fall into a predictable range. Proper stimulus in the right places could manipulate him into doing exactly what MEGA-Man wanted him to do.

As an added benefit, it clashed against Colonel Jeruko's damaging influence. Ambrose sat back and folded his hands. The colonel's outdated form of ethics had been an irritation. He'd considered killing him, but this was better. It avoided a messy affair that might pique the emperor's suspicions.

A reevaluation of eliminating the colonel's interference brought up a new possibility. Thanks to General Nezumi's desire to curtail Colonel Jeruko's influence, all Ambrose had to do was show him this recent conversation.

Ambrose tapped his chin. The general would undoubtedly tell the emperor. Would this trigger another bout of psychosis? The emperor had killed one of his sons already. MEGA-Man wouldn't like it if Terkeshi died too.

Ambrose filed the recording away for further consideration.

38
The Emitter

3791:105:17:09. Terkeshi crossed his arms and leaned back, ignoring the cyborg in the copilot seat beside him. The riff of one of his favorite songs played from the electronic device attached to his ear. The bone-crushing chords throbbed through him, matching his mood.

As the battle-music blared, he waited for his part in the next stage of insertion. The *Fire Breather* dominated the view outside his construction ship. Men and cyborgs in space suits crawled around it. They either completed the assembly of the emitter inside or performed the technical tasks necessary to make it operational.

The musical tempo made by metallic tapping reminded Terk of a ticking timebomb. Once they finished housing the perantium device in *Fire Breather*, that's what it would be—a bomb of sorts, set to destroy their enemies.

The closer the project came to completion, the lighter Father's mood became. Terk's, on the other hand, darkened by the day. *Father's getting what he wants. What do I get? I get turned into a damned robot.*

Maybe Jori's death was a good thing. Sensei Jeruko had done him a favor. Anything was better than this.

Terk's temper flared once again. Was Sensei Jeruko really to blame, though? Yes, but so were the cyborgs and his father. *It's my fault too. I shouldn't have let Jori save those prisoners.*

"Sir," a voice cut through the comm.

Terk sat up and wiped his eyes. "Go ahead."

"We're ready for you, my Lord."

"On it." Terk manipulated the helm and maneuvered his ship. He extended the claw that held one of the emitter's primary components. Using the features of his cybernetics, he opened the program the cyborgs had installed to help him put the piece in place. Lines of multiple colors flashed across his vision as his eye scanned outside. The resulting information appeared in the top right of his view.

Terk moved the claw as prescribed.

The cyborg next to him smiled in that annoying way of his. "You are point-five degrees off."

"Yes, I can see that," Terk replied irritably. "I'm correcting it now."

"You must be careful," Ambrose said. "One wrong move and it will explode."

Terk winced, jerking the device out of alignment. "What? Why?" He quickly corrected it and glared at the man next to him.

"Someone sabotaged it. It is unstable."

"Fuck! Why the hell didn't you fix it before I moved it?"

"We can only repair it when it is connected to the STK regulator."

"Are you saying just moving it wrong might trigger an explosion?" Terk's irritation came out in a high-pitched tone.

"Yes."

Chusho. He'd known Jori had sabotaged the emitter before his death, but did he intentionally make it so the device would explode? It seemed unlikely. Jori hadn't wanted it built, but he wouldn't have risked the lives of his own people.

It must've been one of those Cooperative prisoners. The only reason Father had seized them was so they could fix it. They had probably taken advantage of the Toradon workers' ignorance and broke it instead.

Terk gritted his teeth. Damn them—and the cyborgs for not telling him. He wouldn't have volunteered if he'd known his life would be at stake. Then again, it would serve Father right if he died while putting this damned device together.

"How long after the connection is complete will the danger be gone?" he asked.

"One day, five hours, and twenty-two minutes."

Terk scowled. "Chusho. I hope you're using your own people to repair it."

"Yes. The work is too precise for your workers."

Good. Terk made another slight adjustment. Perspiration built on his upper lip. An ache ran from his grip on the helm up to his shoulders. His neck corded with the effort of keeping the device on the prescribed trajectory.

"When you get the rest of your enhancements," the cyborg said, "your hand-eye coordination will be vastly improved."

"I'm not getting any more enhancements," Terk replied through his teeth.

"Oh? I thought you liked your new abilities."

"I don't like that you or my father can watch me from them. And I certainly don't like being remote controlled."

"We wouldn't do that," Ambrose said.

Terk concentrated with his sensing ability to determine if the cyborg had told the truth, but all he felt was a metallic-like essence. "Liar," he replied anyway.

Ambrose seemed unfazed by the accusation. "You'd be a greater warrior than any of your brothers. You would be the greatest Mizuki emperor of all time."

Terk huffed. "So you can see the future, too?"

"I can see a new age is coming. You view us as outcasts, but we are technologically advanced. If you choose to remain as you are, we will evolve and ascend above you."

"You are not better than me. You're just a machine," Terk said sourly.

"I am more than you will ever be," Ambrose replied.

Terk glowered. *I should mess up on purpose.* He'd rid the world of these arrogant machines, stopping them from turning him into a robot at the same time.

"You are point seven inches too far to the left," the cyborg said.

Terk growled. "I know."

With a slight nudge of the controls, he grudgingly moved the component back in line. Killing himself, Ambrose, and a few of the cyborgs wouldn't achieve anything. *Other than making me an even bigger failure.*

*****

3791:105:18:25. Ambrose detected the prince's annoyance but didn't comprehend what had caused it. Although the reason was inconsequential, his curiosity got the better of him.

While maintaining focus on the task at hand, he opened another program. With a mental prompt, he accessed the prince's brain activity and analyzed his emotions.

Interesting. Even though he had turned off the anger stimulation for this assignment, the young man's mood remained elevated. Fifty-seven-point-two-three percent angry, twenty-three-point-five-eight percent sad, and nineteen-point-one-nine percent ashamed.

Psychological analysis indicated his temper likely derived from the sadness, shame, or a combination of the two. Of course the analysis itself was ambiguous. Although the numerical values had a precision to them, the standard deviation was high. Even with today's technology, pinning down specific emotions remained difficult.

He glanced at the prince's tight expression, recognizing how it matched his internal measurements. Ambrose indulged in the contempt that sparked within himself. These ordinary humans came with countless chaotic and illogical emotions and reactions. How could they attain even their most mundane objectives while being plagued with these inexplicable moods?

Becoming a MEGA had simplified his own life. Without the obstacle of emotional interference, he easily achieved his goals.

If only he could convince the prince. Terkeshi's insistence on not being further enhanced could create complications if he didn't embrace the transformation. Someone as potentially powerful as Prince Mizuki must ally with MEGA-Man.

39
Disposable

3791:106:05:28. Terkeshi followed the cyborg through the belly of its advanced vessel. He hadn't realized how oppressive his own ship was until he'd come here. Instead of the darker metal walls, this one was bright titanium. The corridors weren't as wide, but the cleanliness gave the illusion of spaciousness.

His admiration stopped there. Not only did it seem like he stood in the center of a spotlight, but the surrounding silence disturbed him. The only noises were the occasional clopping of metal feet as he passed some cyborg or another.

Very little tickled his senses either. The meager lifeforces from these freaks set his teeth on edge. He sensed nothing from the robotic being in front of him now. Hell, he couldn't even tell its sex. Androgynous subcultures existed throughout the galaxy, including in Toradon where many still frowned upon it, but this creature took it to a whole new level.

The cybernetic being came to a set of wide glass double doors. Windows lined either side, revealing a vast room full of both robotic machines and machine-like people. Nearly everyone wore white. One cyborg had on blue gloves and white goggles, though the eyewear might be part of his face. Another ran a scanner over a piece of equipment. Rows of beds lay further back, each holding a patient with a convoluted mess of tubes and wires coming out of them.

Terk craned his neck to get a better view. Whatever was being done didn't appear to be the same procedure as when they'd enhanced the senshi. A clear but sparkly liquid pumped into them. Most attachments connected to the tops of their heads.

Is this the next level of enhancements? He sure the hell hoped not.

Ambrose met him with a flat smile. "Thank you for coming, Prince Mizuki."

Terk crossed his arms. "What is it you wish to show me?"

"Come with me." Ambrose turned, leading him inside. "I want you to see all cybernetics can do and ease your worries."

Terk huffed through his nose. *If this chima thinks he'll convince me by showing me people with no lifeforces, he's wrong.*

Ambrose brought him to a rear section that hadn't been visible from the windows. The place resembled both a gymnasium and a lounge. While a pair of cyborgs played a table game in one corner, two others nearby ran on treadmills. At the back wall, a cyborg man with four arms competed in a dart match against a woman with metallic eyes. Another cybernetic man with bulky metal arms lifted weights—perhaps twice what Samuru could lift. This cyborg didn't seem to break a sweat, nor did any strain show on his face.

Without the benefit of sensing emotions, one might assume they enjoyed themselves. Yet Terk felt very little from them. The two at the table emitted a trickle of interest as they played, but they might as well be putting on shoes compared to the intensity Jori used to radiate whenever he'd played a strategic game. The woman at the dart board trickled a pinpoint of satisfaction, but the man accepted his loss with the same obliviousness as a computer.

"This is our training-slash-recreation room," Ambrose said with a tiny prickle of pride. "Look at our people. They are at peace."

"How can they be at peace if they don't feel anything?"

"They don't feel afflictions either. Aren't you afflicted?" Ambrose cocked his head. "I sense it in you. You're hurting. Is this how you wish your life to be? Join us and all your pain goes away."

Terk glowered and put up a mental wall to keep the man from reading him. Still, Ambrose had a point. Acid seemed to eat at Terk's intestines. The tightness in his shoulders pulled at the tendons in his neck, creating a permanent ache. Something agitated inside him and sprang out at the slightest provocations. How much better would he feel if he no longer worried about failing, didn't care when Father spoke disparaging words, or didn't break down whenever he thought of Jori?

His gut rolled. Not having any emotions at all meant he'd be as braindead as these people. "Perhaps, but this isn't what my men signed up for. They assumed they were just getting enhancements. If they knew they'd lose themselves, they might've declined."

"They all wanted to be better, and now they are," Ambrose replied. "They are the ultimate warriors."

Terk shook his head. "Their free will is gone. Not only can they no longer choose happiness, but they also can't choose their own actions. I don't want to be like that."

"Their enhancements differ from yours. You still have your free will. We're not here to take that from you."

Terk tensed. "But you'll give my father that ability?"

"Perhaps that was a mistake."

"Damn right it was."

Ambrose's brows drew together. "But he is your father. Shouldn't children do as their fathers tell them?"

"I don't want him to have that kind of power over me!"

Ambrose blinked, then he remained frozen as though caught in an infinite loop where every attempt to solve a problem confronted the same issue. He finally conceded. "I will limit his control, but I cannot take it all away at this time. Please understand."

Terk crossed his arms. "Why not? Why can't you do it now?"

"Our contract is with him. When he is gone, it will be with you. You will have full autonomy over your cybernetics."

"You have no right to force this on me."

Ambrose pressed his palms together. "Again, you are missing the benefits."

Terk ignored him. "How do I know you're not also controlling me?"

"We don't want to control you, my Lord."

Something contradictory flickered in Ambrose's words, but Terk couldn't pinpoint it. "But you control my warriors."

"We merely turned off a function."

"That implies you can turn it back on. You still manage his features, and you've given my father that ability as well."

"Don't you want to maintain control of your soldiers?"

Terk almost answered yes but then Ambrose would be right. He pinched the bridge of his nose. If only he had the intellect to refute him.

"Not everyone who receives cybernetics will be like your soldiers," Ambrose continued. "There will always be those who must be governed. It is no different from what the Mizuki Empire does with their slaves. Some people are in charge, the rest obey."

Terk frowned. "So these people here, did you convert them because they needed to obey?"

"Many chose this life. Some, however, did not."

"Those you forced, was it because they didn't share your ideals?"

"Perhaps. There are several factors to consider."

The pit of Terk's stomach curdled. If he embraced their lifestyle, they'd have no reason to control him. But if he did so, he'd lose himself and likely make decisions he never would've made for himself if he had been whole. And if he didn't do what they wanted, they might force him. He was trapped.

"Do not concern yourself, Prince Mizuki," Ambrose said without emitting an ounce of reassurance.

Terk refocused on his mental wall. If only he knew how to emit a false emotion.

Ambrose swept out his hand. "Have a look around. Ask my people anything you'd like. You'll see just how remarkable they are—and how remarkable you can be."

Terk departed the veneer-faced man to explore on his own. He kept his emotions subdued as he visited the area where the tubed and wired cyborgs lay. They could've been sleeping, but not a single one emitted a lifeforce.

"Are they alive?" he asked the pale woman tending to them.

"Yes."

Terk bit the inside of his cheek. A fully human doctor would elaborate. "What are you doing to them? Are they getting more enhancements?"

"We are repairing them, so, yes, we are adding more enhancements."

"What do you mean by *repairing* them? They're broken?"

"Some didn't conform, some resisted the treatment, and some malfunctioned."

Terk's jaw dropped. So many questions ran through his head, he didn't know where to begin. "H-how often does this happen?"

"Nineteen-point-seven-eight percent of the time."

Terk nearly choked. Why didn't they tell Father about this? Surely, he wouldn't have insisted on the enhancements if he'd known one in five would end up like this. Father may think him incompetent, but incompetent was better than whatever the hell this was.

What did this creature mean *didn't conform* and *resisted treatment*? Did these subjects consciously resist augmentation or did their bodies reject the implants? If Terk didn't embrace his cybernetics, would his chances of becoming like this increase?

He opened his mouth to ask but stopped the flood. The answers didn't matter. This was monstrous. These people were insanely dangerous.

*****

3791:106:06:47. A strange feeling coursed through Ambrose's veins as he headed to his office. Showing the prince his potential should have worked. He ought to be eager to get rid of his hard feelings, yet an inexplicable horror and disgust held him back.

Ambrose replayed the scene from the prince's eye. The conversation with the medic triggered the strongest emotions. But why should a nineteen-point-seven-eight percent be so troublesome? So what if a few inferior beings didn't make it. Evolution was all about survival of the fittest. Toradons knew this better than most.

This required further evaluation. The prince must embrace his potential.

He stepped into the conveyor, then accessed his program to run a new analysis. Data from his psychology microchip, information from other evaluations, and notes from observations poured in. With little thought, everything coalesced into an organized stream.

When the conveyor doors opened, Ambrose had an answer. The prince cared about people, even ones he didn't know. This compassion certainly didn't come from the emperor. That man understood the necessity of sacrificing the unworthy.

The prince's mother probably contributed to this infirmity, but the most likely culprit was Colonel Jeruko. He'd been a large part of both princes' lives.

Ambrose must do something about him. Unfortunately, the analysis he'd competed after overhearing the prince and Jeruko speaking indicated going to General Nezumi with the recording wouldn't be enough. Even after all that had transpired, the emperor still trusted the colonel.

Ambrose turned the corner and smacked his head into the chest of a black-garbed warrior. He shook himself off and looked up at the rat-faced general before him.

"My apologies," General Nezumi said with oily emotions that made Ambrose's insides curdle. "I was hoping to run into you, but not literally."

Ambrose put on a fake smile. "It's alright. How may I help you?"

"Can I speak with you in private?"

"Certainly." Ambrose pointed down the hall. "My office is there on the left."

They entered the room. Nezumi looked around with a frown. "It's rather small."

Ambrose dipped his head. "All I need is a computer and a desk."

The general grunted.

"But you didn't come to me about my office," Ambrose added.

"No." The general's mouth widened, and deviousness wafted off him. "I'm here about Colonel Jeruko. He's trying to turn the prince against you."

Ambrose raised his brows at the coincidence. This man might still be of use, but he opted for discretion. "I'm not surprised."

The general's emotions flickered in annoyance at the simple reply, but he kept a straight face. "I may not know everything you hope to gain by helping us, but I suspect you need Prince Terkeshi to side with you just as much as you need the emperor—perhaps more so."

"It's true." Ambrose clasped his hands in front of him. "It will do us no good to ally with the emperor, only to have the prince as our enemy in the future. We're looking for a long-term alliance."

"Then maybe we can help one another."

"What do you have in mind?"

"I need a way to discredit the colonel, get the emperor to realize he's no longer his friend."

"I fear that may make the emperor more unstable than he already is."

"He trusts me more every day. And I'm confident that showing him Jeruko's disloyalty will help him realize who his real friend is."

Ambrose had his doubts but didn't argue. "Give me a moment to think."

He ran a new analysis, this time stating that the general had come to him rather than the other way around. He also calculated the chances of Nezumi discovering further damning evidence and accounted for the potential effects on the emperor's mental health.

Ambrose returned his focus to the general. "I can give you a device to spy on the colonel."

Nezumi huffed. "I already have spy equipment. He's too cunning to get caught."

"Your scanners can't detect this, nor will cancellation devices interfere with it."

The general tilted his head. "Tell me more."

"First, I need to know your plan."

Nezumi puckered his lips and narrowed his eyes. "How do I know you won't sell me out to the emperor?"

"It just so happens I agree with you about the colonel's influence. However, there's still the risk that exposing his treachery will cause the emperor to lose control over his sanity. Neither of us can afford for him to turn on the prince."

"That doesn't answer my question."

"I need you. If the emperor threatens the prince, protect him—even if it means taking the emperor's life."

Nezumi barked a laugh. "The emperor gives me my power. I'd be a fool to go against him."

"If the emperor dies, Prince Terkeshi will take his place. And guess who will have control over his cybernetic implants?"

"You."

Ambrose smiled at his insight. "Yes, that's true. We will maintain some control, but we are not warriors. We do not have the skills to manage your armies. You, however, would make an ideal regent."

Nezumi's eyes brightened. "Tempting, but why me?"

"The prince needs someone strong at his side… And someone ambitious. General Samuru has great strength, but he's not ambitious. Nor does he have your intellect. You and I both know you are the best candidate."

Pride emanated from the general, but so did skepticism. "Why not use this spy tech yourself?"

"If the emperor found out we were spying without his permission, he'd turn against us. He trusts you, though. You are his most loyal officer."

The general's expression brightened. "It's a deal. You give me a way to discredit the colonel and I will assassinate the emperor."

Ambrose raised his finger. "No. My superior still has plans for him, so only kill him if he becomes a danger to the prince."

General Nezumi agreed. After he left with the bug-sized device, Ambrose allowed a grin to spread across his face.

40
Death Sentence

3791:106:07:29. Terkeshi ground his teeth as he stood before Father's desk and waited to be acknowledged. His hands sweated. The tension in his upper body had not abated since he'd moved the emitter components into the *Fire Breather*.

The task had been nerve-wracking, yes, but he couldn't quiet all the memories ricocheting in his head. When he pushed one away, another popped up in its place. Jori's murder turned to the slaughter of the people on the *Shadow Croc*, which changed into the cold and unsettling way the cyborgs destroyed humanity.

Most of the people the cyborg enhanced lost a portion of their lifeforce and twenty percent died. The muscles in Terk's back constricted as a sensation of a thousand ice picks pierced his spine. A one in five chance of death meant nothing to his father, so Terk didn't bother bringing up what he'd seen. The only way to keep Father from adding upgrades was to prove himself.

Father's head snapped up. "What do you want?"

Terk pulled his shoulders back and braced himself. "I want to captain that ship."

"That won't happen." Father returned to his work as though the matter were closed.

"Why not?" Terk pushed.

Father exhaled loudly. "Because I can't trust you to obey orders."

"All I ever do is obey orders. And if I don't, you'll just make me."

Father glowered, but otherwise ignored him. "Plus, I saw how you almost botched the perantium project."

Terk clenched his fists. He should have known Father would watch through his cybernetic eye again. He should have worn the disruptor device but didn't want to prompt the cyborgs to repair him. "I didn't even come close to botching it. I got all the pieces in without a single incident."

"You went out of alignment more than once."

"I did better than any other pilot would've."

Father drummed his fingers. "Perhaps it's best we let the cyborgs finish their enhancements."

Horror chilled Terk to the marrow of his bones. "You can't be serious! I succeeded in both missions."

"You hesitated!"

"I didn't see the point in killing perfectly good workers."

His father slapped his hand on his desk. "Workers can act as spies as well as anyone, you fool—better than, in some cases, because people hardly take notice of them."

Terk huffed out of his nostrils. "If they make such great spies, why kill them?"

Father shot to his feet. "Your damned sentiment makes you weak—just like your pathetic little brother."

Terk bristled. "For someone who believes emotion is weakness, you sure get pissed off a lot."

Father darted from behind his desk with the rapidity of a charging blackbeast. Terk stepped back, but not fast enough to avoid the open-palmed slap.

"Watch how you speak to me, boy!"

Terk resisted the urge to rub his burning cheek. "It's the truth! You let your emotions get away from you when you killed my brother."

Father raised his hand, ready to strike again. Terk stood his ground as the man's rage barraged his senses.

Father leaned in. His hot breath reeked of fury. "He defied me," he finally said in a low rumble. "*You* would be wise to not do the same."

Terk swallowed. "I'm not trying to defy you. I did what I was told, and I will obey next time. Let me captain that ship and you will see. I can be even deadlier than Dokuri."

Father's glare lingered. Terk's mouth dried.

Father eventually sat back down. He eased his hands into a serene position, yet his anger still flared. "If you want to be a captain, you must prove you can follow orders without question. I have two prisoners from the *Shadow Croc* who are no longer useful. Execute them."

Terk staggered as though someone had stabbed a nail into his heart. "Yes, Sir." He worked the dryness from his mouth. "Should I bring them to the arena?"

"No. Take them to the nearest airlock and release them."

A shiver ran down Terk's spine. Shooting them would be easier and faster, but he didn't argue. "Yes, Sir."

"Now go."

Terk gulped, then turned on his heel and withdrew.

*****

3791:106:08:05. The discomfort Terkeshi had been sensing increased with each step. By the time he entered the lower decks, the sensation reached an agonizing threshold. Although Terk had received training to tolerate pain, this was different. He'd much rather suffer an open fracture to his femur than take on someone else's prolonged suffering.

General Nezumi met him in the hall with a condescending smile. "I'm looking forward to seeing how you handle this, my Lord."

Terk gave him a side-eyed scowl. The smartass remark on the tip of his tongue vanished with the signal that came in through his cybernetic eye.

"I'm watching you, boy," Father broadcasted.

Terk considered using his disruptor. It would be pointless, though. Nezumi would tell Father everything and it would give Father a reason to activate the remote control. Besides, those prisoners would die regardless.

He entered the cell block with his gut rolling like giant waves. The long hall before him was deceptively serene, but horrors lurked within. He plodded down past quiet rooms, following the thread of suffering.

Despite the hints the terrible sensations provided, he nearly choked at the sight of the prisoners. No wonder their agony had penetrated the inside of his head so strongly. They teetered on the edge of death.

One man lay in a fetal position in a puddle of his own piss, the other in a mangled heap. Dried blood caked their bodies. The man hugging his knees had been flayed from face to torso. The other had two, possibly more, bones jutting from his limbs.

How are they still alive? Terk doubled over.

"Are you alright, my Lord?" Nezumi mocked, patting him on the shoulder.

Terk retched on the man's boots. "What the hell did you do?"

Nezumi's mouth twisted as he tried to shake off the bile. "I did what needed to be done. And then some—for good measure."

"You're a monster," Terk croaked as he wiped spittle from his lips.

Nezumi puffed out his chest. "I am a senshi."

A sweltering intensity that surged through Terk's body gave him the strength to stand upright. He flicked his hand at the prisoners. "You're no senshi. What you've done is inhuman."

Nezumi shrugged. "That's a matter of opinion."

Terk gritted his teeth. For a moment, his anger smothered the prolonged pain of death these prisoners suffered. Then their torturous emotions resurged, making him close his eyes against the onslaught.

"Take them to aft airlock eight," he ordered his personal guards with a rasp.

Tokagei unlocked the cell. While the fully human guard carefully lifted the flayed man and helped him hobble out, the cyber senshi yanked the broken prisoner up and dragged him.

The moans emanating from the prisoners echoed against the walls and penetrated the marrow of Terk's bones. Their sensations blinded him as he followed.

Their arrival at the airlock didn't come soon enough. A glacial sweat saturated Terk by the time the senshi dropped the tortured men inside the compartment. He shivered at the relief they radiated as death loomed beyond the outer doors.

Nezumi stood before the door panel with a patronizing smile. "Are you sure you don't want to punish them a little longer first?"

Terk shoved the man aside. His finger poised over the controls. *You can do this. It's only a mercy killing.* Still, he hesitated. He closed his eyes and swallowed, then jabbed the button.

The outer doors opened. A hiss flooded his ears. Although he didn't see the prisoners fly out into space, he felt the pain of their deaths intensify.

The moments that passed seemed like hours. Terk's heart stabbed rhythmically in agonizing slowness. The contents of his gut swirled like excrement in a toilet.

Their emotions blinked out at the threshold of their demise. Terk leaned his palm against the wall to keep from falling. His chest heaved until the lingering sensations finally dissolved into emptiness.

He opened his eyes and straightened. "There, Father," he broadcasted through his cybernetic eye. "It is done."

Terk marched away with his chin out and shoulders pulled back. Inside, he withered like a spider sprayed with pesticide.

41
Reflection

3791:106:15:50. Terkeshi crawled out from under his covers with a groan. He eased his feet to the bare floor and cradled his head in his palms. Nausea tumbled in his gut as remnants of his nightmares lurked on the fringes.

He rubbed his eyeballs, trying to ease the dull ache left over by his fitful sleep. When the lights in his room illuminated to their full strength, he stood and yawned. His fatigue lingered as he rolled the crackling from his neck and shoulders. He reached his arms overhead and stretched, bringing about a momentary surge of energy.

With it came the memory of his nightmare where he'd mechanically shot down a horde of innocent people. Weariness sped back in.

He gave up and ambled to the bathroom. Leaning onto the counter, he groped for the cloth hanging by the sink. After putting it under the humidifier, he rubbed his face. Usually, the dampness refreshed him. Not so today.

At some point in his dream, he'd changed from a robot into the monster, onihitokuchi, and ripped people apart instead. The pain of death his victims had suffered enraged the beast within him until he'd woken with a scream.

Terk shook off his unease and put paste on his toothbrush. After lethargically brushing, he took a swig of astringent mouthwash and swished it around. His eyes remained unfocused as he stared into the depths of the drain. Eventually, he spit the stuff out. Bubbles lingered at the drain's edge until he pressed another button that sucked it all down.

He checked the mirror for the first time that morning. The mechanical parts of his eye weren't visible, but he imagined them turning and grinding like an industrial engine. A memory from his waking life popped up. With teeth bared and the rage of a monster storming inside him, he relived that moment when he had slaughtered all those workers.

Terk forced the gory afterimage from his mind and refocused on his reflection. The angry face glaring back at him triggered a burning deep within. His jaw bulged as though he held rocks between his teeth. Dark eyes blazed beneath his hooded brows, and his frown remained fixed despite his attempt to correct it. He might as well be his father.

His fists tightened and his nostrils flared. He didn't want to be like that man, perpetually angry and never with anything good to say. Nor did he want to be Father's little puppet.

Viscous saliva filled his mouth as the most recent deaths flickered through his thoughts. He didn't regret ending the suffering of those tortured men. After what Nezumi had done, they deserved peace. But damn it, why had he allowed himself to be pushed into doing it? *Because I'm a fucking coward, that's why.*

Terk clenched his fists. Father had found yet another way to control him, but no more. His chest constricted. Next time he saw Father, he would stand up for himself. No giving in and killing people just because Father told him to. He'd be as courageous as Jori.

Terk flinched. All this time he'd been thinking his little brother had been a coward for succumbing to his emotions and sneaking behind Father's back to save those Cooperative prisoners. That wasn't it at all. Jori's actions had been brave. Even in the face of Father's deadly wrath, he'd resisted with stubborn determination. He stood up to Father to do what he'd felt was right—consequences be damned.

"Oh, Jori," Terk said quietly. "I understand now." *Too bad I don't have your bravery.*

Jori had died a hero's death. Not only had he saved the Cooperative prisoners, but he'd also attempted to sabotage the perantium emitter. What had Terk done since then? Betrayed his brother's memory by murdering people and enabling Father to slaughter even more by helping with that stupid device.

He glowered at his reflection. Burning liquid built at the rims of his eyes. "I hate you, you fucking coward."

Jori wouldn't have submitted to cybernetic augmentation. He never would've murdered innocent men and women. Nor would he have allowed Father to fix the emitter.

One thing Fujishin had said popped into his head. *"You'd be wise to separate yourself from him as well, young Prince, before he makes you do something you regret."*

Too late. Terk's nails bit into his palms. His list of everyone to blame—the cyborgs, his father, and even Jori—fell away, leaving only one person at fault. Terk could have stopped all this. He should've done a better job of supporting Jori and keeping him from being killed. Instead of being quick to please Father, he should have resisted the way Jori had done. He never should've surrendered to cybernetic surgery. Rather than help with the emitter, he should have sabotaged it when he'd had the chance. Yes, he would have died, but so what? The universe was better off without him.

Terk let out a low growl that escalated into a roar. He punched the mirror with his palm. The resulting pain did nothing to quell the intensity of his emotions.

His reflection wavered, then the plexiglass repaired itself. Terk's chest heaved. Something had to be done. He couldn't change the past, but he had the power to change his future. His mother was out of reach, Jori was dead, and he'd pushed Sensei Jeruko away. What remained was a weak-minded nobody.

Well, no more. He shoved back from the mirror and activated his disruptor. Despite his assurances to Sensei Jeruko the other day, he wasn't sure if it thwarted the technology of the cyborgs. So without looking, he went through a drawer in his desk. When his hand found the cold metal handle of his utility knife, he clutched it with sweaty palms.

His heart throbbed as he eased onto the edge of his bed. The weapon warmed in his palm. Deep breaths prepared him for the one option that remained.

"Music on!" he called to the computer. A piercing wail filled the room, then turned into a rough singing voice.

"Louder! Level fifteen."

The music blared. Still not looking at the blade, he lifted it to his face and pressed the tip under his eye. Sweat beaded on his forehead.

215

You can do this. You must *do this.* Terk swallowed the dryness from his throat. He sank the point in further, his heartbeat increasing with the stinging sensation. His arms quivered, but he kept his breathing even to maintain control.

The blade slid under his eyeball. He shuddered and loosened his grip lest he cut more than intended. His perspiration thickened. His chest moved in and out as he gulped in air.

Once it was deep enough, he mentally prepared for the next move. He wiped his hands on his thighs, then clamped them onto the handle.

He thrust it downward with a scream. His flesh ripped and spots flashed through his consciousness. A crunch more felt than heard resounded in his head and blackness fell.

*****

3791:106:16:32. Ambrose replayed the feed from the prince's eye. Terkeshi was upset, but nothing indicated the cause of the disconnection. The music was loud, sure, but not loud enough to break the receiver.

He filtered out the awful, screaming music only to hear Prince Terkeshi's respiration. It sounded like he exercised. However, the video showed no movement before his eyes closed.

Ambrose checked the prince's vitals. An increased heartrate. *Exercise. It must be.* It still didn't explain the broken link. A brain scan would tell him more, but it was too late to run one. He ran an analysis instead. Nothing concerning came up.

With a mental nudge, he accessed the emperor's surveillance. Not a single camera fed from the young man's room. Surprising, considering the emperor's paranoia. Perhaps there used to be one, but the prince had disabled it.

He dared not ask the emperor since he shouldn't have access. This would remain a mystery for now. He'd question the prince later. Getting this emitter set up was the priority, especially at this sensitive junction.

42
In Memory Of

3791:106:16:56. Terkeshi awoke on the floor. His cheek rested in a puddle of something sticky. He eased onto his elbows. His head throbbed, each beat sending out a fresh surge of blood. The intensity of his pain made his gut roil.

He tapped the comm behind his ear. "Sensei Jeruko."

"Yes, my Lord," his master said in a formal tone.

Terk swallowed at the emotional hurt. "I need you. Please."

"Of course," Sensei Jeruko replied less formally.

Terk struggled to his feet and lurched across the small room like a drunkard. When he stepped on his bloody knife, he lost his balance. His arms flailed until he crashed on his hands and knees.

A howl escaped his throat as more blood gushed out.

His door beeped. "Enter!"

Sensei Jeruko entered and gasped. "Chusho! What happened? Secur—"

Terk flung out his hand. "No! No security! Lock the door."

"My Lord! You need medical care."

Terk pointed to his bathroom. "Get me that towel."

Sensei Jeruko hesitated. The tromp of feet belonging to Terk's personal guards approached.

"Don't let them see," Terk begged.

His mentor shut them out and hastily retrieved a cloth. With a firm grip, he pulled Terk up. "You must rest. Lie face up, not down."

Terk let him ease him onto the bed. Every movement sent a twinge through his skull, but he managed to settle without crying out. Then Sensei Jeruko pressed the towel down over his eye, and Terk shrieked.

Sensei Jeruko patted Terk's chest with his other hand. "It's alright. I'm here. I'll help you however I can."

Terk whimpered. "Thank you."

"Chusho, boy. What happened? Did the cyborgs do this to you?"

"No," Terk replied with a sniffle. "I cut it out. I don't want it. Never did. I'm a coward. I should've—"

"This isn't your fault. I should have done a better job of trying to convince the emperor not to do this."

"No. I am to blame. I must make up for my mistakes." He reached for Sensei Jeruko's hand. "Help me?"

"Of course. Anything."

Terk swallowed the lump in his throat. "Are you sure? You could be killed."

"Ask me. If it's not something I can do, I will say no. But I won't tell anyone about our conversation. Whatever happens, I shall always do my best to protect you."

Terk's healthy eye stung as it filled with tears. "I know. You're too good to me."

Sensei Jeruko patted him again. "That isn't your fault. You've suffered so much lately."

Terk warmed at the emotions emanating from the man. "I should've listened to you. Forgive me for being stupid. I thought I didn't need you anymore, but I was wrong."

Sensei Jeruko gripped his shoulder. "You're a fine young man, Terke-chan. Don't ever believe differently."

"Thank you." Terk reined in his emotions. "I want to finish what Jori started... And destroy the perantium device. I have an idea." He took in a ragged breath as a wave of agony rippled through him. "But it will be dangerous."

Sensei Jeruko's throat bobbed, and his eyes darted around the room.

"There are no listening devices in here. Jori showed me—" His voice quavered. "—how to deactivate them."

Sensei Jeruko exhaled. "You're right. We must do this."

"In memory of Jori," Terk added. "So his death won't be in vain."

Sensei Jeruko nodded. "For your mother, as well. Your father plans on using his new weapon on Lord Enomoto's estate. Although that's just a small area of the continent, I don't trust his sanity enough to believe he won't use the weapon at higher power.

Not only could it affect the island your mother is living on, but it will also kill millions, possibly billions, of others living on the planet."

Terk's throat caught. Despite knowing Father's plan for Lord Enomoto, it had never occurred to him to consider the consequences for the entire planet. "Then we must do this soon, before it's too late."

"Tell me what to do, and I will do it, Terke-chan, no matter what it takes."

Terk sighed with relief. "I'll set an explosion. You get our people off that ship."

"Your father will kill you."

"The blast should hide what I've done. Father will blame the cyborgs."

"And if he doesn't, I'll protect you. I won't let him do to you what he did to Jori."

Terk swallowed against the lump in his throat.

Sensei Jeruko's brow furrowed. "What will you do, exactly?"

"Ambrose said one piece is unstable. I'll set the bomb there."

After he labored through the rest of the plan, Sensei Jeruko squeezed his hand. "Let's do this, then—for Jori."

Terk gripped his master's hand in return. *For Jori.*

43
Good News Meets Bad News

3791:106:22:09. The deathly quiet of the communications room made the skin on Jin Jeruko's neck prickle. The stale air lay as static as a corpse. Empty chairs faced consoles with dead screens.

Being alone didn't ease the feeling of being watched. He'd run into General Nezumi while retrieving medical supplies and a special tech item, and half expected the chima to peer inside at any moment.

Jeruko shook off his unease. The man could spy all he wanted, but he wouldn't learn anything. After he had stabilized Terkeshi's wounds, they discussed the plan to sabotage the emitter. Included in that hastily made scheme was disabling the surveillance cameras. Maintenance would have them repaired soon, so this was Jeruko's only chance before chaos erupted.

The screen of the communication console came alive, the hum breaking the silence of the room. He glanced out the windows once more, seeing no one.

Terkeshi had gone elsewhere. He'd ditched his personal guards and headed to the far side of the ship. Worry wriggled in Jeruko's gut. It shouldn't be too difficult for the young man to use his authority to retrieve an explosive device. But between the cyborgs and the emperor's paranoia, something was bound to go wrong.

What worried him most was that the emperor would blame Terkeshi for the disaster. If that happened, Jeruko would do what he should have done all along—assassinate him.

He returned to the screen and held his breath while logging into his account. Several messages popped up. Scrolling through them revealed reports needing his review. A few questions from subordinates had come in as well.

One from an unknown sender caught his eye. Jeruko cupped his chin in one hand while the other poised over the open command. No visitors had entered the room, but he glanced around anyway.

With a flick of his finger, the message opened. His stomach danced while his decryption program converted the video. *Please let this be it.*

As soon as it finished, he jabbed the play button. Commander Hapker of the Prontaean Cooperative popped up. Jeruko sighed with relief, but his tension remained.

"Sensei Jeruko," the commander said in a despondent tone. "I'm glad you've contacted me. I have good news and bad. I'll start with the good news." He paused and folded his hands, causing Jeruko's heart to pound so hard that he worried it would break through his chest. "Jori is alive."

Jeruko plopped backward, making his chair creak. *Alive! Thank goodness!*

"You were right in guessing the Cooperative has organ regeneration capability," Hapker continued. "Although that technology is not widely available, we have it on this ship. Doctor Jerom is our resident expert."

Jeruko tapped his foot as he waited for the bad news.

"However, there's still a chance he won't make it," Commander Hapker said.

Jeruko swallowed, trying to wet his suddenly parched throat.

"He's been in an induced coma so his body can heal. We've had two scares where the heart we implanted acted up. Doctor Jerom thought we'd need to grow another new one, but no further incidents have occurred. Jori's heart is beating normally now, though still mending. I pray he'll wake soon. I'll keep you posted."

The message ended. A fluttering sensation ran through Jeruko's body. He closed his eyes and added his own prayer. Tears spilled, leaving droplets on the console.

Jori is still alive! He had to tell Terkeshi right away.

After carefully erasing the message and logging out, he sprang from his chair. The entrance to the room swished open, revealing General Nezumi wearing a smug smile.

Jeruko made his expression go blank. "May I help you, General?"

Nezumi swaggered past the threshold but not far enough in for the door to close. "I bet you didn't notice my little spider cam."

He pointed over Jeruko's shoulder. Jeruko turned and studied the wall, almost missing the tiny, camouflaged device. His gut tumbled. *Chusho!* How much did he see?

"I've noticed you in here too many times not to be suspicious," Nezumi continued. "I had to know what you were up to, and now I do."

Jeruko swallowed. "Did you tell the emperor?"

Nezumi broadened his smile. "Not yet. I've been wondering what I should do with this information. On the one hand, I can hold on to it until the most opportune time arises."

You mean use it to blackmail me. Jeruko's panic waned as his temper sparked.

"On the other," Nezumi continued, "I can finally be rid of you."

"You might be a hero for a while, you rat, but exposing me will increase his suspicions. He'll see enemies in every shadow, and it won't be long before he sees you for what you are."

"I am loyal."

"To yourself! You have no honor."

Nezumi barked a laugh. "Says the man who goes behind the emperor's back to send secret messages."

Jeruko flinched, but not at the man's attack on his honor. What he'd done held more honor than what Nezumi and the emperor could ever muster together. "Do you know what's in that message?"

"Oh yes. I know it all."

An icy tidal wave surged from Jeruko's core. If Nezumi ever told the emperor, Jori would be in great danger. That couldn't happen. He would not allow this power-hungry chima to hold Jori's fate in his hands.

"I do not regret my choices. I have lived my life with honor." Jeruko approached, taking calm yet deliberate steps. "And I have one honorable thing left to do."

Nezumi cocked his head. "And what might that be?"

In a swift motion, Jeruko lunged and withdrew the knife from his belt.

Nezumi jumped back from the thrust, through the open door and into the hall. Jeruko missed by a hair and leapt forward with another swing.

Nezumi dodged. He pulled out his own blade and took a fighting stance. With a teeth-baring grin, he beckoned with his free hand. "You don't stand a chance, old man. I know your weaknesses."

Jeruko cursed to himself at the loss of his advantage. It didn't matter. Giving up was out of the question. The emperor couldn't learn about Jori. The boy deserved a decent life away from this madness.

He gritted his teeth and reversed his grip. His eyes remained on his opponent's blade as he circled. When Nezumi reached for his comm with his free hand, Jeruko feinted an attack. He kept him on the defense, just enough to evaluate his options. Nezumi's skill rivaled his own. The man was swift and ruthless while Jeruko barely dodged. His bad leg slowed him down, but the quick-wittedness of his mind made up for it.

Mushin.

Nezumi stepped in with a slash. Jeruko ducked, spun, and swept out his foot into a low sweeping kick to the back of the knee. Before his opponent recovered, he jabbed his knife into the man's thigh.

Nezumi roared and fell but rolled out of the way of Jeruko's next attack. Blood drizzled from Nezumi's leg, but he managed an upright position.

"You're not the only one who knows the weaknesses of others," Jeruko said. Nezumi tended to swing wide, forgetting he didn't need all that power to inflict damage. A simple slice or jab would do.

Nezumi bared his teeth and attacked with fury. Jeruko twisted his torso, avoiding the blade by centimeters. More slices and thrusts followed. Jeruko danced out of the way. He cut twice into Nezumi's arm, but not deep enough to stop him.

Nezumi pulled back with a huff. "Fight me, you coward."

Jeruko didn't bother replying. While the chima predictably went for the throat and torso, Jeruko aimed for the limb that held the knife. *Get rid of the danger, then get rid of the man.*

An ache blossomed in Jeruko's bad leg.

He didn't think he'd let it show, but Nezumi's smile broadened as he lunged. Like a relentless rapid-fire weapon, Nezumi never let up. He slashed and stabbed, forcing Jeruko to fall back.

A beep sounded in Jeruko's ear. Terkeshi... It must be. It was time for Jeruko to end this and help people get off the *Fire Breather* before it exploded. *Damn this rat-faced chima!*

He took a risk and counterattacked. He missed. The move cost him. A sting swept across his forearm as Nezumi forced him to block. Blood splattered. He deflected into a cut of his own, but barely made it through Nezumi's leather armor.

Madness glittered in Nezumi's eyes as he continued his frontal assault. Jeruko's leg gave way and he stumbled. Nezumi went in for the kill. His knife drove into Jeruko's gut. Jeruko twisted, slicing at Nezumi's wrist at the same time.

Nezumi dropped his weapon with a yell. "You fiend! I'll k—"

Jeruko swiped his blade across the man's throat. Nezumi's last words cut off as blood spewed from his neck. The madness in his eyes turned into desperation.

Jeruko stepped back, panting, but didn't let down his guard. *Zanshin.* Remaining mind. Make sure it's over before walking away.

Bloody rivulets ran down the front of Nezumi's uniform and puddled at his feet. Jeruko remained captivated as it grew into a pool. Nezumi fell to his knees, then smacked the floor, sending out red splatters.

Jeruko straightened, then doubled over from the twinge in his gut. *Damn it!* He pressed his hand to the wound and pulled it away. Red goo stuck to his fingers.

He glanced at Nezumi's fallen blade. Redness coated it up to the hilt. *Chusho.* He was in trouble but had no time to fret. Terkeshi needed him.

With steps that sent jarring pangs through him, he retrieved both the spider cam and Nezumi's MM from his wrist. Hopefully, the tablet was the only place this communications room recording existed.

As he ambled down the hall, he called the emperor. "Sire, General Nezumi tried to kill me."

"What! What the hell are you talking about?"

"Something's happening, Sire," Jeruko said, changing the story he and Terkeshi had concocted. "Nezumi made threats to the Mizuki line. I believe the cyborgs are involved. Terkeshi is in trouble."

He passed a senshi in the hall. The warrior's eyes popped as he looked him up and down. "What happened, Colonel? Are you alright?"

Jeruko waved him away and kept on. Every step made his insides feel like they ripped further, but he couldn't risk slowing.

"Where is he?" the emperor asked. "I can't access his camera."

"He's on the *Fire Breather*."

"What the hell is he doing there?"

Jeruko paused, trying to think of a way to answer without lying. "It's those cyborgs, Sire. There's more to it than what they're telling us."

"I'm sending Samuru."

"No need, Sire. I'm headed there myself. Just tell our people to get off that ship."

"What did Nezumi say, exactly?"

"He made vague references only. I don't know the extent of his part, but I'm sure it'll be bad."

"Damn that chima to hell," the emperor mumbled, then ended the conversation.

Jeruko entered a conveyor and slumped against the wall. This plan was out of control. They'd made it in haste, but it couldn't be helped. Once the emperor discovered what Terkeshi had done to his eye, which would be soon, there would be hell to pay. Sabotaging the emitter provided a cover. Terkeshi could say he did it because he thought the cyborgs were controlling him. All this broke his rules about lying, but he finally realized there were worse disgraces.

The conveyor opened to the shuttle bay. Workers eyed him with furrowed brows, but he ignored their concerning remarks. "I need a ship. Now!"

A shokukin led him to the nearest one. "It's ready, Sir. I can come with you if you'd like. Help you with the medical kit."

"That won't be necessary. Just get me inside. I'll do the rest."

A few groans and shuffling of his feet later, Jeruko sat in the pilot's seat with a first aid box in his lap. Not long after that, the shuttle was underway.

He took out a cauterizing tool and opened the private comm to Terkeshi.

"My Lord, I had a run-in with Nezumi. He's dead. I've told the emperor and mentioned the cyborgs."

"Thanks for the heads up. Don't worry. I've got this under control."

"I also advised him to get our people off that ship. I'm still on the way to assist, though."

"Like I said. Don't bother. This will be over soon."

Something about the youth's defeated tone triggered a rise of goosebumps on his arms. "What do you mean?"

"I can't live like this anymore, Sensei."

Blood drained from Jeruko's head and settled into an icy knot in his gut. "Terkeshi, no. You can't."

The communication ended. Jeruko attempted to call him back but got no reply. *Chusho!* He hadn't told him about Jori yet. He willed his shuttle to go faster, praying he'd get there before it was too late.

*****

3791:106:22:51. Kenji Mizuki commed his son for the fourth time. Still no answer. What in the hell was going on? Nezumi and the cyborgs? Terkeshi in danger? It made no sense.

He drummed his fingers on his desk, then called the bridge. "Samuru! I need you to go over to the *Fire Breather* and find out what's happening." *The more people sorting this out, the better.*

"Yes, Sire."

He contacted Ambrose.

"Your Eminence. How may I be of service?"

"What the hell happened to my emitter?"

"Everything is proceeding as planned."

"What do you mean, *as planned*?"

"We've nearly repaired the perantium emitter. We have a few more days of work and—"

Mizuki slammed his fist onto his desk. "That's not what I'm talking about. I'm told you're colluding with my general and have nefarious intentions with my son."

"I assure you, Sire, there is no colluding with anyone. And your son is fine."

"Then why the hell can't I access his cybernetics?"

"I'm not sure. We have the same issue and are looking into it."

"Have you seen him? With your eyes, I mean?"

"No, Sire. But we received a notification that he's on the way to the *Fire Breather*."

"Have one of your people tell him to get over here."

"Of course, Sire."

The video communication flickered off. Mizuki growled and called Terkeshi using the comm that should be adhered by his ear.

"Yes, Father," the boy transmitted.

"It's about damn time. I've been trying to call you. Why can't I do it through your cybernetics?"

"Unknown."

Mizuki flinched. "What do you mean, *unknown*?"

"I do not have adequate data to formulate a response," Terkeshi replied in a monotone voice.

"*Adequate data*? What the hell is wrong with you, boy? Why are you talking like that?"

"Nothing is wrong, your Eminence. I'm merely responding to your inquiry."

Mizuki's neck prickled. *Did he just call me* your Eminence? *What have those damned machines done to my son?* "Get back here at once."

"Yes, Sire."

Chusho.

Mizuki frantically returned to the call button. "Samuru! Implement Operation Offline. Take a few squads with you and kill every cyborg you encounter."

"Yes, Sire."

Chusho! Mizuki slammed his fist onto his desk. He knew those freaks would betray him eventually, but this was much sooner than expected. Operation Offline had only the primary aspects outlined.

Plans zipped inside his head as he pulled up the stats from the *Fire Breather*—double-checked the data from his own ship—

verified none of the readings were off—and raced through the information on every other operation he could think of.

Everything seemed ordinary, but something was definitely amiss. He glanced at the case in the corner. The helmet mocked him. His grandfather had been in a tight spot back then, but he hadn't let that stop him. He'd won the day, regardless of the difficulties.

Mizuki balled his fists. He was better than his grandfather. He'd defeat every single one of his enemies, no matter what it took. Fujishin. Enomoto. And even the cyborgs. No one crossed a dragon and got away with it.

44
Suicide Mission

3791:106:23:06. Terkeshi smirked, priding himself on how he made it seem the cyborgs had taken control of him. If cameras caught him sabotaging the emitter, Father would still believe the cyborgs were to blame. He'd never trust them to complete the emitter, and millions of people wouldn't be murdered.

A metallic clank followed by squeals locked Terk's shuttle into the *Fire Breather*'s bay. While the air pumped back in and the pressure stabilized, he took a moment to study his appearance. The nanite mask worked but didn't fit perfectly. The copy from one side of his face matched the other, but the alignment was off. His eyes appeared closer together and his nose had a funny dip on the bottom.

Good enough for now. It wouldn't matter soon anyway.

His comm beeped again. He pulled it from behind his ear and dropped it.

After powering down the shuttle, he carefully lifted the lead-lined case holding the bomb. No one paid him any mind when he entered the main hall. A few shokukin glanced at him as they evacuated. Their emotions emitted uncertainty, but none seemed to notice his off appearance.

It wasn't until he reached the center corridor leading to the perantium emitter that Brian stopped him. Terk masked his thoughts the way his mother had taught him, not knowing whether Brian read them like Ambrose did.

"Prince Mizuki. We wish to speak to you about your—is there something wrong? I'm getting strange readings from—"

Terkeshi shoved past him. "I'm busy."

"My Lord! Your father wishes for you to return to his ship."

Terk flicked his hand and kept going. "Later!"

229

It took him a few minutes to find the unstable piece he'd moved the other day. "What's the status here?" he asked the nearest cyborg.

The machine-man using his metallic claw to manipulate the circuits of an open panel answered without looking away from his work. "Stabilization in two hours, forty minutes, eighteen seconds."

Good. Cutting it short but still plenty of time.

He returned to the device and knelt. The case clanked on the floor and the lid opened with a squeal. If his actions had raised suspicions, he didn't sense it.

He fiddled with the controls. A green light flashed on, indicating the bomb had synced with his detonator. Terk closed the case and stood. His breath shortened. He ran his hand down his chin. This was it. The final moment had arrived.

He glanced about. No sign of his own people. He shut his eye to minimize distractions. The movement made his other one twinge, but not bad enough to interfere. He spread the tendrils of his senses out, concentrating first around him then in each direction of the ship. The distilled emotions of some cyborgs brushed by, but no familiar sensations stood out.

He couldn't reach all the way through the vessel, but hopefully, Sensei Jeruko had gotten everyone out.

"Sir, Ambrose wishes to speak with you."

Terk flinched and snapped open his eye. A cyborg he didn't recognize stared at him with mechanical eyes.

"Where is he?" Terk asked.

The man pointed up over his shoulder. "In the observation room."

Terk followed his finger to the window where only the top of a few heads appeared. He didn't sense anything from the man. Usually, he felt a little of his lifeforce. Perhaps he blocked him as well. *Does he know?*

The cyborg departed. Terk scanned the bay. The others seemed to have their attention elsewhere, so he left the bomb there. It'd be nice to die knowing Ambrose was here to perish too.

His hands sweated as he climbed the ladder to the upper level, but he maintained a brisk pace. By the time he met Ambrose and Brian inside, his brow dripped with sweat and his heart raced.

Ambrose's veneer forehead wrinkled. "What did you do to your eye?"

Terk's nervousness vanished, and he flashed a smile. "I broke it. No one will ever take control of me again."

Ambrose cocked his head. Terk pressed the detonator. He had time to see the man's eyes grow before the floor rumbled and a roll of fire smashed through the observation window.

Terk's body slammed against the wall. Bones cracked. Heat seared over him. He ducked under the console instinctively.

Then everything went black.

45
Evacuation

3791:106:23:37. Terkeshi choked as dense smoke permeated his lungs. He pressed his hand to his throat and gasped. Each breath sent stabbing sensations into his chest.

Chusho! He was supposed to die. Now he would slowly suffer instead. His body heaved as it fought to stay alive despite his intentions. He sat up, still gasping.

The blast hadn't taken out the artificial gravity. He stood on shaky legs and opened his eye. Smoke stung it back shut. He touched it, intending to rub it. A searing sting exploded as his hands and face burned.

Everything hurt, but how bad off was he? He forced his eye open. Pure greyness surrounded him. He held up his fingers. Outstretched, he couldn't see them. Halfway in revealed his black and red charred digits.

Terk groped for the way out. His hand struck the console and sent a spasm up his arm. He gritted his teeth and moved toward what he hoped was the exit. As he did so, emergency extinguishers shot from the ceiling. The air vents sucked out the smoke.

Terk found the door and stepped out. The device loomed through the haze below like a sleeping dragon. Spots of orange glows indicated parts of it still burned.

The faint lifeforces of cyborgs stirred but most lay deathly still. Terk's neck muscles tightened, stinging him as his burnt skin stretched. He considered the sheathed knife at his side. Ambrose and his unfeeling cohorts were dangerous sociopaths. They deserved to die.

His conscience had barely troubled him when he'd devised this plan, yet he hesitated now. As far as he could tell, Ambrose was unconscious. The prospect of killing him when he lay helpless like this made his insides squirm.

What's the matter with me? It's just one more death on my hands. He growled, then turned his back on the man.

Now what? If the explosion hadn't been enough to kill him, had it been enough to destroy the device? Probably not.

He hardened his resolve and decided facing Father was the only option left. If Father blamed him for this disaster, so be it. He wanted to die anyway.

Perhaps this would still work out. Father would be a fool not to think the cyborgs had something to do with this. Surely he'd consider their agreement broken and the perantium emitter project would be abandoned.

Terk exited the bay and entered a parallel corridor. This area wasn't as smokey, but still made him cough. Two cyborgs marched by him as though nothing was wrong. He passed another who stood like a statue. Even her eyes remained motionless. Terk shivered at the thought of what all this smoke would do to them if she didn't blink.

Strong lifeforces grabbed his attention. *Chusho!* A few of his people hadn't left yet.

He followed the sensation until he came to a dark heap on the floor at an intersection. He knelt and smacked the person's face, making the burns on his hand smart. "Wake up!"

"Uh?" Malkai blinked, revealing green eyes dulled with smog.

Terk shook him. "Wake up! We must get out of here."

Malkai groped the wall, but his legs didn't lift him. Terk pulled at his arm, straining his own hurting body, and steadied him.

Malkai stumbled, but eventually found his feet. "Sir? What happened?"

"The cyborgs betrayed us."

Malkai's mouth fell open as he seemed to see Terk for the first time. "What did they do to you?"

"Too damned much," Terk grumbled. "Now go. If you find more of our people, get them out."

"What about you, Sir?"

Terk pointed. "I sense more shokukin this way."

"I can help you, Sir."

"No. Just go. I've got this."

"But you're hurt."

"I gave you an order," Terk replied mildly. "Now get your ass out of here."

Malkai glanced around, squinting his eyes as though trying to peer through the smoke. "I have to get Benjiro."

Terk's heart leapt. "He's here?" He concentrated and found his uncle's unique essence. "This way."

He raced ahead as Malkai ambled along. Though his vision was limited, his ability led him to a figure in a fetal position rocking against the wall. "Ben!"

The man covered his head with his arms. "Benjiro scared. Benjiro scared," he said over and over.

"It's alright. Malkai is here."

The shokukin arrived and squatted next to him. "It's me, Ben. Let's get out of here."

Benjiro forgot all about his fear and stood. "We go?"

"Yes, we go." Malkai placed his arm over Ben's shoulder and patted him.

Terk sighed with gratitude. It was good to know his simple uncle had someone who cared for him. He silently vowed to look out for the man in the future, maybe even find a way to get him home.

The two men left. Terk concentrated on their lifeforces until he was sure they were safe. He puffed, then refocused his ability to find others. The lifeforce of one person struck him.

Sensei? Chusho! What the hell was he doing here? And why was he going the wrong way?

As Terk turned to go to him, a rumble and vibration threw him sideways. He caught himself against the wall, but still slipped. A resounding boom popped his eardrums and he slammed to the floor. A red fireball rolled rapidly, headed right for him.

"Sensei!" Terk yelled as he jumped to his feet and sprinted down the hall. "Go back!"

Terk's prayers that the man had heard him cut off as a blast of heat flung him forward. Ribs cracked. Skin sizzled. His mind slipped.

At least I'll die the way Jori had done—a hero.

46
Escape

3791:106:23:45. Jin Jeruko spotted Terkeshi down the hall. His heart leapt then lurched when a painful eruption shook the walls and struck his ears.

A tsunami of flames followed. The scene unfolded in slow motion. Jeruko bounded to the youth with all his strength. His bad leg twinged, and he almost tumbled as his knee twisted the wrong way. He nearly dropped onto the young man when the heatwave smacked him and propelled him backward.

Jeruko crashed against the wall. Boiling air bombarded him. He both heard and felt the hair on his head and brows singe. His vision flared red, then black.

The heat dissipated and he fluttered his eyes open against the seething fumes. Jeruko pushed himself up, forcing air into his lungs despite the burning. He attempted to straighten but a sharpness cut through him. A glance at the wound Nezumi had inflicted revealed a new injury. Shrapnel stuck out of his abdomen. The blood gurgling from it smoldered.

Jeruko hunched over as he staggered over to where Terkeshi lay. "Terke-chan," he said with a strained breath.

Instead of kneeling, he fell. His bad knee struck the floor and the pain jarred up to his tormented stomach. He closed his eyes and breathed steadily until the worst of the agony passed.

When he opened them again, he nearly choked at the sight of Terkeshi's charred face. The nanite mask appeared to have burned over the top left side and resembled a bubbling tar pit. Red and black patches covered his skin, especially over his nose and forehead.

Jeruko put his hand on the young man's chest. Several thumps pounded. He sighed. Terkeshi still lived.

He inspected the rest of his body. Spots of blood indicated flying debris had struck Terkeshi, too. Unless he had internal injuries, he could pull through.

Jeruko pushed aside the soreness in his own body and grabbed the youth by his shoulder. The wounds in his gut ripped when he tried to lift him, so he dragged him instead.

Little-by-little, he scooted down the hall with his charge. Every movement sent out shards of pain. Sweat broke out over his forehead, but immediately dried in the blistering air.

He mustered on. Losing Jori had been hard enough. Losing Terkeshi would send him over the edge.

A cyborg with a mostly metallic head walked by.

"Help me!" Jeruko called out.

It stopped and turned. "How may I be of service?"

Jeruko shivered at its computerized voice. "Pick him up and take him to the shuttle bay."

Its cybernetic legs released a hydraulic hiss as it lifted Terkeshi. Jeruko winced when it tossed him over his shoulder.

Terkeshi seemed not to notice. His body hung lifeless as it swayed while the cyborg walked. Jeruko fought off a wave of dizziness and hobbled after him.

It reached the shuttle bay before he did and marched to the remaining vessel. Jeruko gasped with each step. *At least the air is clearer here.*

His vision clouded but he pushed on until he caught up. He nearly collapsed at the ship's entrance. He forced himself upright and slapped his hand against the keypad. Its doors slid up and the gangway extended.

"Put him on the healing bed," Jeruko said.

The cyborg promptly complied, then met him before he'd reached the top of the ramp. "May I be of further assistance?"

"Did you set up the healing bed?"

"No."

"Then do it," Jeruko replied with exasperation.

The cyborg obeyed.

"Will that be all?" it asked.

"Yes." Jeruko considered allowing it to go with him but remembered how other cyborgs could watch through his eyes. "You may leave now."

It left without protest.

Jeruko updated the bed's program with instructions to avoid Terkeshi's damaged eye. *We don't want to give his cybernetics an opportunity to fix themselves.*

He groped along the walls. After reaching the cockpit, he dropped into the chair harder than intended. A twinging spasm sent his head spinning. He grimaced and prayed he'd stay conscious long enough to get the hell out of here.

The sensation subsided. He closed the shuttle doors and activated the instrument panel. The automated system accepted his request for departure and his ship lurched forward as the conveyor track pulled it to the exit tube.

Jeruko willed his heartbeat to keep going while the red light of the airlock flashed. It seemed an eternity passed as the air sucked out and the pressure equalized.

As soon as the light turned yellow, Jeruko pressed the remote to open the door. He silently begged it to move faster as his head bobbed with lightheadedness.

A beep sounded from his console, jerking him awake. A green light shone above the bay doors. Jeruko applied the throttle and the vessel jolted into motion as the mechanism lugged him out and away. Once he reached the proper distance, he engaged the thrusters.

Jeruko's stomach cringed as the force pushed him back into his seat. An alarm sounded. He glanced at the controls. His ship was off trajectory and the radiation light flashed. Jeruko switched the viewscreen from digital to outside visualization. His eyes bulged at the sight of the *Fire Breather* erupting with an orange glow that was quickly snuffed out by the vacuum of space.

His vertigo increased as his shuttle spun out of control. Each turn revealed further destruction of the place he'd just left. Another Toradon ship approached the *Fire Breather*. He couldn't be sure, but it looked like a Sidewinder-class vessel from the *Dragon*. The emperor must be sending senshi troops over. Hopefully, the pilot would be smart enough to stay away from the ensuing chaos until it settled.

Blackness danced across his vision. He blinked, attempting to keep it at bay. The instrument panel lurched and blurred. Since automated controls would eventually stabilize the ship on their own, he concentrated on entering the coordinates. After triple-checking them, he engaged the autopilot.

The dizziness swept him away. A coldness washed over him as his body slipped into shock. Blackness flickered in and out, then finally enveloped him.

47
Plans in Flames

3791:106:23:56. Kenji Mizuki glowered at the viewscreen. His nails dug into his armrests as details of an explosion on the *Fire Breather* came in. It seemed to come from the location of the perantium emitter.

He sent out a general broadcast. "Where is Terkeshi?" No one responded. "Has anyone seen the prince?"

"Sire!" Niashi said. "There's been another blast."

Mizuki jerked forward with a growl. *This is a fucking disaster!* He called Ambrose but got no reply. The same for his assistant. All he could do was watch his plans blow apart. *What the hell is going on?*

"Sire, I have a shokukin on the comm."

"Put him through."

"Sire," a weak-voiced man commed. "The prince was injured, but not badly. He said the cyborgs have betrayed us."

Mizuki clenched his jaw. *Those traitorous chima!* Why have they done this? What could they possibly gain from it? "Is my son with you now?"

"No, your Eminence. The last time I saw him, he went to help more of our people escape."

"What the hell for?" Mizuki asked, more to himself than the shokukin.

"I-I'm not sure, your Eminence."

Mizuki ended the communication and shook his head. What was that boy thinking?

"Sire," General Samuru transmitted. "We're close enough to dock on the *Fire Breather*, but it doesn't look safe. We're seeing more explosions."

"My son is still on that ship, General. I need you to find him and get him out of there." *Damn it, boy. Why did you have to be the last Mizuki heir?*

"Yes, Sire. Docking n—Chusho! We've been hit!"

Mizuki jumped to his feet. "By what? Are you under attack?"

"No. Another explosion. Shrapnel damaged our engine. We're in trou—"

"General!" No response. "General!"

He dashed to the operations station and gripped the back of Niashi's chair. "What the fuck just happened?"

Niashi tapped away at the controls. "A larger eruption. It doesn't look good, Sire."

"Any sign of an attack?"

"No, Sire. It appears internal."

"What is the cyborg ship up to?"

"They're just sitting there, Sire."

"Call them!"

He stormed to his chair and sat with a thump. Ignoring the growing ache pounding in his skull, he assessed the situation. Sensors indicated multiple explosions. The *Fire Breather* had broken in half and chunks of it hurled into space. The damage had clearly come from within, but how? And by who?

"Sire, I have someone from the cyborg ship on the comm."

"Put them through." *Let's get to the bottom of this.*

"Your Eminence," an unfamiliar monotone voice said. "How may we assist?"

Mizuki slammed his fist on his armrest. "You can tell me what the hell is happening!"

"The *Fire Breather* is damaged."

"No shit. How? What happened?"

"Unknown, your Eminence. We are gathering information now."

Useless. "Get Ambrose on the line."

"We have lost communication with him. He was on the *Fire Breather*."

Bullshit. Those backstabbing liars. How dare they do this to him. He'd been so close. Perhaps too close. That's why they'd done it. Well, they made an enemy of the wrong person.

He turned to his tactical officer. "Target the cyborgs and fire! Take those freaks out before they activate their shields."

"Target acquired. Firing cannons now."

"Give it everything we've got." Mizuki ground his teeth as a jolt under his feet indicated weapons were underway. "Half view of the cyborg ship and half on the *Fire Breather*."

The viewscreen split into two images. All that remained of the *Fire Breather* was chunks of twisted metal. If anyone had survived, it'd be a miracle. If Terkeshi hadn't gotten onto a shuttle or escape pod, he was dead.

Mizuki attempted to contact him again. Still no response. *Damn it, boy.*

This couldn't be happening. Everything he'd worked so hard for had fallen into shambles. He was left with nothing, not even an heir.

The energy cannons struck the cyborg vessel and created a gaping crater. An orange glow within indicated they, too, would experience a series of explosions.

"Sire," the tactical officer said. "Escape pods are being ejected from the cyborg ship."

"Retrieve them all," Mizuki ordered. Those cowards would pay for their treachery. He would torture them in the worst ways imaginable. And if Ambrose was there, he'd suffer the most.

"Then send teams to investigate the *Fire Breather*," he added. With the perantium emitter destroyed, the only hope for the Dragon Empire rested on his last surviving heir.

I must find my son.

48
End of an Era

3791:109:02:37. Light. Blurry light. Terkeshi strained his eye. Blobs of color coalesced. *Where am I?* He blinked. His vision cleared, but only a little—enough to see he was in a tiny room.

He glanced around. A medical monitor sat on his right. He turned sluggishly through the healing nanite gel. Another machine blocked his view of the door.

The sophisticated devices cramped into every available space triggered a familiarity. He was on a shuttle. Not just any shuttle either—a top-of-the-line vessel capable of traveling long distances. How did he get here?

Terk rose. Dizziness overtook him. He held his head and rolled slowly into a sitting position. He kept his eye closed and waited for the room to stop spinning.

Touching the left side of his face found his eye remained injured. Whoever healed him had not fixed this. *Thank goodness.* With any luck, the cyborgs had zero access to his eye or his brain.

Terk's dizziness abated. He examined his surroundings once more. *Where is everyone?* He extended his sensing ability. Not a single lifeforce pricked his senses. His heart skipped a beat. Had the cyborgs taken him?

He hopped off the bed, then grasped the edge for balance as vertigo struck again. With careful steps, he reached the door. It slid open.

So they hadn't locked him in. That was good.

The bright hallway laid deathly quiet. No cyborgs. He ambled down the aisle, checking each room as he passed. All the beds were empty. The small kitchen, too. If anyone had cooked in it, they'd cleaned up after themselves. This certainly wasn't a Toradon senshi trait.

His heart thumped with every step until he made it to the cockpit door. A vibration from his feet told him the engines were running. Someone must be flying this thing. He held his breath and pressed the button to open it. It slid with a hydraulic hiss.

He peeked inside and his throat caught. "Sensei!"

When he grasped the man's shoulder, a weak lifeforce trickled through. *He's alive!*

Terk gently pried Sensei Jeruko from the confined cockpit. With effort, he hauled him to the healing bed. His strength wavered, but he finally laid his mentor down and reset the nanites. The medical monitor flickered. Shallow irregular waves rolled across the bottom.

"Chusho!" *What do I do?* A healing bed wouldn't work on this. Sensei Jeruko needed surgery.

His eyes darted around the room until he found something to press against the wounds. The one with a metal object sticking out worried him the most. He knew enough first aid to leave it there. But pressing down on one injury made blood come from the other. How could he stop it without putting pressure on it?

Sensei Jeruko's face was pale, his breathing shallow. Terk gripped his hand and squeezed. Worry gnawed at his gut.

He rushed back to the cockpit. The viewscreen showed the stats as well as the camera view where space sprawled out before him. Where were they? Maybe someone else out there could help.

A tap at the controls revealed their location. His heart skipped a beat. They'd been traveling for two days already. The *Fire Breather*, the *Dragon*, and the cyborg ship were nowhere in the vicinity. This shuttle's arc drive had brought them a great distance.

He checked navigation. They were headed to Meixing. More specifically, the destination was Hisui Island where Sensei Jeruko's consort lived, and where Washi, Michio, and Terk's mother lived in exile.

Blood drained from Terk's face. As much as he wanted to see his mother, heading this direction meant Sensei Jeruko had taken him and escaped. But why? Did Father discover Terk had destroyed the emitter? Did the cyborgs find out and attempt to destroy the *Dragon*?

The possibilities swirled in his head. He had no way of knowing what happened, so returning carried a risk. If he contacted anyone, Father or the cyborgs would find him. Did he want either of them to? No, but Sensei Jeruko must get medical attention.

A sensation stirred. Sensei Jeruko's lifeforce grew. Terk abandoned the cockpit and rushed back to the infirmary.

Sensei Jeruko still slept. Terk found a med-scanner and waved it over him. His internal damage was in danger of reaching toxicity. Terk let out a despairing cry. He had no idea how to treat it. He grasped the man's hand and squeezed.

Sensei Jeruko stirred. His eyes fluttered.

"Sensei," Terk said softly. "Wake up. Please, Sensei. I don't know what to do."

"Jori?" Sensei Jeruko replied groggily.

Terk swallowed down the lump in his throat. "It's me. Terk."

Sensei Jeruko's brow furrowed. "Terke-chan?" He raised his hand to Terk's face. "You're alive. Blessed be, you're alive."

"I am, but you're not doing so well. You have internal injuries. I don't know how to treat them. We're days away from help."

"Terke-chan. I need to tell…" Sensei Jeruko took in a labored breath. "I'm so proud of you."

Terk's heart leapt to his throat.

"You did the right thing," Jeruko continued. "Jori will be so proud."

Terk's eyes burned. "I'm not worthy of your praise."

Sensei Jeruko patted his cheek feebly. "You are worthy." He wheezed.

Terk squeezed his hand. "Hold on, Sensei. Rest."

"No. I have—" He coughed. "—to tell you… Jori is—"

Sensei Jeruko choked, then his body convulsed.

Terk held him down. "No! What do I do? No!"

The convulsions stopped. Sensei Jeruko rasped. His lifeforce evaporated.

"No!" Terk burst into a sob. "You can't go! You can't. I need you!"

Sensei Jeruko stilled. He was dead.

"No, no, no," Terk cried. "What will I do without you?"

Terk dropped his head on Sensei Jeruko's chest and wept. Everyone he'd ever truly cared about had gone. He was alone.

49
The End?

3791:109:09:28. A metallic scream echoed throughout the arena. Who would have believed that a machine could be so afraid of pain and death?

Kenji Mizuki watched as an interrogator dismantled the mechanical parts on the cyborg's face. Its metal arms and legs had already been taken. The only external part left was the eye.

"It wasn't us," the cyborg said in a monotone voice that belied its previous anguish. "Someone else did this."

Mizuki didn't bother to reply. Talking with this thing was useless. It repeated itself, as though playing a recording. Either it truly knew nothing, or it had been programmed to say this.

Numbness replaced Mizuki's mood. Not even anger pestered him. He glanced at the dragon banners strung along the walls. Meant to inspire pride in the senshi and instill fear in their enemies, they hung limply now. With the arena mostly empty except for the prisoners and a few guards, any sound echoed as though in a tomb.

It was over. The Mizuki Empire would soon be no more. When the other lords found out about his setback, there'd be war. Fujishin and Lord Enomoto would undoubtedly be at the head of it.

Even if Mizuki defeated them, his line would end. All his sons were dead. Dokuri, his most dangerous warrior; Jori, his most intelligent and promising son; and now Terkeshi. Perhaps the boy didn't have Dokuri's brutal strength or Jori's skill, but with a little more training, he could have been great.

Mizuki scanned the few senshi who lined the walls of the arena to watch the torture. Their grim expressions reflected what they thought of Terkeshi's death. It was the end of an era. The Dragon Empire waned. Only Mizuki remained to face the wolves alone.

Five senshi stood out. Mizuki's gut soured at their empty looks. The chimas couldn't even spare a frown for the loss of their prince. They'd probably been a part of this disaster.

Mizuki reflected on the report about a lot of blood being found in Terkeshi's room. With surveillance down, he had no explanations. Ambrose's cyborgs weren't on his ship at the time, but these cyber senshi were. One of them must have done something.

He called Tokagei over. The man approached without even a flicker of emotion.

"What happened to my son?"

"I do not know, Sire."

Mizuki clenched his jaw. "Aren't you his personal guard? Why did he go to the *Fire Breather* and why weren't you with him?"

"I do not know. I did not accompany him because I was off duty."

"Well, who the hell *was* on duty?"

Tokagei didn't reply right away. "I do not know."

Mizuki balled his fists. "Do you know anything? Do you know what the hell happened on the *Fire Breather*? Or why the cyborgs betrayed me?"

"It wasn't us. Someone else did this."

Mizuki's eyes widened as a shiver ran down his spine. The shudder shifted into a boiling rage. *Us?*

He turned, expecting General Samuru and found Colonel Bakuto instead. The senshi was competent, but the strangeness of entrusting his tasks to a different subordinate made his insides writhe.

His Five Talons were no more. The elderly Sensei Aki lay ill and likely wouldn't recover. Fujishin betrayed him. Nezumi too, and he was dead. Then Samuru died in the *Fire Breather*'s explosion. Jeruko likely had as well. And Terkeshi too.

Their bodies hadn't been found, but hardly surprising considering the damage done to the *Fire Breather*. Although he'd held some hope that they'd escaped, the reports said otherwise. Several men claimed to have seen them both alive just before the culminating blast. Hoping they remained so was foolishness.

He composed himself, then faced the interrogator. "This one next," he said, pointing at a cyborg rescued from the *Fire Breather*.

"It wasn't us!" the cyborg said with more humanity. "You must look within."

Mizuki froze at the new words. "Hold on," he told the interrogator. "What do you mean?"

"It was sabotage."

"Sabotaged by your cyborgs!"

"Why would we fix the device just to sabotage it? It is illogical. Evidence has surfaced that shows your son was with Ambrose and Brian during the first explosion."

"They brainwashed him!"

"He disconnected from our network prior to the incident."

"Bullshit. You took control of him."

"Illogical. Illogical."

"What's illogical is that my own son turned against me." Doubt of his own words crept in.

A ghosted figure appeared to his left. This time, he faced Jori and didn't waver from the fury in his eyes. Mizuki's knife handle protruded from his chest. His lips didn't move, but Mizuki imagined him speaking. *And you wonder why people betray you.*

Terkeshi had said that once. Mizuki forced himself to focus on the cyborg. *No. Not Terkeshi.* That boy was incompetent, but he wouldn't have done this. He pushed the thought aside, not wanting to believe it.

"I want nothing to do with you or your people," Mizuki raised his hand, intending to rub the muscle by his eye to quell the spasm, but decided against it. "If you come into my territory again, I will obliterate you."

"You can't get rid of us," the cyborg replied.

Mizuki's neck prickled. He dismissed the feeling and pulled out his phaser. With a roar, he shot the thing in its face. The machine-man fell without so much as a whimper.

"We are everywhere," a waiting cyborg added.

Mizuki showed his teeth and fired at him too. He dropped with the same dead weight.

"We can side with you or we—" yet another said.

Mizuki shot him.

"—can side with—" the next one continued.

Another blast.

"—your enemies."

247

Mizuki pulled the trigger once more and the last cyborg collapsed. His chest heaved as rage and fear swirled inside him. The entire room hushed. A dragon banner fell, crumpling like the empire itself.

*****

3791:109:11:57. MEGA-Man analyzed all the data that streamed in. None of the reports from his disciples clarified what had transpired. One thing was clear. They were all now either dead or disabled.

It had begun with Prince Terkeshi Mizuki. His cybernetics were the first to disconnect from the Great Commune. MEGA-Man instructed the devotee designated as Ambrose to get him reconnected, but the following feed indicated it wouldn't happen.

MEGA-Man examined Ambrose's final visual sensor data. No emotions bothered him as he watched Prince Mizuki appear by the emitter. The youth held a case but left it there before meeting with Ambrose.

Ambrose's sensors picked up an anomaly on the prince's face. It had a strange energy signature in the place where his cybernetic eye should have been.

"What did you do to your eye?" Ambrose had said.

The prince smiled. "I broke it. No one will ever take control of me again."

A feed from another cyborg revealed the explosion had probably originated from the case. If MEGA-Man had still been human, he would have been angry. Thanks to his enhancements, logic allowed him to understand that this was but a minor setback.

Prince Terkeshi might no longer be his, but a Mizuki heir remained—a much better one. That his disciples had told him he was in Cooperative territory meant little. MEGA-Man's devotees resided on every world. And he had time. Lots of time.

*****

Terkeshi stared numbly at the viewscreen. The appearance of a blue planet should've raised his spirits. He was finally free of his father, and free to start over with a new life. But the cost of his freedom had been too great. With Jori dead and Benjiro abandoned, what would his mother think of him? And what would Washi and Michio do to him when they found out Sensei Jeruko had died saving him?

He almost didn't want to face them, but he had nowhere else to go.

The thought of suicide no longer appealed to him. Such a sacrifice would no longer have any meaning. His only choice was to own up to what he'd done and hope his mother would forgive him—Washi and Michio too.

And who knew? Maybe this new life wouldn't be so bad.

Dawn Ross

Did you enjoy this novel? Leave a review. Authors love reviews!

Next:
Isle of Hogs: A Dragon Spawn novella – After escaping the madness of his father, Prince Terkeshi must adjust to his new life as a farmer. The worst part isn't the smelly livestock or the lack of respect that comes with being a mere peasant, but the ghastly injuries that have diminished his fighting ability. When cyber-pirates kidnap people from his village, can the once-promising warrior overcome his disabilities and fight to save his new friends?

And:
Warrior Outcast: Book Four – The Cooperative and a sneaky cyborg make trouble for the surprise reappearance of another beloved character from the first two books.

Sign up for my newsletter by visiting my website, DawnRossAuthor.com, and get great deals!

The first thing you'll receive is an exclusive Prequel to Book One. You'll also get access to the first few chapters of the current books plus upcoming books. There may also be more free short stories related to the main story.

Connect with Dawn Ross online:
DawnRossAuthor.com
Twitter.com/DawnRossAuthor
Goodreads.com/author/Dawn_Ross

Dawn Ross

Glossary

Abira – The Battle of Abira is where Emperor Kenji Mizuki's grandfather had won a battle with a sword.

Aboru – A star system in Toradon territory.

Aki – Sensei Aki is the emperor's old teacher. Before passing away, he served as one of the emperor's Five Talons (aka advisors). He also served two previous emperors.

Ambrose – The lead cyborg who comes to visit Emperor Mizuki.

Arashi – A planet that has swirling storms.

Arc drive or arc reactor – This is one of the largest components of a spaceship. It is the engine that allows a ship to travel many light years away without violating the speed of light by bending space-time.

Arc gauge – A gauge that measures the amount of power the arc-drive is using.

Asp – A small Toradon space fighter.

Bakuto – Colonel Bakuto is a Toradon senshi serving under General Samuru. He heads the division of senshi foot soldiers.

Bantam – A small ship used primarily for hauling small loads of cargo.

Benjiro – A shokukin who is a genius at engineering but doesn't have the capacity to articulate himself well or to do everyday things. It was discovered in book 2 that he is the brother of Terk's mother and Lord Enomoto, making him Terk's uncle.

Biskol – A Toradon senshi who has skills in programming.

Blackbeast – An animal that Terk often refers to. It is never described but it is hinted that it might be a large wolf-like predator.

Black Gharial – A Rhinian ship that attacks the *Dragon* and the *Fire Breather*.

Bō – A fighting staff used in martial arts.

Bokken – Wooden swords used in martial arts practice.

Bolin – A Toradon senshi.

Botan - Emperor Botan Mizuki is Emperor Kenji Mizuki's father.

Brevak –General Brevak is the captain of the *Basilisk* warship.

Brian – A cyborg who assists Ambrose.

Buru – A man who bullied Jeruko while he was at the Senshi Dragon Academy.

Chima – Means vile one or hated enemy in Terk's language.

Ching – Captain Ching sometimes works the tactical station on the *Dragon*'s bridge.

Chusho – Means shit in Terk's language.

Comm – A communication device.

Communication hub – A form of communication that uses quantum entanglement technology for an instantaneous exchange.

Conveyor – An elevator-like car on a spaceship that moves vertically and horizontally.

Cooperative – The Prontaean Cooperative is an agency that governs space. It has numerous treaties with various worlds that provides its charter to keep space safe, ensure peace, regulate fair trade, and colonize new worlds. Its powers are granted by several planets, and the number of planets that are part of the Cooperative continues to grow. It does not include Toradon territory. Toradon's consider the Cooperative their enemy.

Defuser – Technology that renders phaser rifles and other energy weapons ineffective within a certain range.

Deskview – A desktop computer.

Disruptor – A device that can disrupt surveillance cameras and listening devices within a certain radius.

Dojo – A place to practice martial arts.

Dokuri – Jori and Terk's older half-brother who was killed by a rebellious Toradon lord about a year ago.

Dorb – A remote-controlled hovering ball that shoots bursts of low-level energy.

Dragon – The Toradon emperor's primary warship.

Dragon Emperor – Emperor Kenji Mizuki is the ruthless ruler of the Toradon Nohibito/Dragon People and is often referred to as the Dragon Emperor.

Dragon Warrior – Toradon senshi who have graduated from the Senshi Dragon Academy and directly serve Emperor Mizuki.

Edo – Edo is a bridge worker on the *Dragon* warship.

Enomoto – Lord Enomoto is a powerful Toradon lord who serves under the emperor but is dangerously close to being stronger than the emperor. He rules nearly the entire planet, Meixing, in the Toradon territory. His sister is Jori and Terkeshi's mother and his brother is Benjiro.

Fairyfly drones – Small flying drones that record a scene and send the feed to a military visor. The wearer of the visor eye-clicks the remote functionality of the drones.

Fire Breather – The spaceship the emperor will use to house the perantium emitter.

Five Talons – The emperor's five advisors, also known as the Emperor's Claw. They are Samuru, Jeruko, Nezumi, Aki, and Fujishin.

Flying Fish – The name of a Bantam-class cargo ship captained by Captain Tobiuo.

Fujishin – Fujishin used to be one of the emperor's Five Talons until he betrayed him and is now leading a band of rebels.

G-LOC - G-force induced loss of consciousness.

Geun – A Toradon senshi who serves on the Toku station in Toradon territory.

Gravity wheel – This is the part of a spaceship that creates gravity for its passengers. It is one of the largest components that give a spaceship its circular shape.

Great Commune – The wireless network connection composed of all the cyborgs who fall under MEGA-Man's rule.

Hamaki – A cigar.

Hapker – Vice Executive Commander J.D. Hapker is a Cooperative officer who had been held prisoner by the emperor until Jori helped him escape.

Hisui Island – An island on the planet Meixing where Terk's mother and Jeruko's sons are exiled. It is ruled by Lord Qing.

Jeffston – A cargo captain mentioned by Captain Tobiuo.

Jerom – Doctor Beck Jerom is one of the primary doctors on the Cooperative ship that Commander Hapker serves on.

Jeruko – Sensei/Colonel Jin Jeruko is one of the emperor's Five Talons. He is also Jori and Terk's primary military teacher and head of their personal guard.

Jin – Sensei Jeruko's informal name.

Jinsekai – The primary planet in Toradon territory.

Jori – Jori is the ten-year-old youngest son of Emperor Mizuki.

Kelar – A Toradon senshi.

Kenji – Emperor Mizuki's informal name.

Kiai – Kiais are short shouts made when performing an action move in martial arts.

Kortsu station – A space station in Toradon territory.

Koshu – Aged saki.

Kyunayama mines – Titanium ore is mined from this location on one of the moons in Toradon territory.

Laohu Dunes – A desert area ruled by a Toran lord.

Lazarus shield – A shield within a shield where the depletion of one initiates the other as it regenerates.

Lifeforce – The essence of a living thing that Terkeshi can sense using his sensing ability/sixth sense.

Malkai – A shokukin, man from the Toradon worker caste.

Maru – Lord Maru Jeruko is Sensei Jeruko's father.

MEGA – Stands for mechanically enhanced genetically altered.

MEGA hunter – A slang word for a MEGA Inspection Officer.

MEGA Injunction – Some decades ago, it was popular for rich people to get genetic and biometric enhancements. Common people felt such enhancements were unfair, especially since these enhanced people considered themselves superior and tended to seek positions of power. Protests became violent. As such, governments all over the galaxy stepped up. People with unnatural abilities were ejected from positions of power and strict laws were made to protect future generations.

MEGA Inspection Officer – This officer works for an organization that roots out MEGAs and makes sure they get filed in the intergalactic database. Many officers are fanatic about their work as they strongly believe that alterations to the human body is immoral.

MEGA-Man – A cybernetic man who has made himself into the most advanced man-machine in the galaxy. He is the leader of a race of cyborgs.

Meixing – A Toradon planet ruled almost entirely by Lord Enomoto.

Michio – Michio was Jori and Terk's personal guardsman as well as Washi's brother and Jeruko's son.

Midori sector – An area of space in Toradon territory.

Minashi – The Rebellion of Miniashi was a battle in which Emperor Kenji Mizuki's grandfather fought blindly because his helmet stopped working.

Mizuki – The family name of Jori and Terk, and their father the Dragon Emperor. The emperor refers to himself by this formal name.

MM – Stands for Mini Machine. It is a computer that is most often worn around the wrist like a brace but can be flattened and held like a tablet.

Montaro – Jori and Terk's older half-brother who was killed by their father for being grossly incompetent.

Mushin – Means no mind in Terk's language. No mind means to do your task so well that you don't need to think about it.

Nanite mask – A device that can be worn over the face and can be used to make someone look different and defeat facial recognition software.

New Nishiki Market – A space station on Toradon territory.

Nezumi – Nezumi is a retired general and is one of the emperor's Five Talons. He used to be one of Dokuri's personal trainers and personal guard.

Niashi – Major Niashi works at the operations station on the *Dragon*.

Night Mugger – A Rhinian ship that attacks the *Dragon* and the *Fire Breather*

Nohibito – Means people in Jori and Terk's language. It is often used together with Toradon Nohibito, as in Dragon People.

Onihitokuchi – A monster from Japanese lore known to kill and eat people.

Pachin – A Toradon senshi.

Parvati – A distant star system that the cyborg race is believed to come from.

Pentaduna – A powerful energy source traded on the black market because the emperor is the only one who should have it.

Perantium emitter – A powerful wave emitter that is powered by a crystal called perantium. It was designed to temper the plate tectonics of the planet Thendi, but Emperor Mizuki stole it so that he can convert it into a planet killing weapon. The perantium device is also called a wave-emitting device, perantium emitter or just emitter.

Prontaean – It is a word that describes the known galaxy. It is believed the word derived from an ancient Earthen Indo-European language where the prefix pro- means advanced or forward and the suffix -anean means relating to.

Prontaean Cooperative – An agency that governs space. It has numerous treaties with various worlds that provides its charter to keep space safe, ensure peace, regulate fair trade, and colonize new worlds. Its powers are granted by several planets, and the number of planets that are part of the Cooperative continues to grow. It does not include Toradon territory. Toradon's consider the Cooperative their enemy.

Porcupine bomb – A grenade-type bomb that shoots out super-heated metal darts. These darts can sometimes overwhelm energy shields and sear through armor.

Pulcrate – A planet under the Prontaean Cooperative's jurisdiction.

Qing – Lord Qing rules the small Hisui Island on the planet Meixing.

Reactables – A type of musical instrument.

Relativistic jet - an astronomical phenomenon where ionized matter is emitted from certain cosmic bodies and approaches the speed of light.

Repulse Monkey – A tai chi move.

Rhinian – A proper adjective defining people or things from Rhinus, in this case, mercenaries.

RR-5 – A phaser rifle with multiple settings and functionalities.

Rushiro – A Toradon senshi.

Ryu – Emperor Ryu Mizuki is Emperor Kenji Mizuki's grandfather.

Sakon – General Sakon is the captain of a Toradon vessel called the *Brimstone*. He is known for great violence.

Sam – Chief Sam Simmonds is a Cooperative officer who had been held prisoner by the emperor until Jori helped him escape.

Samuru – General Samuru is one of the emperor's Five Talons and is considered the emperor's lifelong friend.

Sarcosuchus – A Rhinian ship that attacks the *Dragon* and the *Fire Breather*

Senshi – Means warrior in Jori and Terk's language.

Senshi Dragon Academy – A renowned school for warriors who want to serve in the emperor's army.

Serpent – A small transport ship with some firing capabilities. It is often used by the Toradons for raids or pirating.

Shanliang monk – A respected culture in Toradon, known for their good virtues.

Shiu – Lord Shiu was a rebel killed by Fujishin.

Shodo – Japanese calligraphy art.

Shokukin – The term for members of the Toradon worker caste.

Sidewinder – Toradon infiltration ship.

Sika – A type of deer on one of the Toradon planets.

Simmonds – Chief Sam Simmonds is a Cooperative officer who had been held prisoner by the emperor until Jori helped him escape.

StarFire – The name of the Serpent-class ship that Jori and Terk had crashed on a Cooperative planet in book 1.

Stealthware suit – A garment that can make the wearer look invisible.

STK regulator – A component of the perantium emitter.

Sunsu – A docking master on the *Dragon* warship.

Superstrat – A type of guitar.

Tablet – A small hand-held computer device much like the tablets of the 21st century, but with more functionality. Some tablets can be folded around the wrist, and are then called an MM.

Talons – The emperor's five advisors, also known as the Emperor's Claw. They are Samuru, Jeruko, Nezumi, Aki, and Fujishin.

Tanto dagger – A military grade dagger worn by senshi warriors.

Terk – Short for Terkeshi (see below).

Terke-chan – The -chan at the end of a name denotes affection.

Terkeshi – Terkeshi or Terk is the fourteen-year-old eldest son of Emperor Kenji Mizuki.

Thao – Lord Thao had been one of Emperor Kenji Mizuki's friends.

Thendi – A planet that is having trouble with plate tectonics. The emperor stole their perantium emitter from it.

Tiger Knights of Tora – The senshi who served the Toran lord.

Tobiuo – Captain Tobiuo is the captain of the Bantam-class cargo ship called *Flying Fish*.

Tokagei –Terk's personal guard who gets cybernetic enhancements.

Toku station – A space station in Toradon territory.

Tora – A stronghold on one of the Toradon planets. It was ruled by a lord who rebelled against the Mizuki Empire.

Toradon – Means dragon in Jori and Terk's language. It is often spoken as Toradon Nohibito, which means Dragon People.

Toran - Anything that comes from the Tora culture.

TTAC Room – Acronym: Tactical Training Action Center. This room is used for simulated military training and exercises.

Viewscreen – A large computer screen.

Wang – Captain Wang is a Toradon senshi who gets cybernetic enhancements.

Washi – Washi was Jori and Terk's personal guardsman as well as Michio's brother and Jeruko's son.

Yujio – A Toradon senshi who gets cybernetic enhancements.

Zanshin – Means remaining mind in Terk's language. Remaining mind means make sure it's over before you walk away.

Books by Dawn Ross:

The Dragon Spawn Chronicles
StarFire Dragons
Dragon Emperor
Dragon's Fall
Isle of Hogs (a novella)
Warrior Outcast

Connect with Dawn Ross online:
DawnRossAuthor.com
Twitter.com/DawnRossAuthor
Goodreads.com/author/Dawn_Ross

Dawn Ross

About the Author

Dawn Ross currently resides in the wonderful state of Kansas where sunflowers abound. She has also lived in the beautiful Willamette Valley of Oregon and the scenic Hill Country of Texas. Dawn completed her bachelor's degree in 2017. Although the degree is in finance, most of her electives were in fine art and creative writing. Dawn is married to a wonderful man and adopted two children in 2017. Her current occupation is part time at the Meals on Wheels division of a senior service nonprofit organization. She is also a mom, homemaker, volunteer, wildlife artist, and a sci-fi/fantasy writer. Her first novel was written in 2001 and she's published several others since. She participates in the NaNoWriMo event every year and is a part of her local writers' group.

Made in the USA
Monee, IL
02 December 2024

70406918R00148